Drew glanced at]

She squinted through icy slits. Even though she stood right beside her son, she didn't matter. He sought Drew's assistance with a snow angel. Despite the cold, her temperature rose. She needed to stop Drew's game this instant.

"Come to this clean patch of snow. Now lie back." Drew held Noah's small hands until he leaned nearly horizontal and then released. "Now flap your arms." He demonstrated the right technique.

Noah flapped and jumped before Drew finished instructions. "Hey, I made an airplane," he shouted, flinging up his arms.

His exuberance stabbed Erin. She forced a fist against her achy stomach.

Drew stared at the snow and shrugged. "Yeah, I see an airplane."

Noah's eyes glittered between his hat and his scarf.

She needed to stop this foolish talk. Until this weekend, Noah had never paid much attention to planes, and she hadn't encouraged any interest. Since he'd met Drew, he played airplane games, talked about flying, and made snow airplanes.

Praise for Margot Johnson

"Margot Johnson makes an impressive debut with this heart-warming love story of two people who cannot possibly belong together—but do."

~Mary Balogh, New York Times Bestselling Author

~*~

"Margot Johnson hits all the right notes in her debut novel, *LOVE TAKES FLIGHT*. The hero and heroine are likeable characters that made me root especially hard for their happy ending. The author shines at bringing family dynamics to life with all of their love and imperfections."

~Donna Gartshore, Harlequin Love Inspired Author

~*~

"This story will set your heart beating and your fingers crossing as you hope for the very best ending for Erin, Drew, and Noah. A bonus for Canadian readers is the recognizable setting, and for readers around the world, it is a lovely introduction to Canada."

~Annette Bower, Award-winning Romance Author

~*~

"Filled with relatable characters, descriptive narration, and heartwarming moments, it's an absolute must-read for any dog lover!"

~Carolyn Cyr

Love Takes Flight

by

Margot Johnson

Love Takes Flight

Cover Art by *Tina Lynn Stout*

The Wild Rose Press, Inc.
PO Box 708
Adams Basin, NY 14410-0708
Visit us at www.thewildrosepress.com

Publishing History
First Sweetheart Rose Edition, 2019
Print ISBN 978-1-5092-2636-8
Digital ISBN 978-1-5092-2637-5

Published in the United States of America

Dedication

For my precious girls, Lindsay and Laura,
in honor of "we three"
and
my caring mom, Diane,
with love always

Acknowledgements

Many people helped me achieve my author dream.

~

Thank you to my wonderful husband, Rick Johnson, the most patient man alive, for making me laugh every day and being eager to read—and enjoy—this romance, not his typical genre.

~

My late dad, Ian Bickle, inspired my love of books and writing, and I'm forever grateful.

~

I appreciate the encouragement and feedback from Carolyn Cyr, Andrew Michener, Chris and Lindsay Vandermeer, Laura Almas, and other family and friends.

~

My mom, Diane Bickle, offers endless support and delicious dinners, freeing my time to write.

~

Finally, thank you to my dedicated editor, Leanne Morgena, for valuable insights and guidance along the way.

Chapter 1

Wind howled an eerie soundtrack mixed with dog pants, whines, and yips as Erin handled late afternoon kennel chores at Canine Corner.

At her hip, five-year-old Noah doled out dog treats. "What kind is this guy, Mom? He's hungry."

"He's a beagle." Erin paused, and despite the unsettling weather, forced a smile. "I like his brown and black patches."

"I like his soft ears." Noah squatted and held out a hand. "Shake a paw. Good dog." He shifted to the next dog.

Ominous tension hung in the air and prickled the back of Erin's neck with the late winter prairie blizzard bearing down on her small acreage just west of Moose Jaw, Canada.

They worked their way from stall to stall and fed, patted, and played with each dog for a few minutes.

As she bent to fill a water bucket, Erin laughed and wiped her cheek from a chocolate Lab's lick, but uneasiness still tiptoed near. She took a deep breath laced with a musky mix of kibble and damp dog and squatted to soothe a shaking poodle. "You're okay, pup."

The building siding rattled, and her young son straightened and widened his brown eyes.

She hugged him close and ran a hand over his

wavy, brown hair. "We're almost finished. You're a great helper."

Her parents and brother's family should have arrived by now. If the storm blocked their way, she'd be stuck on her own with Noah and the dogs all weekend with no one to help with the chores. She should never have given both her assistants the same weekend off. At a sharp knock at the door, she jumped and nearly tipped a water bucket.

Noah tapped her arm. "Are Grandma and Grandpa here?"

"Probably another dog needs a place to stay." Her family would have burst right in, so the visitor must be a client. Still, her torso muscles tensed and yanked the growing knot in her stomach. She swung open the door, and a whoosh of icy air rushed in past a man and a border collie covered in snow. "Come inside. The storm is wicked out there." She forced the door shut against the wind and led them to the kennel office-reception area accompanied by a chorus of barking. "Hi, my name is Erin Humphrey, and this helpful guy is my son, Noah." She stuck out her hand.

The man hesitated before he shook it. "I'm Drew Dixon. I made a booking for my dog, Jake."

He brushed snow off his cropped, brown hair, wrinkled his brow, and scrutinized the surroundings.

"Please, sit here. I half expected you to cancel in this weather." She gestured to a chair and perched opposite. "Noah, please give Jake a dog treat."

"Where's Ray?" Drew glared over his shoulder.

"He's probably somewhere in Arizona—at least, if he's smart. As soon as he handed over the keys to this place, he left prairie winters behind." Erin met his gaze and smiled, forgiving him for missing the former owner.

"Ray's on vacation?" Drew pinched his mouth into a hard line.

"He's not on vacation. He retired and sold the business. He said he told all his clients." Erin thrust her chin forward and sat taller, prodded by more than a tinge of pride in her new venture. "I took over the operation a couple of months ago." Her client's eyebrows arched like two agitated caterpillars.

"I had no idea." Drew flattened his eyebrows.

A shadow crossed his face.

She bit her bottom lip and pressed on her touchy stomach. He questioned her ability. She didn't measure up as a caregiver for his dog. She didn't expect every client to be pleasant, but she didn't need an issue today of all days. Her cheeks radiated heat, and she sat forward and tossed back her hair. "I assure you I love dogs, and I offer the same care and attention as Ray. I spent a couple of weeks working alongside him, and he showed me the ropes before he left."

"Jake is a little skittish. He doesn't take to everyone and definitely not to other border collies." Drew darted his gaze around, and he bent to pat his dog.

Noah held a dog biscuit toward Jake.

The dog sniffed and nibbled.

Noah waited until Jake swallowed, plopped down, and patted him like an old friend.

"Don't worry. We'll treat him well." Erin tipped her head. Her client should relax. "See, they're already bonding." Irritation at his curt, skeptical manner scratched her throat, and she swallowed. "Jake will stay in his own private, indoor-outdoor space like always. Everything is the same...except Ray." She met her client's flashing, brown eyes.

"What's your experience in the kennel business?" Drew wrinkled his forehead and checked his watch.

Erin took a deep breath and blotted her damp palms on her thighs. "I'm new to the business, but I know dogs. I've owned dogs all my life." She'd bought herself a fresh start with Eric's life insurance. She might be a kennel rookie, but if she could get past her beloved husband's death, she could handle anything. Her marketing degree rounded out her natural entrepreneurial streak, and she worked hard. Drew's distrust insulted her capability.

"I didn't expect this change at all." Drew shook his head and narrowed his eyes.

"Please, don't feel you have to leave Jake here." Erin bit her bottom lip and stood. "In fact, you should probably find another kennel. I won't charge you a cancellation fee, but you better get on the road again before the weather gets any worse."

Drew opened his mouth and closed it, and he swept his gaze from Erin to Noah to Jake.

The dog wagged his tail and panted.

Noah bent to pat him.

"How much attention will he get?" He flipped up his wrist again to check the time.

"I treat all the dogs like they're my own." Erin rubbed Jake behind his left ear. She took a deep breath of the damp, fur-infused air. In the background, a dog woofed. "I give them attention in the kennel and outside several times a day."

"I don't know..." Drew hunched his shoulders,

stood, and stomped to survey the row of stalls.

Erin followed Drew out of the office into the main kennel area. "I won't talk you into leaving your dog here. You need to make sure you feel comfortable." She turned to gauge her young son's reaction, who was fortunately, preoccupied with the dogs.

Drew glanced at his watch. "I better go. I need to catch a flight out of Regina. I can't miss it. I, uh, need to get away to my dad's place, so Jake can stay for a few days."

"He will adjust. Will you be satisfied leaving him?" Erin barely curved her lips around her crisp words. "Because if you don't trust me, you need to find another place for Jake." She straightened.

"The problem is Jake doesn't know you. I don't know you." Drew's dark gaze speared. "But I don't have a choice right now. I need to catch my flight."

"You do have a choice." She had to remain pleasant with clients. Her face burned, and she stayed firm yet polite, even though his words snapped like an elastic band, and his jaw hardened to a stiff line.

"I can't arrange other care at the last minute." Drew shifted and flicked his gaze between Jake and her.

"I suppose you're right. So, Jake is welcome to stay this time, but I suggest you find another kennel the next time."

"Maybe I will." Drew patted his dog. "I'll be back on Monday night. You'll be okay for a few days." He flipped his gaze from Erin to Noah, and his left eye twitched. "You help your Mom take good care of him, okay, Noah?"

"Okay, I will." Noah rocked onto his toes and nodded.

Erin held out her hand with a firm handshake. Drew's cool hand matched his manner.

He passed her Jake's leash, patted his dog one last time, and hurried outside.

The cold nipped Erin like his attitude, and she banged the door shut. Too bad he wasn't nearly as nice as his dog, but at least, she had a few days before their next encounter.

She settled Jake in his individual dog run and finished the last of the afternoon chores. Then she cozied Noah's hat low over his eyebrows and his scarf high to cover his cheeks. As she opened the door, a frosty blast hit. She held Noah's hand and led him into a whirlwind of snowflakes.

"Where'd the house go, Mommy?" Noah tugged her arm.

Erin shivered and squeezed reassurance. The wind whipped a snowy veil. "We'll find it. C'mon, let's run before we get stuck in a snow bank."

Inside, she laughed at how much snow collected on their heads and jackets in just a couple of minutes. She brushed off Noah's red hat and finger-combed her hair, loose around her shoulders. The house's warmth enveloped them and melted the snowflakes.

Their golden retriever, Sam, greeted them with a full body wag and licked snow off their mittens.

"Will Grandma and Grandpa and Uncle Mitch and Auntie Claire and Luc and Anna still find us?" Noah scrunched his face into a frown.

"They should be here soon." Erin unzipped Noah's jacket, placed a hand on his rosy cheeks, and kissed the tip of his nose. Instantly, a deep ache clutched her throat. His daddy would never again see his expressive, little face.

Erin hung up their coats and peered out the front window through the curtain of snow. She squinted and tightly hugged her arms around her middle. Swirling snowflakes blurred the gate at the end of the driveway into nothing but a hazy shadow. She could handle the kennel chores alone if she had to, but she could use a little moral support in the storm. Besides, Noah would have a lot more fun playing with his cousins and grandparents than tagging along while she worked.

The answering machine blinked, and she listened to another cancelled booking. The phone rang, and a woman, stuck at home in the driveway, arranged to pick up her dog tomorrow instead. Erin switched on the news, and the announcer warned against highway travel. The roads might get blocked. Concern stirred her stomach into a whirlwind.

She busied Noah with a pile of favorite books while she chopped onion and browned meat for spaghetti sauce. The savory aroma of onions and garlic wafted through the kitchen but didn't give her an appetite. She paced from the stove to the front window and back, until the faint outline of a van plowed up the driveway. At last, her family was safe. She placed her hands on her chest and heaved a giant sigh of relief.

"They're here." Noah squashed his nose on the window.

"Come in." Erin waited until the last moment to open the door and usher her family inside along with a current of frigid air. "I'm so relieved you made it. The weather is nasty."

They spilled into the entrance way, laughing and shivering.

Erin backed up, gathered coats, and hugged them. "Noah, give Grandma and Grandpa a hug."

Noah threw his arms around their waists. "I'll hug Uncle Mitch, and Auntie Claire, and Anna, and Luc." He stepped sideways and squeezed them all.

"The drive took twice as long as usual in this weather." Mitch stomped snow off his boots and lifted the hats off Anna and Luc. "We couldn't have driven much farther."

He stretched to his full six-foot stature and brushed snow off his dark, wavy hair.

Claire shook snow off her curly, blonde bob and then smoothed Anna's blonde curls and Luc's dark, brown waves.

"I counted seven cars in the ditch." Luc played scarf tug-of-war with Sam.

"Yum, the food smells good in here, sis. I'm starved." Mitch rubbed his belly.

"I hope you're all hungry. Dinner's almost ready." Erin brushed off snow and hung coats.

Sam gathered as many mitts and hats as he could carry in his golden retriever mouth.

"I baked." Gayle held out a pan of brownies.

The chocolatey aroma lured her close. "Thank you, Mom." Erin hugged her again. "You make the best desserts." She stepped into the hallway and waved everyone to follow.

"Come, and I'll give you a quick tour." Erin smiled, and her pride welled. Her face flushed as she showed them her comfortable, cozy, and appealing bungalow home. Down the hall, she pointed out the three bedrooms. "You can leave your suitcases here."

"You get to sleep with me in my room." Noah

poked his cousins and clapped.

"We'll be very comfortable here." Claire smiled and nodded, surveying the surroundings.

Erin's parents and brother echoed agreement.

"You kids better actually sleep." Brian chuckled and tickled his grandchildren's tummies.

"Now, I'll show you the rest of the place." Erin led them to the spacious living and dining room, decorated in muted gray with a variety of bright, accent colors. "During the day, I like the prairie view out the front window." Snow swatted the glass.

"I hope we can enjoy the scenery tomorrow." Gayle shivered and crossed her arms.

"Last stop is the kitchen." Erin flung wide her arms in the bright, white space. "The previous owner renovated and upgraded everything." She appreciated the long countertop, new appliances, and round table in the corner.

Her parents, brother, and sister-in-law followed her and filled the room with a happy jumble of voices.

"I agree with Mom and Dad. Your place is great." Mitch surveyed the room and gave a thumbs-up.

"Thanks, Mitch. We like it." Erin flashed a wide smile, shining with pride. Her brother usually supported her decisions, and his approval always counted. "Make yourselves at home." She lifted garlic bread from the oven.

"Wait until you see the set-up for the dogs." Her dad, Brian, planted his hands on his hips.

He motioned his graying head toward the back yard.

"I'll give you the outside and kennel tour later. I'm just so thankful you could come to help this weekend."

Her parents and brother had discouraged her from purchasing such a labor-intensive business, but when she asked for help, they were all gracious enough not to say, "I told you so." Operating a kennel wasn't exactly a cakewalk for a single mom, but she'd show everyone. She'd prove she could run a successful business and build a secure future.

"Helping is a handy excuse to get together." Mitch shrugged his broad shoulders and ran a hand through his thick, damp hair.

Just two years older than Erin, they could pass for twins. Growing up, she always had a partner in mischief.

"Family never needs an excuse to get together." Brian slapped Mitch on the back, leaned against the fridge, and crossed his arms across his thick chest.

"I'm just glad you're not alone with Noah in this storm." Gayle stirred the spaghetti sauce.

The spicy tang of tomato and oregano drifted through the room.

"I'm relieved you have company, too." Claire flipped back her curls and stood on tiptoe to lift dishes from the cupboard to set the table.

"We would be fine, but I'm glad you're here." Ice crystals swept across the kitchen window like fine sandpaper, and she hugged her arms around her waist and shivered. "Come for dinner, everyone…Noah, Anna, and Luc."

They all found a spot around the dining room table.

Sam sprawled underneath, ready to snatch a napkin and any tasty morsels that tumbled his way.

"To your new home and business." Mitch raised a glass of red wine, and everyone joined the toast.

"How's business going anyway?" After grabbing a slice, he passed the garlic bread.

Erin handed the bowl of pasta to Claire. "The dogs and most of my clients are great." She wrinkled her nose.

"Sounds like you have a story?" Brian scooped sauce on his pasta.

"The last client of the day grilled me on my credentials and nearly fired me on the spot. He only left his dog here because he desperately wanted to catch a flight." Erin raised her eyebrows. "On the bright side, his dog behaves well." She sighed, tore her bread into small pieces, and twirled a giant knot of spaghetti around her fork. Her family sat safely cocooned out of the storm, but her uneasiness still percolated.

"You'll meet all kinds, and I'm sure you'll charm most people." From Eric's spot at the table, her dad winked. For a few seconds, a sorrowful pang filled her chest, and she blinked back tears before anyone could notice. Her dad had sat before at the end of the table opposite her, but she never forgot who really belonged there. Three years ago, crushing an idyllic life together, she had lost Eric. Now, memories and their son lived on as proof, and her excruciating wound had healed into a dull ache nestled in her bones. Life struggled on, and an exciting new path beckoned.

As her family chattered away, Erin glanced around, appreciation swelling in her chest and nearly crowding out challenges with clients and weather. She filled her mouth with spaghetti and savored the rich tomato flavor. The blizzard raged on, but her family weekend held the promise of fun. Nothing could possibly interfere.

****

Drew kept his car to a crawl toward the east side of Moose Jaw, fishtailing around icy corners. He switched the heat to defrost, clicked the windshield wipers to high speed, and leaned forward in his seat. Poor Jake, abandoned with the new owner and her look-alike son. The boy couldn't have been more than five, and the pair hardly inspired confidence. They were nothing like Ray who boasted forty years of dog-care experience.

He glanced at the clock and punched a button to find another radio station with better weather news, but no, the same terse report warned against travel.

A wave of distress raced to his temples. He desperately needed this weekend away to clear his head and regroup from the crushing pressures at the Air Force base. Now, weather threatened to bury his plans. He needed moral support from someone, and maybe a weekend with his dad would help him face his daunting career threat.

Drew gripped the steering wheel, and tension shot to his shoulders. Hearing the commanding officer threaten to remove him from the elite SnoWings aerobatics team had flipped his life upside down like a midflight loop. Every time he replayed their conversation, the imposing image of the CO's stiff shoulders and stern face haunted him, and sweat trickled down his sides.

"I'm sorry, sir. I won't make another serious mistake." Drew barely met the commander's piercing glare of green eyes as sharp as broken glass.

"You're right. If you want to call yourself a SnoWings pilot, you will never again make the mistake you made today."

Drew had flushed, nodded, and hurried from the office.

He stared at the snowy road and shivered. The memory chilled him to the core. The military had catapulted him from a chaotic home life, and flying meant everything. He couldn't lose his coveted spot on the team. He had to do whatever the team demanded to get past his near-deadly mistake in the air. The *incident* threatened to shatter his SnoWings dream and ruin his life.

As he neared the edge of the city, he spotted a blur of flashing blue and red lights signaling trouble ahead. A cluster of police vehicles blocked the road, and Drew pounded the steering wheel. *Not another delay.* A little nasty weather couldn't stop him. He had to catch his flight and escape. He slowed and lowered the radio volume.

Exhaling a foggy haze, an officer flagged him over.

Drew opened the window a few inches, and a gust of frigid air rushed in.

The uniformed man leaned to face him. "Sorry, visibility is near zero, and we've closed the road."

"But I've got a flight to catch..." His voice cracked. Frustration boiled in his chest.

"Sorry, sir, you can't proceed tonight. We're not letting anybody through. I mean nobody." The officer shook his head and made a sweeping gesture to point him back toward the city.

He slapped the dash and spun the car into a jerky U-turn. His breath puffed in and out in frosty clouds, and his wipers squeaked a protest against thick snow. A block later, he stopped to make a call. The phone clicked straight to message manager, and he squeezed a fist so hard his knuckles turned white. "Hi, Dad. I looked forward to our visit this weekend." His voice wavered. "But a blizzard just hit, and I can't get to Regina to catch my flight. Uh…I guess we'll talk later."

Disappointment pounded his temples. He needed to confide in somebody and boost his confidence. Frank never was a father a son could count on, but he quit drinking a year ago, so maybe now he could be a steady influence.

Drew braked and crept around stuck cars. Snowdrifts narrowed the streets, and blowing snow swirled cars and houses into a blurry haze. His heartbeat throbbed in his chest as he manoeuvred through snowdrifts and pointed his car west into the city's outskirts toward Canine Corner. He puffed a frosty sigh of relief. The police only blocked the main exits out of the city, so he could rescue poor Jake as soon as possible from the kennel full of strange dogs and an inexperienced, new owner. Now, the weekend loomed long and empty, and he needed Jake's company more than ever.

Chapter 2

The doorbell interrupted the laughter around the dinner table.

"Pizza's here," Mitch joked, and he lifted his napkin and wiped his chin.

"Who's here on a night like this?" Erin jumped and headed for the front door. "I'm not expecting any more clients tonight."

The chatter around the table stopped.

When she opened the front door to the last person she wanted to see, she clenched the doorknob, her smile freezing.

Drew stood on the doorstep like a glum snowman bracing himself against the wind.

"You changed your mind? Come in, so we don't let in all the cold and snow." Erin shivered. "You're half frozen." She waved him inside and shut the door.

"The road to Regina is closed." Drew brushed snow off his shoulders and huffed. "I came for Jake. I'm also stuck just outside your gate, so I'll need to call a tow truck." He shook off a shiver.

"You're not going anywhere tonight, young man. Hi, I'm Erin's dad, Brian." He stepped forward into the entryway and shook Drew's hand. "No one in his right mind is out on those roads tonight. I highly doubt if even tow trucks are still working. We left Regina just before police closed the road. If we hadn't been worried about Erin and Noah on their own, we would have returned home."

"Any chance of a push?" Drew's whole being drooped. He wiped the bridge of his nose.

"I don't know…" Erin raised her eyebrows. Ice and snow melted and dampened his cropped, dark hair and thick eyelashes and dripped huge drops onto his thin cheeks. She glanced at her dad for an opinion.

Brian planted his hands on his hips and shook his head.

Mitch joined them in the entrance. "No way, man." He shook hands with Drew. "I'm Erin's brother, Mitch. I'd like to help you out, but the weather is insane. Even if we dig out your tires by the gate, you'll be stuck again before you hit the main road, guaranteed."

"I know you." Noah joined the growing semi-circle of family near the door. "You're Jake's dad." He bounced in place.

"Yes, I sure am. I'm here to pick up Jake and head home, so you can finish your dinner." Drew flickered a smile at Noah before he let the corners of his mouth sag.

"Come in, and join us. I insist." Brian gestured for Drew to pass him his jacket. "We'll finish dinner and then take stock of the weather."

"Yes, we have plenty of food." Erin nodded, but resistance squeezed her throat and cooled her tone. "Maybe later the storm will blow over, and we can dig your car free." She didn't want him here, but she didn't really have a choice.

"No, thank you…really…" Drew frowned, grabbed the doorknob, and shook his head.

The family's coaxing drowned out Drew's protests,

and Erin directed him to a seat at the dinner table between Noah and Brian.

"I'm glad you're here out of the storm." Mitch grinned at Drew and continued his story about the time they built a snow fort in the backyard.

Erin stared at her food. She didn't need a stranger interrupting her family visit. The wind howled, and she shuddered. The storm better subside soon. If it didn't, she might have an extra and unwanted guest overnight.

****

Lassoed into the family circle seasoned with garlic and basil, Drew shifted in his chair and twisted spaghetti around his fork. His mouth watered. He was hungrier than he'd realized, and a hot meal might calm his impatience and sooth his jangled nerves.

At the Air Force base, he wore the awkward role of outsider, and now, he skirted the edges of a close family gathering. His head ached, and he jiggled his leg under the table, anxious to leave. As soon as they finished their meal, he'd get on his way home. He rubbed his temple. The family took their time eating, and their laughter and quips lobbed around the table like a tennis match where he acted as the lone spectator.

Apparently, Erin didn't have a Mr. Humphrey—at least, no one mentioned a husband. He scanned the family members seated at the table, and his hostess tilted her head to one side and laughed. Her thick, cocoa hair flowed around her shoulders and framed her rosy complexion and perfect white smile. His pulse jumped, and he took a deep breath to calm his surprising reaction.

Dinner finally ended, and Brian surveyed the view from the front window. "Weather's plain ugly. I can hardly see the van now. A real, old-fashioned prairie blizzard just blew in."

"I'll just go and check the state of the road by my car." Drew put on his jacket.

"Can we come?" Noah and his cousins jumped and wiggled.

"You better stay warm in here." Brian swept his grandchildren into a group hug and tickle.

"Dad and I'll go with you." Mitch grabbed their jackets out of the closet.

"I appreciate your help. I'm sure the three of us can get me on my way." Drew yanked his hat low on his forehead.

"Shovels are in the shed around back." Erin stood leaning on the kitchen doorway, giving instructions.

Drew's pulse spiked. Her sweater and jeans hugged her tall, lean shape, and he couldn't tear away his gaze. He blinked and forced his attention to his boots. She should be the last thing on his mind.

Mitch bent to pat the retriever wagging his tail by the door. "Okay, Sam, you can come, too."

Outside, the snow piled knee deep on the sidewalk and drifted to hip level along the bushes dotting the yard. The cloak of snow over the shrubs transformed them into eerie snow ghosts outlined with the reflection from the front porch light.

The three men and Sam trudged toward the gate, and Drew puffed and squinted against pricks of whipping snow. Just through the gate, he stopped and pointed. "That hill up ahead is my car."

Brian and Mitch both laughed and leaned on their shovels.

Drew groaned. Heavy snow buried his car—beyond

digging, beyond towing, beyond rescue—until the blizzard ended. Inside his jacket, he tensed his shoulders. He had no choice but to stay. The storm definitely and completely stranded him with strangers in unfamiliar surroundings away from the city. He couldn't go anywhere tonight. The realization struck him harder than the pounding wind, and he clenched his jaw into a vise grip.

"I can't believe it." Shoulders hunched, Drew kicked at a snowbank as hard as he would a football. Then he kicked a second time, and his boot flew off into a pile of snow. Drew balanced on one leg and pointed. "Go get the boot, Sam. Go fetch. Good dog, Sam."

"Check out the arctic flamingo." Brian chuckled and swung an arm toward him.

Mitch laughed and stomped in circles to keep warm.

After a couple of false starts, Sam delivered the stray boot.

"If I can unbury the trunk at least, I can grab my bag." Drew tromped toward his car.

The three men used full arm swipes to clear off the trunk enough to open the lid without filling the inside with snow.

"C'mon, let's get back to the house." Brian led the way.

With every step, Drew braced himself against the howling wind and bemoaned his rotten luck. His breath puffed in icy bursts, and he shivered, hunching his cramping shoulders. Face facts. He was trapped here until morning.

Brian led the guys in the front door and clamped a

hand on Drew's shoulder. "Say hello to the newest member of the family, everyone. Drew's here to stay."

Drew shuddered while he brushed snow off his jacket. He barely knew Erin and her family. How would he cope with strangers for an entire evening and night?

****

In the kitchen, Erin sipped coffee with her mom and Claire and traded family stories. Her dad's announcement smacked her harder than the storm. She set down her mug and rubbed her tense arms. Having her reluctant client, Drew, as a dinner guest was bad enough. Now, she had to put up with his company for the entire night. His presence disrupted everything and infringed on a precious family weekend. She kneaded her middle and wrinkled her nose, dismayed at the turn of events.

"Where will we put him?" Gayle crinkled her hazel eyes and clasped her short, auburn hair.

"Maybe I could put him in the kennel." Erin's idea burst out with a kernel of a wish.

Gayle reacted with wide eyes and open mouth. "Oh, Erin, you should be nice."

Claire smiled and tilted her head. "He's handsome."

Erin shrugged and bit her bottom lip. She hadn't noticed. Honestly, she hadn't paid attention to any man since Eric. Raising Noah drained much of her energy, and no man could ever replace the dad he lost. Plastering on a pleasant hostess face, she greeted wet, exuberant Sam and dragged herself to talk to the men in the foyer.

"Nobody's driving anywhere tonight. I haven't seen in years such a wicked storm. You're stuck with us, Drew." Brian slapped him on the back and sprayed snow in all directions.

Erin had a different take on the situation. Her family got stuck with Drew, not the other way around. She clenched her teeth and forced a smile. "Mother Nature has her own plans. Don't worry, we'll find you a bed."

"Believe me, imposing on you is the last thing I want. But, I, uh, don't have any alternative." Drew shook his head, and his jaw jutted a hard edge.

"We'll just have to make the best of the situation." Erin shrugged, raised her hands, and flipped up her palms.

"I always say the more the merrier." Gayle dried her hands on a kitchen towel. "Come in, Drew. Join the fun."

The kids ran by, and Sam wagged his tail and entire body so hard he bumped Noah into his cousins, and they all tumbled like human dominoes.

Drew grimaced and backed out of the way.

"Welcome to our world." Mitch chuckled at the chaos. "I gather you don't have kids?"

"No, I'm single. No kids." Drew shook his head and fisted his hands.

For an instant, his eyes clouded.

"You might decide you never want them after an evening in our chaos." Mitch squatted to pat the dog.

Drew laughed and raised an eyebrow. "You might be right."

"Okay, you goofballs. How about if we play for a while in Noah's room?" Brian gathered up his grandchildren and scooted them away.

"I hope you like board games. Our plan is to get

the kids to bed and break out a little competition." Mitch pumped a fist in the air.

Drew stretched his lips into a straight line. "Can't say I've played many board games lately, but when in Rome…"

"We better find you a place away from the chaos." Erin handed Drew sheets, blankets, and towels then showed him the sofa and bathroom in the basement. "Sorry, I can't offer you a real bed, but the sofa is pretty comfortable."

"I appreciate anywhere to sleep for the night. I'm sorry to trouble you for a place to stay."

"You can't help the weather." Erin shrugged. His apology made him slightly more appealing.

Drew lowered his gaze and cleared his throat. "Can I, uh, ask…another favor…?"

"Yes?" She faced him. He had a lot of nerve to ask for more.

"Jake's out in the kennel." He cleared his throat and met her gaze. "Would you mind…? Could he join me inside for the night?"

Her inner ice cube melted a little, and she smiled. "Aw, you miss him. Of course, he can join you. I told you I love dogs, so I understand why you'd rather have him close and don't want to leave him in the kennel any longer than necessary."

"Thank you." Drew nodded and gave the barest hint of a smile.

The firm line along Drew's jaw softened, and in a flash, she saw what Claire had noticed earlier. When Drew's chiseled features relaxed and his expression warmed, he verged on handsome. She clutched at her nervous stomach and blinked. She shouldn't notice a man's appearance, no matter how attractive. Over Drew's shoulder from a picture on the wall, Eric's gentle, curved face smiled. "I'll soon make my evening kennel rounds, so I'll rescue Jake then. The kids will welcome him, and Sam won't mind, will you, Sam?" She patted the dog's head.

"Thank you." Drew stood straight and rubbed his forehead. "I really appreciate your understanding."

"Jake's a good dog. Now, I'll let you get settled." Erin spun and headed for the stairs. Drew actually sounded humble and appreciative. His attitude had improved. But he should show plenty of gratitude because he had invaded her personal space and family time. She would give him the benefit of the doubt this evening. But tomorrow when he dug out and said good-bye, she would remind him he should find another kennel where he trusted the owner. He didn't belong here and never would.

****

Drew surveyed his basement home for the night and sighed. He gauged the length of the sofa and tested the cushions. His accommodations weren't exactly ritzy, but they would suffice. He couldn't have asked for more as an unexpected, and probably unwelcome, guest. He rubbed his throbbing temples. One night wouldn't kill him. He would wake early, dig out his car, and escape down the road. He'd block the whole experience like a bad dream.

"Come and join us up in the living room, Drew." Brian's voice boomed down the stairwell.

He scanned the room and zeroed in on the wall covered in a collection of family pictures. Stepping closer, he recognized Erin's parents and brother. Like the atmosphere at the dinner table, the pictures of Christmas and holidays shouted their closeness. He scanned the collection and stopped on a picture of Erin and a man with their arms around each other, heads tipped together and smiles glowing. Their obvious love oozed.

"Oh, you're right here." Brian moved close.

Drew flinched at the unexpected interruption and faced him.

"Her husband, Eric, passed away three years ago." Brian's jovial face drooped.

"Oh, no. How terrible…with a kid and all." Drew swallowed and lowered his gaze. When his parents split, he'd lived the pain of loss. Erin's pain over losing her husband and young son's father must have been unbearable. His head throbbed, and he pressed on his temple. He might need to check his bag for pain medication to tame the nagging tension. He cleared his throat and glanced from the picture to Brian and back.

"The situation devastated Erin. But she's strong and determined. For Noah's sake, she fights through her pain. She's really bounced back with the kennel to keep her busy." For a silent few moments, Brian rocked on his heels. "Well, shall we?" He gestured toward the stairwell.

"Sure." He didn't really have a choice. Drew followed him up the stairs, shaking off the sobering exchange. Erin was a young widow. What had happened to her husband? His throat clutched, and he erased an image of Erin's pretty face. How on earth would he survive an evening interacting with a room full of strangers?

In the living room, Brian and Mitch crouched in

front of the fireplace, adding kindling.

"Anything I can help you with?" Drew stood to the side and scrutinized their work.

"Nah, we got this. I'm a camper." Mitch added a couple of logs.

After checking on the dogs and retrieving Jake, Erin and Claire joined the group in the living room. Erin laughed. "The wind nearly blew us over." Their red cheeks beamed, and their eyes blinked icicle lashes.

Jake shook a spray of snow in all directions and returned his coat from mostly white to its usual black and white patches. He wagged his tail, circled Drew a few times, and took off in a game of chase with the kids and Sam.

"The dogs are all set, and we can stay inside until morning." Erin blew on her hands and rubbed them together.

"Can we have hot chocolate and marshmallows now?" Noah and his cousins skidded to a stop.

"Yes, you may." She clapped once. "Go put on your pajamas, and we'll get the snacks ready." She went to the kitchen and returned with a big bag of the fluffy, white treats.

Drew perched on the edge of the sofa and patted Jake just as the kids, dressed for bed, tumbled into the room.

"Hey, are you sleeping here, too?" Noah dropped to his knees and hugged Jake.

Jake wagged his whole body and slathered Noah with licks.

Noah giggled and used the back of his hand to wipe his cheek.

"Yeah, Jake and I are stuck here for the night."

Drew rubbed his temple. Much as he longed to escape, he was trapped. A bit of a loner, he often struggled to feel comfortable around people he didn't know well. Growing up in a dysfunctional family had taught him early others were unpredictable, and he couldn't rely on just anybody.

"Oh, cool. Do you like hide-and-seek?" Noah leaped to his feet, bounced, and stared.

"I haven't played that game in a long time." Drew scanned the room for another adult's support.

Erin placed her hands on her hips. "Sorry, no hide-and-seek tonight. Busy kids need sleep." She tapped Noah's shoulder.

In front of the crackling fire, Gayle and Claire served cups of steaming hot chocolate topped with whipped cream.

"Time for your snack." Erin stepped across the room and gathered roasting sticks from the dining room cabinet. Smiling, she passed them to everyone. "Careful you don't poke anyone."

"I've never roasted marshmallow indoors." Drew slid off the sofa and knelt close to the fire. He adjusted the stick's angle to avoid the flames.

"You haven't lived." Brian winked and popped a gooey marshmallow into his mouth.

"Didn't know what I missed all these years." Drew eased his golden treat out of the fire. So far, snack time was bearable. He scanned the semi-circle around the fireplace and rested his gaze on the three excited children. The firelight glinted on their bright, sticky faces. Surrounded by their loving parents and grandparents, the kids had no idea yet of the value of their warm family circle. He blinked a few times and swallowed. "Excuse me. I need to help myself to some water." He hurried to the kitchen, ran cold water, and lifted the cool glass to his forehead. Before he rejoined them, he drank a full glass.

Erin's face glowed, and her eyes sparkled. She patted the children's backs. "Okay, one more marshmallow each, and you need to brush your teeth and tuck in bed."

Drew couldn't tear his gaze from Erin, gently guiding her son and showing she cared.

"Can Drew roast one for me, Mommy?" Noah squished a marshmallow in his small hand.

"Maybe Grandpa or I…?" Erin speared a fresh marshmallow.

"Sure, I will. I need the practice. I mean, if your mom doesn't mind, I can help." Drew searched Erin's gaze for approval, and heat surged to his face. His life was consumed by practice. On a weekend off, why did he have to remind himself how much he needed repetition? Yes, he definitely needed to drill on precision flight patterns. Intense training flights and his tenuous position with the SnoWings were an ever-present burden.

Erin hesitated for a second and nodded. She passed him a marshmallow, and the tips of their fingers touched.

He closed his fingers, and intense warmth jolted up his arm to his chest. The instant attraction grabbed his breath. Swallowing hard through his dry throat, he stared at the fire. He needed to escape. His life already had more than enough complications. He forced a slow, deep inhalation, but before he could regroup, the lights flickered and died.

Everyone reacted to the sudden shadowy cloak at once.

"Mommy?" Noah's voice shook.

"Oh, no." Claire gasped.

The fireplace threw dancing orange and yellow patterns across the room, a muted reprieve from total darkness.

Erin squeezed Noah's shoulders. "Let's all stay calm."

"Not a power outage." Brian groaned and slapped his knee.

"We'll be okay." Gayle encircled the children in a hug.

As reality sank in, nervous energy pulsed.

Snowballing misfortune made Drew's shoulders ache. The blizzard raged on, and now their warm little island had only the fireplace for heat.

Chapter 3

"Everyone, just sit tight, and I'll get flashlights and candles." Pulse racing, Erin moved through the darkness and groped her way to the kitchen closet where she kept the emergency supplies.

The fireplace would help keep them warm in the living room, but if the power didn't soon return, the rest of the house would chill. Inhaling calming breaths, she handed out flashlights and candles.

"I'll help." Mitch hurried to light candles, and soon the house glowed with flickering light.

"What about the kennel? Will the dogs stay warm?" Drew paced to the kitchen window.

She clenched her teeth. Of course, he would question her contingency plans. "Fortunately, the kennel switches automatically to a backup power generator. I'll head out to check the heat right away, but first, this sleepy crew better go to dreamland."

Erin swept Noah and his cousins into a group hug. She'd have suggested they all bunk in and have a pajama party by the fire, but not with a total stranger in the house. No way would she show Drew her plaid, flannel pajamas. "Grandma will take a flashlight and read you stories in bed. As soon as I return from checking the dogs, I'll come in and give you another hug."

"But we're not tired…" Noah rubbed his eyes and

yawned.

"Of course, you're not." Erin kissed his tousled head.

"Erin, you stay with the kids. Mitch and I'll go." Brian stretched tall and raised his thick hands to his hips. "Drew, feel free to come."

"No, I don't need help. I mean, thanks, Dad, but as part of my job, I check for trouble. I need to handle everything." In the tangerine candlelight glow, she straightened and squared her shoulders, but her insides churned. She'd show them her strength and demonstrate she could handle a challenge. She curled her hands into firm fists. Even if she had been alone with Noah in the storm, she'd have found a way to cope.

"If you insist on coming, let's get going." Her dad motioned toward the door.

"We don't all need to go." Erin rested her gaze on Drew.

"I'd like to help. Strength in numbers, and pitching in is the least I can do." Drew stood tall.

"I'm fine, really." But when he put on his jacket, she didn't resist.

A faint light beamed from the direction of the kennel, a sign the auxiliary heat worked. Just to be sure, Erin and the three men waded through thigh-high drifts to the kennel. She squinted against the driving snowflakes and shivered inside her parka. Apprehension along with cold seeped past her warm layers.

The beagle nearest the door set off the barking alarm, and the place echoed with yaps and woofs, large and small.

Through the dim lighting, Erin confirmed the

heater and fans operated properly. Then she and the men made their way from dog to dog with soothing voices, treats, and reassuring pats until the atmosphere calmed. The familiar aroma of damp fur hung in the air.

So far, so good. Erin's heart rate slowed to a normal, steady pace. "Everything's under control out here. Thanks for your moral support, guys!" Thank goodness, she didn't have to deal alone with the storm's impact. But she still had to cope with Drew, and a long, dark night stretched ahead.

****

Back in the house, Drew settled himself in the armchair beside the fire while Erin tucked in the children. The orange flames and flickering candlelight lit the room with a shadowy glow, and the semi-darkness protected and made him less conspicuous as a stranger among close family. Erin showed cool courtesy, and her family welcomed him, yet he didn't really belong.

"What do you do in Moose Jaw?" Brian stretched and yawned.

Erin returned to the room, plopped onto the end of the sofa, and folded her arms.

In front of the fire, Mitch sprawled on the floor with his head resting on Claire's feet, and the two dogs snoozed nearby. The cozy scent of burning wood swirled, and Drew took a deep breath. "I'm with the Air Force, uh, a pilot training with the SnoWings."

"Why didn't you say so? I'm retired from the Forces." Brian sat forward. "I worked as a communication specialist. You and I must have a lot in common."

Erin hugged her arms around her and stared at the

fire.

"What a coincidence." Pain tapped at Drew's temples. First impressions showed Brian could boast an outgoing personality, successful career, and close family. If only he and Brian had more in common.

"Being selected for the SnoWings is quite an honor. That achievement says a lot about your skills as a pilot." Brian sat forward and swooped his hands together in a loud clap.

"Flying's in my blood. For as long as I remember, I've wanted to be a pilot." Drew rotated his stiff shoulders and searched for a way to change the subject. A wood log snapped, and the flames flared. He needed a total break from the pressures at the base and a chance to muster his confidence and return with a game plan. He glanced at Erin gazing at the fire.

"Why did you choose military life?" Brian slapped his hands on his thighs.

"I liked the idea of doing something for my country and, at the same time, pursuing something I loved." Drew stared at the licking, orange flames. The full story was a little more complicated, but the abbreviated version worked. Flying had lifted him from an unstable home and given him goals and purpose.

Brian beamed. "I felt the same way. Army life suited me…both of us." He sat back, put his arm around Gayle, and squeezed her shoulder. "Making the SnoWings is a very impressive accomplishment." He nodded and pursed his lips into a quiet whistle.

Now, Drew barely hung onto the coveted opportunity. *Somebody else jump in and change the subject.* He glanced at Erin snuggling a blanket past her chin. Did he imagine a change or did her pretty face pale underneath the fire's glow?

He cleared his throat. "Thank you. When I joined the Forces, I dreamed of making the SnoWings team–perfecting the formations, performing around the country, and inspiring kids. Last fall, I finally got selected." Drew lowered his gaze and massaged his left temple. He needed to get off this topic and away from the spotlight.

"The SnoWings are the definition of absolute teamwork in action." Mitch made a zooming motion with his hands parallel to each other.

"Yeah, teamwork's pretty key." Drew glanced and caught Erin squeezing her eyes shut. Obviously, she had no interest in his flying career, but he didn't mind. He didn't want to talk about flight anyway.

"Teamwork is critical, and military life can be pretty challenging." Brian pointed at Erin and Mitch. "These two are the proverbial base brats. Our family relocated nine times."

"Dad, Drew doesn't need to know our life story." Erin put a hand on her dad's arm.

"I don't mind, really. Tell me more, Brian." The more he kept Brian talking, the less he had to reveal. He didn't need Brian or anyone prying into his SnoWings life. Once the team allowed him to stay, he could be plenty proud.

"Dad, please." Erin shook her head. "Mitch, you tell him."

"Hey, you heard the man. He's interested." Brian slapped his thigh. "Now, where did I leave off? Oh yeah, after we moved to Moose Jaw, Erin put her foot down. She wouldn't leave, except for spending four years at University of Regina."

"I wanted to keep the same friends, not lose them." Erin crossed her arms and glared at the fire.

"I know what you mean." Drew tapped clenched fists on his thighs. "You just get settled in at the base, bond with the other pilots, and you transfer to the next posting. With everyone in the Forces relocating so often, you always have to connect with someone new. Of course, friendships aren't automatic. People don't always click."

Heat burned in Drew's cheeks, and he crossed his arms. He shouldn't be sharing his feelings with a room full of strangers. The more he opened up, the more they would pry into his life, and he preferred not to reveal certain details. He couldn't trust strangers.

"Anyway, I stayed in Moose Jaw, and I belong here. I'm never moving." Erin stood and tossed aside the blanket.

Both dogs jumped and wagged their tails, ready for action.

"How about a game? I think we could play Disko by candlelight." Erin smiled at the happy dogs. "Not you, pups. Not your kind of game, so lie there." She patted them.

Drew breathed a sigh of relief. He could have hugged Erin for refocusing the group's attention.

"I like that idea." Mitch swung to a sitting position. His brown eyes lit.

"Should we form mixed teams?" Mitch glanced at his dad.

"Yeah, we better go with couples." Brian stood and smirked. "I know you girls don't like to lose."

Erin groaned and shook her head, rolling her eyes at Claire and Gayle.

Gayle gave Brian a playful punch on the arm.

Drew shrugged and swept his gaze to Erin's serious face. "I guess we're a team." He used the term loosely. A team needed to know each other, trust, and work together in perfect harmony. Without undying commitment and practice, people didn't gel as a true team. He and Erin barely knew each other, and they probably wouldn't click, even over a game. They would be two individuals competing to win but definitely not a true team.

"I better keep the fire stoked." Mitch tossed another log on top, and the flames leaped higher. "The weather report predicted the wind chill would drop to minus forty this evening."

Gayle shivered.

"Definitely feels that cold out there." Brian reached over and rubbed her arm.

"The heat from the fireplace won't reach the bedrooms, so I'll make sure the kids are still covered." Gayle took a flashlight, tiptoed down the hallway, and returned a couple of minutes later. "The room feels a bit chilly, but the kids are snug in their beds."

Drew helped Erin set up a portable table and chairs in front of the fireplace, and they all circled the game board. The fire crackled, and he inhaled a deep, calming breath of the smoky aroma. "You'll have to give me a quick lesson. I've never played this game." He picked up one of the round disks and flipped it.

"You'll catch on quickly. Flick a finger to shoot." Erin demonstrated. "Now, lean my way."

Drew tilted to his right, and his shoulder bumped Erin. The surprise connection jolted him straight, and a current sizzled down his arm to his fingertips. He bent to listen for instructions, and as she fixed her gaze on the disk and poised her finger, he sensed her face too close. He jerked upright, and his heart rate jumped.

"See. Watch my finger." She demonstrated a flick, and the disk ricocheted across the board.

Drew caught her glance.

She focused quickly on the game.

The fire reflected on her creamy, smooth skin, and suddenly a hint more color pinked her cheeks. Maybe just light from the flames added color. He couldn't be sure, and warmth rushed to his chest. "Okay, here goes." His pilot life demanded precision, but the recent talk of the SnoWings and teams jetted his concentration off course. The disk hit a peg and bounced right back. He jumped.

Everyone laughed, and the fire snapped.

"Not as simple as flying a jet, eh, Drew?" Brian flicked his disk into the center.

"Apparently not." Drew faked a laugh. During his weekend off, he didn't need a reminder of the cockpit. Spending the night with strangers already added enough stress. "Nicely done." He nodded at Mitch's expert shot to the center hole.

An extra strong gust of wind swatted blotches of snow onto the window.

Erin stood to scan the yard. "The storm's not showing any signs of letting up. Brrr, the draft by the window is chilly." If the power didn't return soon and restart the furnace fan, they'd need to bundle up in jackets and blankets.

After a few more practice shots, the three-team tournament started. In the ring of laughing, teasing family, Drew did his best to participate. He let the inside jokes roll past and forced some chuckles from the edge of the caring circle. They oozed love and belonging. How must forming part of such a caring circle feel? Would he ever experience the same comfort? His chest squeezed with regret, but a few shots into the game, the shield of dim lighting sprinkled with laughter eased the ache in his temple.

A couple of hours passed quickly, and the fire cozied the room with crackling and a rustic aroma. Based on their winning records, Brian and Gayle challenged Drew and Erin in the final round.

"Okay, you two. Your mom and I saved our best shots. The competition is serious now." The fire caught the twinkle in Brian's eye. "This game decides the gold medal."

"You're on. Don't let me down now, Erin." Drew plunked his fist on the table, bantering like the others.

"Of course, you can count on me." Erin bent and focused. "But don't disappoint me." Flexing her shooting finger, she teased right back.

Disks flew, and Mitch and Claire cheered for both teams.

Finally, Drew readied for his last shot for the win.

"You can do this." Erin curled her hands into two fists and stared at his hands.

Focus, Drew. He could make the shot. He lined up, took a deep breath, and snapped his finger. The disk spun toward the center hole, wavered, and dropped.

"Yes, you scored the winning point." Erin flashed a wide smile and slapped a high five.

For a second, his chest inflated so full it nearly burst. He thrived on performing well and gladly accepted congratulations from Mitch, Claire, and

Gayle. If he had to be stuck somewhere, he could have done worse than this friendly group.

Brian exaggerated a groan. "Beginner's luck. I'm sure of it. I guess you two earned the gold medal." He yawned. "Well, the hour is late for an old guy, but we can't sleep until the heat's back on. We need to make sure the people and the pipes won't freeze. What's next to keep us alert? How about a midnight dance party?"

When everyone groaned, Brian chuckled.

"I'll stay up and tend the fire." Erin added another log, and the flames leaped brighter, and the wood hissed.

"I can, uh, keep you company." Drew took a deep breath. "I'll work for a night's room and board." Anyway, he probably couldn't sleep. As the long, dark, cold night and the reality of his situation closed in, he rubbed his temples because his nagging headache had crept back.

"No, really, I'll be fine." Erin waved him off. "You can go to bed."

"Let me tend the fire." Mitch stirred the embers.

"Go get some sleep." Brian pointed toward the hallway. "We'll take shifts until the power turns on."

Just then, footsteps padded down the hallway, and sleepy-faced Noah and his cousins appeared in the living room doorway, greeted by the dogs jumping and wagging.

Noah ran shivering to Erin's open arms. "Mommy, I'm freezing."

The kids cuddled by the fire with their parents. Even though the rest of the house cooled, the crackling flames kept the living room warm enough for now.

Meanwhile, Gayle found blankets to cure their

chills.

"You'll be warmer soon." Erin soothed them and tucked the blanket tighter under Noah's chin.

"We'll make you three a cozy bed right in front of the fire like a campout in the living room." Brian headed for the bedroom. "I'll get your pillows."

"Is everybody camping in the living room? Are Grandma and Grandpa? Are you?" Noah pointed at Drew.

"Uh, no, I won't stay by the fire. I'll put on my jacket and sleep downstairs on the sofa."

"Aw." Noah scrunched his face into a frown.

"Why not?" Luc shivered and yawned at the same time.

"Uh…" Drew shifted in the doorway. Maybe his mom or dad should explain.

"Drew's a visitor, so he should have his own room." Erin rubbed Noah's arm and warmed his nose with a palm. "We'll make a family camp here by the fire."

Drew said goodnight and headed downstairs armed with extra blankets. He bundled himself and nestled into the lumpy sofa. "Quite the night, Jake." He stroked the dog's side, taking comfort from his rustling tail.

The chill in the air and taxing evening chased away sleep. He hadn't made a great first impression with Erin. No doubt about it. She was polite but showed only a hint of warmth even during the game. He'd never bask in her wide smiles. If only he could rewind and redo their first meeting. Huffing, he punched his pillow. He couldn't change the past, and now he just had to survive the freezing night. She wanted him to leave as soon as possible, and first thing in the morning, he would grant her wish. He'd never again have to see her or her family.

He rolled over and tucked the blanket around his icy toes. He shut his eyes, and a vision of his dad's weathered face overshadowed Erin's fresh features. Thanks to the weather, plans to visit had fallen through. But his dad probably didn't care. Frank had no idea how much Drew needed a reassuring presence and a confidence boost. Squeezing tight his eyes against his worries, he yanked the covers over his empty chest, high enough to cover his cold nose. Uncertainty threatened, and he better soon find a way to get his life on track.

****

Erin and her family spread blankets in front of the fireplace. She created a fun adventure for the kids, but in the chilly darkness, she shivered. If the wood supply dwindled, they could join the dogs in the warm kennel. Daylight would help bring peace of mind, but right now, morning stretched forever away.

Erin and Claire settled the kids with Sam and took the first shift to tend the fire. They sat in silence until their sleeping children's even breathing hung in the air.

Claire yawned and hugged her arms around her middle. "Poor Drew. This evening, he really got hit with a dose of family."

"Why poor Drew? He crashed our party." Erin crossed her arms. She forced fun during the game, but overall, she didn't enjoy his company.

"You don't like him." Claire blinked and smothered another yawn.

"You heard him talk about his career. I don't want to spend a minute with a pilot." Erin's equilibrium rocked on rough waves. "Besides, when he arrived with Jake, I didn't appreciate his attitude. He thinks he's somebody special, and his dog is too precious to leave with me, a mere kennel hand." She frowned and hugged the blanket closer around her shoulders.

"He's okay. I found him kind of stiff and reserved." Claire wrapped close her blanket.

"If you ask me, he's standoffish and possibly arrogant." Erin stared at the fire.

"I didn't ask." Claire giggled and jiggled her curls.

"He'll leave tomorrow, and I never have to see him again." Erin squeezed the blanket with both fists. Until tomorrow arrived and she reclaimed her space, she'd count down the minutes. Soon, her relaxed family weekend could resume. She just needed the weather to cooperate and Drew to depart.

Then the lights popped on, spotlighting her point, and she blushed. She shouldn't reflect for a second on the stranger downstairs. "Oh, thank goodness." The furnace rumbled, and she jumped and hugged Claire. "Finally, we can sleep."

They tucked the cousins back in bed in Noah's room and put out the fire before they finally headed to bed. Even with the heat on, as relentless wind and snow pelted the windows, Erin tossed all night. Whenever she drifted off, nagging concerns startled her awake. She forced her eyes shut and rolled to a new position, curling her legs to ease her tense stomach muscles. Hard as she tried, she couldn't block unsettling images of mounting snowbanks, kennel chores, and her unwelcome houseguest.

After spending dinner and the evening together, she barely knew Drew, but one fact glared. As part of the SnoWings daring, aerobatics team, he piloted a jet. Even if he had made a better first impression, his profession marked him with a big, fat X.

Her devastating loss rushed back with crushing force, and she wound tighter her quilt around her arms and shivered. A tragic airplane crash had stolen her beloved husband and Noah's dad. Since the trauma, flying still left her with a dry mouth, queasy stomach, and shaky limbs. She wanted nothing to do with a pilot, and the sooner Drew departed, the better.

Erin woke early to do her kennel rounds, and the wind still gusted in a fury. She threw on jeans and a heavy sweater and peered out the front window. With so much snow plastered to the glass, she could hardly see outside, but the evidence glared. Drew would not be free to leave any time soon. The realization hit like a hard-packed snowball. Until the storm blew over, he was stranded, and they were stuck together.

****

Downstairs, Drew opened his eyes to an audience of two.

Panting and wagging his tail, Jake rested his chin on the edge of the sofa.

Noah stared and shifted from foot to foot.

"Morning, guys." He patted Jake and held out his hand for Noah to high five. "What's up?"

"Do you want to come and play with us?" Noah tugged at the blanket.

"Noah, be quiet." Erin hushed her voice as she tiptoed through the semi-darkness. "Don't wake him. Come upstairs."

"Don't worry. I'm awake." Drew flipped back the covers and sat propped by the pillows. "I'd like to play,

42

Noah, but I need to get my car unstuck and go home."

"Aw, darn." Noah backed up, lifted his arms, and threw down his fists.

Erin stood several feet behind Noah. "If you planned to leave this morning, I have bad news. We're stuck with each other a little longer."

"Are you sure?" Drew switched on the lamp and gathered blankets to fold. He blushed and turned as she glanced at his T-shirt and flannel pajama pants. He needed to dress right away in more suitable attire.

"I'm positive. The visibility is still zero with no sign of the wind and snow letting up." She shrugged and took her son by the hand. "Now, come with me, Noah. You can play with Luc and Anna. The basement is Drew's bedroom, so we should give him some privacy."

Drew lifted a hand to his warm face. Labelling the space his bedroom transformed it into a far-too-intimate space to share with a woman he hardly knew. Alarm pinched his temples. Even if he had to fight the weather, he desperately needed to escape.

Chapter 4

Drew let Jake outside and inhaled a sharp blast of snowy air. Erin predicted right. The storm still raged, dumping snow and reducing visibility.

Within two minutes, the dog yipped to be let inside.

He grabbed the towel on the hook by the door and wiped Jake's snowy fur and feet. Then he joined the family in the kitchen.

"Good morning, Drew." Claire cracked eggs. "I guess you'll be here for a while."

He breathed the rich aroma of coffee and maple bacon, and hunger growled in his stomach. He'd eat breakfast and then leave. "Oh, I won't let a little bad weather stop me." He only had to endure being on edge with strangers a few more minutes. He hung back while the others bustled, slicing fruit, buttering toast, and setting the table.

"We won't let you depart until you can travel safely." Gayle smiled and touched his arm. "The weather might improve later today."

"The sooner the better." He clenched tight his jaw. "You've put up with my company long enough." He needed to break out of this stormy trap.

Brian handed him a flipper. "You can make pancakes."

"I'm not much of a cook. You're sure you trust

44

me?" Drew closed his fist in a vise grip around the handle. On top of work and storm stress, he didn't need pressure to perform in the kitchen.

"I have complete confidence in you." Brian slapped him on the back. "Believe me, if you can fly a Tutor jet in tight formation, you can flip a pancake. By the way, those bubbles on top mean you better flip now." He pointed at the pan.

"Okay, here goes." Drew couldn't handle another SnoWings crack. Tension shot from his shoulders to his temples, and uncertainty pinched his forehead. Ever since the *incident*, spending time around his SnoWings teammates produced the same band of tension. He flipped a pancake, and it flopped on an angle, smearing batter on the side of the pan.

"You'll learn. Practice makes perfect." Brian poured coffee.

Drew grimaced, and despite the hubbub reverberating, concentrated on his cooking assignment. He just needed to finish the task, eat, and run.

"Are you having fun?" Mitch grinned and raised his coffee mug. "I like your good effort."

Drew wiped his forehead. "Well, not exactly." The packed, steamy kitchen smothered with action from six adults cooking, three kids popping in and out, and two dogs panting. If he wasn't so hot and busy, he might laugh. He'd never lived anything like this chaos.

"After breakfast, do you want to play hide-and-seek?" Noah tapped on Drew's left hip and grinned.

Luc nodded, and his eyes lit.

Erin stepped near the waiting children. "First, let's have breakfast." She steered the kids toward the table. "You three hungry monsters better eat, and then we'll play a game."

All talking at once, everyone gathered around the table and loaded their plates with scrambled eggs, bacon, fruit, and pancakes.

Drew chewed slowly and swallowed. He sat back in his chair, and the rungs poked his stiff back. He sat forward, took a bite of egg, and glanced at Erin, smiling until she met his gaze. No doubt, she didn't appreciate his company.

"Nothing better on a cold morning than a full breakfast to stick to your ribs." Brian speared another pancake. "Hey, check out the shape. Drew made us an airplane."

"Where is it? Let me see." Noah leaned over to examine his grandpa's plate. "Oh, cool."

Drew chuckled. "You give me too much credit, Brian." Just when he thought he was in the clear, he had to deal with another mention of flying. Tension grabbed his shoulders, leaping to his temples. He needed to escape. "But you're right, those flaps do resemble wings."

Erin clattered her fork and stared at her plate.

Even his gold-medal shot last night had not endeared him to his hostess, but he wasn't here to make new friends. He just had to tolerate the situation a little longer. As long as the weather cooperated, he'd leave soon. "Thank you for feeding me again and letting me stay." Drew swiped a bite of pancake around his plate to soak up syrup.

"You're welcome." Erin sipped her coffee and scanned the table.

"You didn't have much of a choice." His words hung in the air with the scent of buttery toast.

"We didn't want to force you to build an igloo." Brian laughed and spooned more eggs onto his plate.

"Or make you sleep with the dogs out in the kennel." Mitch raised an eyebrow and cracked a crooked smile.

"If this storm doesn't blow over before bedtime, I might consider that idea tonight." Erin tapped her fork and tilted her head.

Drew winced and laughed, but her humor stung. She didn't need to remind him she'd be happy to say good-bye. If the jabs kept up, he'd need a painkiller.

"Sounds like you better figure out how to get on her good side, Drew." Brian furrowed his bushy, gray eyebrows and crunched a bite of bacon.

"Any and all tips welcome." Drew scanned the group, absorbing the joking spirit.

"We'll talk later." Mitch flashed him a thumbs-up and nabbed another pancake. "How should we spend our snow day?"

"You mean, after we dig out the dog runs?" Erin wiped a syrup drip off Noah's chin.

"Oh, right. You invited us here to work." Mitch stretched his face into an exaggerated, fake frown.

"Hey, I actually welcomed your charming company, or I should say Claire's charming company. But the promise of a little work might have sealed the deal." Erin smiled and stood to clear the table.

Their good-natured ribbing was foreign. Drew only knew strained relationships with step siblings.

"Tell you what." Brian gathered a stack of dishes. "The guys will handle kitchen cleanup while you three women relax in the living room." He slid back his chair. "You deserve a break. Afterward, we'll head to the kennels and decide if shoveling makes sense while the weather's still so wild."

Drew gathered plates to clear the table. At least, working would pass the time and keep his mind off the *incident*. If he was stuck here, he'd keep busy.

A few minutes later, the men joined the women in the living room.

"We finished in record time. The men know how to tackle a mess." Mitch jammed his thumbs into his chest.

"I taught you well." Gayle smiled and rolled her eyes at Erin and Claire.

"Too bad you didn't teach him modesty." Erin raised her eyebrows.

"Zing." Mitch jumped and grinned. "Good one, sis."

Drew stiffened at the friendly jab and banter between sister and brother. He didn't know how to handle family fun, and he needed to get away. He pointed at the two dogs, panting and wagging their tails. "I can't refuse the invitation. How about if I take these two for a quick outing? I'll trek out to my car, check the road, and meet you at the kennel."

"You don't need to come and work." Erin zipped her jacket.

"I want to pitch in." Drew meant it. He liked the way her face brightened and broke into a smile. She worked hard, and he didn't mind exercising the dogs and shoveling a little snow in exchange for room and board. He needed to pass the time somehow.

The snowdrifts piled as high as his hips, and he trudged along with Sam and Jake bounding over snowbanks. The snow and wind showed no sign of slowing down, so he couldn't share the dogs' carefree joy. His breath puffed out in frosty clouds, and within minutes, he transformed into a lumpy, snow creature. Snow surrounded and coated his car even deeper than last evening and dashed any hope of going anywhere on wheels this morning. He kicked a snowbank and slogged toward the house.

He had planned a weekend away to give himself a break from work, time to reflect, and talk to his dad about issues they had avoided for too long. Instead, in the company of strangers, he had to fight the weather, as well as his inner demons.

He left the two snowy dogs in the house to warm their paws and joined Erin, Mitch, and Brian at the kennel. They worked in pairs to dig out the outdoor runs but soon realized their efforts were futile. As quickly as they shoveled, the snow and wind erased their efforts.

"I'm warm now anyway." Brian tossed another scoop of snow outside a stall, and most of it blew right back.

"Okay, guys, I vote we quit and shovel later." Erin straightened to catch her breath.

"Haven't seen weather this bad in thirty years." Brian shook his head.

"I've never seen anything like this storm." Mitch leaned on his shovel.

"Weather doesn't get much worse." Drew patted a hyperactive Springer spaniel. Shoveling didn't ease his taut shoulders or racing worries. When would the snow and wind stop so he could go home?

"Since we can't work, maybe we can give the dogs some playtime." Erin showed the men how she took small groups of compatible dogs outside into the large fenced area to romp free. With their fur coats and abundant energy, the dogs weren't bothered by the weather at all.

Drew laughed at the antics of the different breeds leaping, rolling, and transforming their coats to snowy white. He could use a shot of their joy.

"Well, we must be close to lunch and nap time. What do you say, boss?" Brian tugged on Erin's scarf.

"I like the title. I might let you have the afternoon off." Erin pointed and shook her head. "You two, I'm not so sure."

Drew groaned with Mitch and chuckled. She teased him. Maybe he could handle a few more hours here. A sliver of tension dissolved in his shoulders.

The four workers trudged away from the kennel toward the blurred house.

As they approached, Gayle opened the back door and called through the wind. "Have you seen the kids?"

Drew paused, and his pulse tripped. If the kids were outside in the cold and wind, Erin would not be pleased.

Erin increased her pace until her mom's smile and exaggerated side-to-side and up-and-down searching motions tipped the game.

"Lousy joke, Gayle." Brian clomped up the back steps.

"You had me." Drew clapped his gloved hands together to knock off the snow.

"We're just playing hide-and-seek. I guess they're not out here." Gayle raised her voice. "Brrr. Come in and close the door. The weather's not fit for humans."

****

Erin stepped inside, stomping snow off her boots. She laughed at the lively game. Her spunky mom was a huge help with cooped-up kids.

Gayle hurried off in the direction of a trio of giggles.

"Here we are, Grandma," Noah called. "Come find us."

A few minutes later, Gayle joined Erin and Claire in the kitchen. "I let Grandpa, Mitch, and Drew take over hide-and-seek so I could help get lunch ready."

"What do you think of your surprise houseguest?" Gayle patted Erin's arm.

"Pilots are hot." Claire answered first and tucked a blonde curl behind her ear. "Of course, I'm not in the market."

Erin winced. Her family should know by now she shunned airplanes and pilots.

"Oh, Erin, I'm sorry. I didn't think before I spoke." Claire raised her hands for an instant to cover her face and then squeezed Erin's arm.

"You didn't mean any harm." Erin stood, took deep breaths, and stared at the curtain of white out the window. She loaded a basket of buns and caught her mom and Claire exchanging glances. They were concerned, and they meant well pointing out other men existed, but they didn't realize her healing continued. Fond memories and new responsibilities enriched her days. She hugged her arms around her middle and hunched her shoulders. She didn't need any man, let alone a pilot.

Gayle placed a hand on Erin's back. "Should I call the men and kids for lunch?"

She nodded, and soon everyone gathered for

another family meal. She served steaming bowls of minestrone soup and inhaled the savory aroma of basil and oregano. Warm buns and thick slices of sharp cheddar cheese rounded out the hearty noon meal.

"Can we have macaroni instead?" Noah scrunched up his nose and slid his bowl away.

"Macaroni, macaroni, macaroni." Two eager cousins chanted and clanged their spoons.

"Not today but maybe tomorrow. No, show your nice manners." Erin shook her head and tapped her index finger on the table.

Frowning, Noah dipped a spoon into the soup.

"You, too." Mitch pointed at Luc and Anna and furrowed his eyebrows.

Drew's gaze flitted from person to person. "You have your hands full with this place." He tipped his head toward the kennel.

"I chose the business." Erin glared and spit out the words. "I love my work." He had a lot of nerve questioning her career choice.

"I can tell." Drew stared at his soup. "I, uh, didn't mean to suggest otherwise."

"Another bun?" Erin passed the basket. Her appetite ruined, she slid aside her half-full bowl.

Drew reached for another bun. "But do you have help? I mean, besides this capable crew." He swept his arm across her family in a semi-circle.

"You called Mitch capable? Don't flatter him." Claire gave her husband a playful nudge.

"Hey, you stayed inside while I dug." Mitch swiped a hand across his forehead and slumped.

"Somebody had to hold the fort here." Claire smiled and sipped a mouthful of soup.

"Hey, I heard you say fort." Noah set his spoon in his bowl and raised both arms in a cheer. "We can make a fort after lunch."

"Yes, I usually have help." Erin twisted her napkin, justifying her defensive response. "My two employees work part-time. They handle early mornings, evenings, and weekends. But in my dubious wisdom, I gave them both time off this weekend."

"Even with help, you handle a big load." Drew lifted a steaming spoonful of soup.

Erin dabbed Noah's chin. Drew's opinions didn't matter. She managed her busy life, and he should mind his own business. "The kennel work is challenging but nothing I can't handle."

Drew stared at his bowl. "Of course." He clamped his mouth.

After lunch was finished, Brian and Gayle disappeared for a nap.

Followed by Jake, Drew wandered downstairs to read.

Noah and his cousins tore the blankets off their beds to build a fort.

Erin settled with Claire in the living room for a few minutes of quiet time while Mitch started the fire.

"How are you holding up, sis?" Mitch stretched and yawned.

"I'm fine. Why do you ask?" She bit her lip. She couldn't fool her brother, but she still made an attempt.

"Drew isn't your favorite person." Mitch stroked his chin.

"Is my dislike obvious? I put on a pleasant face." Erin flashed an exaggerated smile. Of course, she wanted to be polite, but she didn't need a stranger questioning her capacity to combine motherhood with the kennel operation. Drew deserved to know that he overstepped his bounds.

"Hey, you forget I grew up with you. I know your not-pleased face." Her brother rolled his eyes.

"I didn't appreciate his comments at lunchtime. He questioned whether I can handle my business." She nearly added, "Like the rest of you." Instead, she took a deep breath and twisted a clump of hair.

"Could you have possibly misinterpreted his intent?" Claire smothered a yawn and curled her legs beside her on the sofa.

"Anything's possible but not likely." Erin crossed her arms. The churning lump inside reinforced her opinion.

They sat in silence for a few minutes while Mitch dozed.

Claire knitted, focusing on rapid stitches.

Staring at the fire, Erin replayed the lunch-time conversation. She had seldom met anyone as skeptical as Drew, and he definitely rubbed her the wrong way. She gritted her teeth and switched on the weather to check the latest report.

The announcer droned and pointed to a weather map. "This storm is expected to continue into tomorrow afternoon. If you need a tow truck, expect to wait at least twenty-four hours."

When she heard the bad news, she clicked her tongue in disgust. She ran her fingers through her hair and clenched a clump. The storm would keep Drew stranded here until at least tomorrow. Erin switched off the TV, breathed the calming wood scent, and savored the peaceful crackle. The kids' happy voices faded, and even the dogs vanished. She investigated, and sure enough, the kids abandoned their bedroom fort, so she circled to the stairs.

Partway down, she paused and gripped the handrail. Drew's murmur and Noah's, Luc's, and Anna's excited chatter could mean nothing but trouble. What on earth were they up to? At the bottom of the stairs, she squinted and peered at a flurry of activity.

In the open area by the sofa, Drew and the kids tugged and heaved cushions and blankets into a lumpy contraption anchored by chairs.

Was the creation another fort? Not a fort. She squinted to discern the shape then sauntered over for a closer view. Heart racing, she forced a casual tone. "Hi, guys. What's up? What did you make?"

"Oh, hi." Drew glanced down.

"We made an airplane, Mommy." Noah bounced up and down. "Drew helped us build an airplane."

Sure enough, a crude jet shape stretched across the room. She bit her lip so hard it hurt. "Well, what a surprise. What will Drew instigate next?" She sliced the basement air with a satisfying shot of sarcasm. Concern somersaulted in her stomach, and her face burned. She needed to stop this nonsense immediately.

"We'll go for a ride soon, Auntie Erin." As she circled the project, Anna bobbed her blonde curls.

"We all get to take turns being the pilot." Luc's dark eyes gleamed, and he flipped a blanket over the tail cushion.

"Yeah, Drew will show us how." Noah clapped his hands.

"Oh, will he now?" Erin placed her hands on her hips. She couldn't believe Drew's nerve. He had no business even being in her home, and now he had the audacity to interest her son in airplanes. Of course, she couldn't expect him to read her mind and respect her phobia without knowing the details. Silently seething, she surveyed the situation and reined in her overreaction. "You said you planned to read down here." She crossed her arms but softened her voice.

"I read until this crew visited. I wanted to keep them busy for a while and maybe give you a little down time."

Staring, she flattened her lips into a thin line. "Thank you. But I don't need time away from my life."

"Want to ride in our plane, Mommy?" Noah bounced and flapped a corner of the blanket.

Drew shook his head, crossed his arms, and shifted. "Sorry. I didn't mean to offend." He swept his gaze over the three excited kids and back.

She clutched her middle where annoyance screamed. "Um, tell you what…you go for a ride with Drew, Luc, and Anna, and I'll stand and wave."

"Mommy…please…come with us…" Noah bounced and waved her closer, his exuberance overflowing.

"Okay, okay, just one short ride, and we'll go find Grandma and Grandpa for a game." She shuddered as she forced a step forward. The sooner she ended the activity, the better.

"Captain Noah, you're the pilot. Sit here." Drew pointed to the front chair.

Erin's mouth dried to dust, and her limbs wilted into spaghetti. She took deep breaths and pressed damp palms on her thighs. She shouldn't react with horror to a game of make-believe. Her own basement and furniture surrounded her. Cushions and blankets shaped a pretend airplane. Still, the pounding in her chest didn't ease no matter what she told herself.

"Anna, you can be the co-pilot this time." Drew pointed to a spot beside Noah. "Now, we'll load the rest of the passengers. Luc, sit here. Your auntie can sit beside you, and I'll sit right there at the back."

Erin stepped into the seat over the wing and bit her lower lip. How *dare* he? After one short ride, she would entice the kids to another activity away from Drew and his poor example.

Before she could gracefully lure the kids upstairs, she heard footsteps approaching.

Mitch sauntered in. He yawned, stretched, and chuckled at the foreign object in the centre of the basement. "Hey, you guys are flying high. Can I come for a ride? Zoom." Mitch waved and added loud sound effects.

"Captain Noah, land the plane, and Uncle Mitch can have my spot." Erin jumped out. She lowered her voice and blurted strict instructions. "Keep an eye on things, and as soon as you can, get them interested in something else." She gulped deep breaths, escaped up the steps, and fought to clear her mind of flying images. Real or pretend airplanes caused pain, and so did pilots. No matter what, she needed to steer clear.

****

Drew waited with his head down, staying out of the way while Erin made her quick exit. Her cheeks still glowed from the morning outside, and her hair curled in random places from being squished in a hat. Her natural appearance made his pulse skitter.

He and Mitch took multiple, pretend flights with

the kids. Funny, how different siblings could be. Unlike his touchy sister, Mitch let loose and had a good time. Without warning, she flipped a switch, sometimes smiling and sometimes glaring. Tension vibrated through the room, all because of an innocent game. Maybe Mitch could enlighten him later.

"Okay, guys, time to land." Mitch leaned left and right. "We're running out of gas. Can you thank Drew for playing airplane?"

As he helped the kids climb out, Drew held up his hand for high fives.

"Did you know Drew flies real planes? He's a jet pilot." Mitch gathered blankets and cushions.

The band of tension around Drew's head tightened. Of course, playing airplane landed him right in the middle of more SnoWings talk.

"Wow, flying is cool." Noah paused and flapped the corner of a blanket. "My daddy flew airplanes. Will you take us for a real plane ride?"

Noah's dad was a pilot. He snapped his head to look at Mitch. Naturally, a son would share his dad's interest. Why had Erin rejected a simple, airplane game?

"Oh, please, will you?" Luc clapped.

"A jet ride would be cool, but we can't just invite ourselves onto Drew's jet." Mitch tugged the blanket from Noah and folded it.

Drew gathered cushions and shook his head. "Uh…jet rides are really fun. I wish I could take you, but only grownups can ride in the jets I fly."

"Aw, maybe when I'm a grownup, will you take me?" Noah stood on tiptoe.

"Oh, I'm not sure." Drew scanned the room for

anything that still needed tidying. Erin wouldn't appreciate a mess. "Noah's dad was a pilot?"

"Yeah, he flew a crop duster." Mitch tucked cushions onto the sofa.

So, Noah knew the fact. He gritted his teeth. As an aerial sprayer, he would have flown a small aircraft at low altitude over farmers' fields. Maybe Erin hadn't liked his risky work. Still, she had been married to the guy, and her son loved airplanes, so the game shouldn't have caused any harm. She puzzled him, and he had to fill in the missing pieces.

"Let's go find Auntie Erin. She wants to play a different game. Want to join us, Drew?" Mitch shooed the kids upstairs.

"Sure, in a few minutes. First, I should call my dad." Drew longed to hear his dad lament the missed visit and to know deep down he belonged somewhere, and someone cared. After three rings, the phone clicked to voice mail. His dad probably didn't even miss him. The plan to get together this weekend had been Drew's idea, not his dad's. He'd probably been kidding himself to believe an in-person visit would change anything. In a weekend, he couldn't smooth thirty years of a rocky relationship. He sighed and didn't bother to leave a message.

He cradled his head in his hands, worked his fingers through his hair, and massaged in slow, circular motions. Disappointment chilled him like the weather. Now, he had to again face his unpredictable hostess.

Erin flowed among multiple roles: mother and kennel director; animal handler and hostess; and outside laborer and chef. She balanced a huge load, but he could have bitten his tongue. Clearly, his innocent business questions rubbed her the wrong way. He admired her determination, but too bad, they'd never be friends.

Chapter 5

Erin answered her tenth call of the day. Another anxious client couldn't drive through the storm to pick up his dog. "Don't worry. Your dog is warm and safe here. He's just fine." Business details were easier to handle than Drew. She shook her arms free of tension and joined her family in the living room.

Claire flipped through CDs, humming while she worked.

Mitch and Brian cleared space for the afternoon dance party. After nearly twenty-four hours cooped up in the house, the kids buzzed with energy to burn.

Gayle stretched her arms wide and gazed into the white haze outside the front window. "I can't even see the gate. We might be stranded here 'til spring."

"Good thing we like each other." Erin flopped on the couch across from the crackling fire. Of course, she didn't mean Drew.

"Speak for yourself." Dodging a blue cushion Erin tossed, Mitch chuckled.

Gayle laughed. "Your behavior reminds me of when you were eight and ten."

"Some things never change." Her throat closed. If only some things hadn't changed. Erin had embraced her perfect life with Eric in Moose Jaw. Her high school sweetheart, he charmed her from the day they met until the day he died. Without him, life would never be the same. Before anyone could notice, she blinked her watery eyes.

Grinning, Mitch lobbed a return cushion.

Just in time, she caught it.

Hands in his pockets, Drew hesitated in the doorway. "Mind if I join you?"

Erin stiffened and inhaled the comforting smell of burning wood.

"By all means." Brian waved him into the room. "You don't need an invitation. This weekend, you're part of the family."

"Good timing to help us tear up the dance floor." Mitch struck a disco pose.

"Uh…no thanks. I'll just watch. I'm not much of a dancer." Drew shook his head, and his face flushed light pink.

"Don't worry. Neither's Erin." Mitch ducked another flying cushion.

"Darn, I missed. Oh, brother. Why didn't I have a sister?" Erin smiled and leaped off the sofa. "I want to see who has the best dance moves."

Gayle lifted her leg, put her foot on the coffee table, and stretched.

"What about you, Drew? Do you have any brothers or sisters?" Gayle pointed her toe.

"I have a half one of each. My parents divorced. Then Dad remarried and had a daughter, and Mom remarried and had another son. We never get together. We're not very close."

"You must find the distance…difficult." Gayle wrinkled her forehead and wrung her hands.

"I'm used to our family dynamics." Drew shrugged and crossed his arms. "Being on my own is just normal."

Gayle stretched her other leg and blinked a few times. "Oh, I suppose."

Erin tugged her heartstrings back into place. Drew had a broken family and no real siblings. He must be lonely, but maybe his skeptical manner offended others, too. She blasted the music and rounded up the kids.

"Noah, Luc, and Anna…are you ready?" One last time, Gayle flexed. The whole family sprang into action, twisting and shaking.

As Noah boogied by, Drew shifted in his chair and signaled a thumbs-up.

"Dance, Drew. You should dance, too." Noah jiggled his arms and legs.

"Uh… I don't know…" Drew planted his hands on his knees and shook his head.

In the centre of the room, Brian and Gayle jived, dipping and swirling.

"Noah's right." Brian spun Gayle. "Dancing is good for the soul."

Noah took Drew by the hand and swung to the beat of the music.

Still, he resisted, slipping away his hand and clapping.

Erin bent her knees deep into the twist, tipped her head back, and batted her eyelids. She almost felt sorry for Drew shifting awkwardly in his chair and refusing to participate. Well, he could deal with his own discomfort, and she wouldn't let him ruin her fun.

"Don't be a party pooper, Drew." Mitch clasped Claire's hands, faced her, and spun into the turn-the-dishes-over jive step.

Jake and Sam barked, wagged, and wove in and

out.

The phone rang again, and Erin shimmied out of the room. She'd make the best of a bad situation, but she couldn't stand the tension for long.

****

Luc and Anna skipped over to tug on Drew's other hand, and he finally gave in. Never in a million years would he have predicted he'd sit on the fringes of a family dance party, let alone swing into action. He dredged up inspiration from the music and the others' frenzied movements, and ice crystals beat time on the window.

He shifted from foot to foot, bent his elbows, and snapped his fingers. He wouldn't win a contest, but his rhythm wasn't too bad. He hopped from foot to foot and clapped. Why hold back? Soon, he alternated between digging potatoes and thrashing a butterfly swim stroke.

Erin danced into the room, tipped her head back, and laughed.

He shook loose and, finally, let the tension in his head and shoulders dissolve. Raising both hands in the air, he clapped and swayed. He hadn't had so much fun in ages…since before the *incident* anyway. From the instant he caused the terrifying near-miss in the air, a gray hue dulled his life and shaded everything more serious and less fun. Maybe he could eventually recover, but he had a long way to go.

"Follow me." Brian led a conga line in a circle around the living room, down the hallway, through each bedroom, into the kitchen, and around the dining room table.

Erin kicked her long legs from side to side, her trim

figure outlined in jeans and a fitted white sweater.

Drew glanced at her, gulped air, and turned. Her fresh beauty glowed and tempted dangerously. He couldn't let her distract him from more important issues.

The group danced and laughed until one by one, they sank hot and exhausted into chairs or onto the floor beside the dogs.

Erin filled a pitcher and served glasses of ice water to quench their thirst.

"Whew, I just finished a tough workout." Gayle fanned herself with a hand. Her face beamed magenta.

"Who says you can't dance, Drew? Apparently, flying isn't your only talent." Mitch wiped his forehead and guzzled a full glass of water.

"Don't give me too much credit." Drew shook his head and held his cold glass to his hot cheek. He appreciated the family's enthusiasm, but his dancing needed work. As for his flying talent, he definitely didn't need another reminder his skills wavered. The nagging ache returned to pulse in his head. He needed to rebuild his shaky confidence and the team's trust. Only then would he succeed with the SnoWings.

Finally, only Noah twirled through the room. He raised his arms to shoulder level and zipped around, tilting left and right. "I'm flying. Watch me fly." He spun in circles until he fell into a dizzy heap. "Come and save me. I crashed."

Instantly, Erin paled white as a snowbank.

Drew took a sharp breath and waited. Glances flew among the family members, conversation stopped, and thick silence fell.

Noah sprawled and waved his arms. "Mommy,

Drew wants to take me in his jet."

"I…" Drew raised his eyebrows, held up both hands, and shook his head. She shouldn't blame him for Noah's ideas.

Erin glared, dropped the pitcher on the coffee table, and fled.

He earned another strike against him, yet he did nothing wrong. More than ever, he needed to get away. Now, what could he do to eliminate the strain?

****

Mitch leaned on his shovel to catch his breath. "You're probably wondering about the elephant in the room." He paused and puffed out a frosty sigh.

The three men volunteered to clear a path to the kennel so they could give the dogs some late-afternoon attention. This time, they convinced Erin to stay warm and left her in the kitchen chopping vegetables for dinner.

"We dance a lot around the subject." Frost tinged Brian's gray eyebrows. "Today, we danced literally."

Drew tossed a shovelful of snow and paused to listen.

"Eric…her husband…" Brian stared into the distance. "Late in the evening before dark, Eric took off to aerial spray a section of crops. He might've lost sight of the horizon or dozed off for an instant. He had worked several sixteen-hour days. Anyway, for whatever reason, he crashed."

"Oh, no, not a crash." The revelation hit Drew harder than the blizzard pounding the prairie. As the memory of the *incident* pummeled him, he pushed it away and swallowed a wave of nausea. Despite the cold, under his parka perspiration dampened his shirt.

Mitch forced out a cloud of air. "The plane broke apart and burst into flames. Inspectors recently checked the mechanics, so they were pretty sure the equipment worked fine."

"Yep, the investigation concluded pilot error caused the crash." Brian shook his head, and snowflakes showered off his hat. "The disaster shocked and devastated the whole family."

"You know the risks." Mitch adjusted his flannel face-warmer.

"Yeah, I never forget." Drew took a deep breath of the frosty air. "Mistakes happen so fast up there." A chill, deeper than the bone-numbing cold weather, stabbed him between the shoulder blades. Pilot error stole Erin's husband and transformed her into a single mother. Eric's mistake cost his life and robbed his son of a father. A plane crash rocked Erin's world. "I'm sorry." He didn't know what else to say. He jammed his shovel into a drift, kept down his head, and with a fury, threw snow as far as he could, again and again.

Before they entered the kennel, Brian tapped his arm. "Don't mention this conversation. Erin doesn't like to talk about the crash, and she definitely doesn't want sympathy."

"I understand." He gulped the frigid air. They'd be shocked at how well he understood.

****

The dogs were fed and watered, the kids were tucked in, and the fire crackled. If only the storm would end, Erin's unwanted houseguest could leave, and she could enjoy a perfect, relaxing evening. She scanned the peaceful scene with Claire and Gayle knitting, Brian and Drew reading, and Mitch flipping through a magazine.

Sam stretched out, soaking up the heat from the fire while Jake dropped a ball at Drew's feet.

"Not now, boy. Go lie by Sam." Drew patted Jake's head and flipped a page.

Erin checked the TV weather forecast, and hope glimmered for the first time since the storm struck. The snow should taper off and winds die down by tomorrow afternoon. If the forecast proved accurate, this time tomorrow, Drew would depart forever. She just had to tolerate his presence a little while longer.

"What should we do this evening?" Brian flipped his book on his lap.

"What about playing cards, watching a movie, or playing a game?" Mitch tossed his magazine aside.

Drew kept reading. "Whatever you want to do is fine."

"Okay, talk over options and decide." Erin stood. "I'll be back soon, but I could use a breath of fresh air, so I'll run Sam to the gate and back."

"Jake and I'll come." Drew set aside his book.

Erin froze. She craved a few, peaceful minutes alone. Walking beside Drew wouldn't give her a break.

"He's a bit restless." Drew patted his dog and stood.

Oh, darn. She needed quiet time, not another Drew encounter. "I guess so." Unfortunately, her icy tone didn't deter his interest.

Drew bundled up in his jacket and boots and followed her out the door.

They tromped down the front path, now barely a dip in the white fluff piling up in every direction, while Sam and Jake leaped, rolled, and zigzagged.

"Joy in motion." Erin pointed and laughed at the snowy pair.

"Lucky pooches don't have a care in the world." Drew clomped a jagged track in his large boots.

Did the wind distort his voice or did she detect a slight waver when he referenced the carefree dogs? She took deep breaths of the frosty air and cooled her burning tension. Images of Noah whirling with excitement around his grandpa, uncle, and Drew bombarded her. The men were everything she could never be. Hard as she worked to be the perfect mother, she could never be a male role model. She and Noah shared a happy life, but she couldn't fill the gap where Noah's dad belonged. When Noah had insisted on sitting beside Drew at dinner and told him he wanted to be a pilot, too, Erin wanted to scream, "Never." Instead, she swallowed her horror with a bite of chicken and had glared at Drew, the poor influence. She shook her head free of the disturbing scene.

"I'm sorry." Drew's words nearly blew away.

"Pardon me?" Erin stepped closer to hear.

"I need to apologize." Drew cleared his throat.

"For what?" She stomped past the dog play area. He should apologize for interrupting their family time, intriguing her son, and being a pilot. She could list many things for which he should apologize, but she wouldn't offer suggestions to make his apology easy.

"I never should have doubted you could take care of Jake. You run this place like an expert with a lot of care and attention, probably more than Ray."

The wind whipped his labored breath, and his words rumbled low and sincere. Her companion couldn't be the same skeptical man she met only twenty-four hours ago, now eating a rather large serving of humble pie. "Apology accepted. I'm glad you see I do work hard and take good care of the dogs."

Erin lowered her eyelids against the stinging wind. "These past couple of months, I've learned a lot, and I want to make my business even better. I have plenty of ideas, but one thing at a time. First, I need to retain all Ray's clients."

Drew stopped and faced her, his dark eyes burning. "I'm interested in your business ideas, but hold on. You didn't let me finish. I want to clarify…"

Erin stretched her flannel face-warmer higher over her nose and avoided his intense gaze. Her frustration still percolated, but she listened. He deserved her attention.

Drew thumped his chest with a gloved fist. "I'm in the way. I changed your family weekend and don't mean to ruin your time together."

Erin nodded and steadily trekked around the yard. He had read her mind. She didn't want him here. His presence overshadowed her family visit, but she couldn't agree and make him feel worse. "You don't have a choice. You're trapped. I don't blame you for the weather, and my family likes you."

"Your parents and brother are very friendly, fun, and warm. But I'll stay out of the way as best I can." He stepped over a drift, leaned right, and bumped her side. "Oops, sorry." He laughed. "Obviously, avoiding you is easier said than done."

Erin trudged along. "Do me a favor, though." She finally had a chance to end the airplane talk and rein in Noah's expectations. "Don't give Noah any more ideas about a plane ride. I will never give him permission."

"Of course not. I would never... at least, I didn't mean to suggest I would ever take him on a flight. He might have misunderstood." Drew swung his arms like pendulums coated with snow.

"Whatever you did to grab his interest, I need you to stop." Erin's words pierced the wind, and she swung forward her palms to reinforce her point. The frustration and anxiety simmering since Drew's arrival nearly boiled over on the spot.

"Don't worry. I understand," said Drew.

She would make sure he understood. Her throat ached and grabbed. "Noah's dad...my husband...died in a plane crash."

"I'm sorry." Drew exhaled in a shaky whoosh. He swung his arms harder and higher. "You've lived through a rough time."

"Now, we're fine." She trudged in silence for a few paces and then changed the subject. "If the forecast is right, this time tomorrow, you can leave."

"Yep, with any luck at all, I'll soon wave goodbye." He smacked together his fists.

She clenched her jaw and crunched along with surprising compassion for his situation. "Don't worry. So far, we've coped. We'll make the best of the situation." Still, confusion tempted her to shout words she couldn't say. *Stay away from Noah. Why do you have to be a pilot? Quit being so nice because I want to hate you.*

Nearing the house, Drew cleared his throat. "Anyway, thanks for letting me join you for some fresh air and exercise."

"No problem." Maybe she actually meant it. She wrinkled her forehead and shivered.

"We were just about to send out the search party in case you and the critters got buried." Brian greeted them at the door, and his eyes crinkled with his smile. "Your mom's got hot chocolate ready, and we're ready to play charades."

"Oh, Dad, are you serious you want to play charades?" Erin groaned and stomped her snowy boots. With extra vigor, she bent to brush snow off the dogs' coats and paws before they tracked moisture everywhere. Apparently, despite Drew's good intentions, he couldn't avoid her this evening.

****

Another evening of family games loomed. Drew stiffened. He had just promised to give Erin space. "You all play. I'll go downstairs with my book." He'd intruded long enough, and besides, he disliked charades. He hated making a fool of himself in front of other people.

"We'll play boys against the girls. You're with us, Drew." Brian pointed to the sofa where Mitch sat.

"No, thanks, but I'll let you enjoy a family night." Drew retrieved his book off the coffee table and clutched it. The sweet scent of hot chocolate swirled, and the atmosphere in the room closed in.

"Nonsense, you're one of us this weekend. Besides, we need even numbers on the teams." Brian beckoned him closer.

Erin wrinkled her nose, but she joined Gayle and Claire on their side. "You couldn't talk Dad out of charades?"

Both women shook their heads, raised their arms, and threw up their hands.

"Okay, let's get started." Erin shook her head.

"When Dad sets his mind on a game, nobody can argue."

The invisible band around Drew's head tightened. He didn't have a choice. He'd have happily sat on the sidelines, but they wouldn't let him pass. After he survived one more evening of intensive, family togetherness, he would depart to the solitude of his own home. He read his charade and held up six fingers.

"Okay, we need an answer with six words." Mitch shouted. He sat next to Brian on the edge of the sofa, glued to Drew's actions.

"He means an expression...now, third word." Brian slapped his knee.

Drew outlined a large shape and simulated waves. He floated around the room, and Mitch and Brian followed every move.

"I see a boat." Mitch slammed a palm on the arm of the sofa.

"No, try ship." Brian narrowed his eyes.

"You're a fish." Mitch leaned forward, hands on his knees.

Drew laughed and shook his head. Behind him, Erin snorted, and he doubled his effort. He spun and swished an imaginary tail a little harder.

She tipped her head back, giggled, and pointed.

"You're a whale." Brian snapped his fingers.

Drew clapped his hands and pointed at Brian.

"Okay, after whale, what's next?" Mitch slapped his thighs and leaned forward.

"Sixth word." Drew nodded, made a circle with his finger, and pointed to his wrist.

"Looks like an arm," shouted Mitch.

"No, wart." Brian scrunched his face.

Drew wracked his brain for another angle and couldn't contain a grin. He must look ridiculous leaping and gesturing wildly. Shaking his head, he shaped a bigger circle with both arms and pointed to the wall.

"Maybe a piece of art?" Mitch wrinkled his brow and narrowed his eyes.

"A clock," said Brian.

Drew nodded encouragement and motioned to guess again. They'd get the answer any second.

"No, he means time." Brian shouted and leaped to his feet. "Whale...time...whale...time.... an expression..."

"Having a whale of a time." Mitch threw up both arms.

"Yes, good guess, guys." Drew high fived the guys. He sank into a chair and exhaled in an audible rush. Maybe he could relax now that his turn in the spotlight was over.

The women bemoaned the men's winning point.

Calling the game a whale of a time might be a little extreme, but the laughs temporarily shook away his worries. No doubt about the fun. Erin and her family shared a good time together—just like the winning charade described. But a little fun didn't change reality.

He didn't belong, and he needed to leave. Surely, tonight would be the last night he spent on the makeshift bed in the basement.

****

Erin lay in bed and tucked the covers under her chin. She closed her eyes and popped them open. She rolled her back toward Eric's cool, empty place. Drew hadn't interfered with the fun evening, and without Noah trailing and imitating his every move, she didn't mind his company so much.

She flipped and stared at the ceiling. Drew actually apologized, not once but twice. He regretted their rocky start and didn't mean to irritate. Of course, he'd be a first-class fool to intentionally offend his host. She squeezed shut her eyes and the image of his face floated by. His sharp cheek and jaw lines blurred into softer, gentler contours than when they first met. She yawned and pounded her pillow. Tomorrow, she'd keep Noah and him apart, no matter what. Soon the weather would break, Drew would depart, and she could forget he existed.

Chapter 6

The next morning, as Drew wandered upstairs, the air hugged him with the sharp aroma of strong coffee and burnt toast.

Mitch sipped coffee alone at the kitchen table. "Brian and Claire went with Erin to clean the kennel. Gayle's reading to the kids. The dogs are playing outside. Grab a chair and enjoy the peace while it lasts."

Drew peered out the kitchen window, squinted, and nodded. A tiny surge of hope tapped his chest. "I can see more of the yard than yesterday. Is the blizzard finally winding down?" He poured a cup of coffee and sat opposite Mitch. Quick, he needed a neutral topic, almost anything except flying with the SnoWings.

"Sure hope so." Mitch gulped coffee. "If the storm doesn't let up soon, we'll catch cabin fever."

"I shouldn't miss more than a day of work at the base with all the drills to perfect." Drew rubbed his temple. He clenched his mouth shut, his jaw nearly hard as rock. He wanted to avoid the topic, so why did he mention work?

"What does the experience feel like?" Mitch refilled his cup.

Drew scrunched his forehead. He hated to talk about his flying career. "You mean being stranded with total strangers?" He squirmed and swallowed a mouthful of hot coffee, searching for a way to change

76

the subject.

Mitch laughed and slapped a palm on the table. "No, I mean in the jet. When you fly at high speed and perform all those maneuvers, how does the g-force feel?"

"Extreme pressure." Drew closed his eyes, and the familiar walls of the cockpit loomed close enough to suffocate. Funny how the same answer worked for both questions. A weekend with strangers just added a different kind of weight than piloting a jet into aerobatic swoops. "I mean...extreme maneuvers produce the biggest rush ever, of course. But the pressure pounds your body."

"I can only imagine." Mitch set down his mug and sat forward.

"With positive g-force, pressure five times your body weight squashes you. Your face sags. You struggle to hold up your head. You're hammered into the seat. The blood gets sucked out of your brain, and if you don't tense all your muscles just right, you could gray out. You know, before a person passes out, everything turns hazy."

Drew planted both feet on the floor to steady himself as memories rushed back and tricked his equilibrium into sensing the room tilt. Grasping either side of his chair seat, he took a deep breath.

"Wow, sounds pretty intense." Mitch tipped back in his chair.

"Yeah, you're right. You won't find a more incredible, exhilarating experience." Drew sucked in air and blinked to sharpen his vision back into focus. He gripped his coffee mug. "Being upside down−negative gs−is the worst. A giant force nearly yanks you out of the seat."

"You want to make sure your seat belt's on tight." Mitch jerked left.

Drew jumped at the mock turbulence and lurched his back straight. "Definitely." His pulse raced into overdrive, and his armpits oozed. Mitch had no inkling of the complexity SnoWings navigated and the precision every maneuver demanded.

Just then, the back door opened, and the morning kennel crew blew inside.

"Hello. Good morning. We're back." Brian leaned into the kitchen while he removed his boots. "Get the hot coffee ready."

"Morning, Brian, Erin, Claire." The frigid air blasted Drew's equilibrium back to normal. Nothing could match the rush of catapulting through the sky in a SnoWings jet formation, but ever since the *incident*, more pressure than negative gravity crushed his spirit.

Brian, Erin, and Claire joined Drew and Mitch at the table and sipped steaming coffee.

After the short time outside in forty below wind chills, their cheeks and noses glowed red as apples.

Sporting cold noses and damp fur, Sam and Jake circled the kitchen and bumped into each other and the people seated at the table.

"I volunteer for the next shift." Drew patted Jake. He could repay Erin's hospitality and occupy his mind at the same time.

"No, I don't need your help. I mean, thank you, but let's hope the weather improves soon, and you can head home." Erin hugged her arms around her middle.

Hard as he fought to stay in the moment and joke around with the others, Drew couldn't keep his thoughts from drifting back to the cockpit. He raised his hands and pressed on his temples against the tension vibrating through his head. Momentous aerial challenges threatened. "Sorry, pardon me?" Drew sprang back to the present and focused on Brian's question.

"Will you reschedule your trip to your dad's place for another weekend?" Brian stirred milk into his coffee.

"Possibly. I can seldom take time off from training to visit him in Phoenix, but I'd like to discuss some things." Perspiration seeped onto his upper lip, and Drew wiped it with a finger. Why had he mentioned his need to talk with his dad? Surely, no one would ask him to elaborate. He gulped a large mouthful of coffee and wracked his brain for a new topic.

"Phoenix sounds like a nice place to get together. A little warmth would be welcome, especially after this weekend." Brian rubbed together his hands.

"I agree." The weather in Phoenix might be mild, but the warmth in his dad's place didn't compare to Erin's home. Suddenly, motion caught Drew's eye. Just in time, he set down his mug and held out his arms.

"Zoom, zoom, zoom." Noah flew down the hallway, extended his arms, and aimed for Drew's lap. He leaped and hit the target.

Drew caught him, laughed, and glanced at Erin.

Her glare burned. Hard as he tried, he couldn't stay out of trouble.

****

Erin jumped and put a hand on Noah's arm. "Stop this minute."

"I'm okay. I don't mind." Drew bumped his knees

up and down and side to side. "Ready for takeoff?"

"No, jumping on you is wrong. Come, Noah. Let Drew drink his coffee. You can bounce on Grandpa's knee." Her face burned in contrast with the ice cube chilling her heart. Drew was a terrible influence.

Noah should gravitate to his grandpa and uncle, not latch onto a stranger, even if he just liked the novelty of another guy around. Without a dad or father figure in his life, surely he didn't suffer. She rolled her lips together in a thin line. She couldn't let her son bond with someone who flew jets for a living.

"We better listen to your mom, Noah." Drew stopped and straightened his legs.

"Aw, I don't want to stop." Noah scowled and slid to the floor.

"I want a ride, too." Luc stood on one side of Drew.

"Me, too, please." Anna tugged on Drew's shirt.

"Come here, you two. Drew's not a dad, so he's not a human trampoline like Grandpa and me." Mitch jiggled Luc on one knee and Anna on the other.

Noah climbed onto his grandpa's lap.

Erin calmed her jumping heart. Noah belonged safe with his grandpa. With any luck at all, she'd find the weather would soon break, and she wouldn't have to pry apart Noah and Drew much longer. Now, she better dream up an activity to burn the kids' overflowing energy.

Mitch paused his jiggly lap. "Hey, you three could use a little fresh air and exercise. Let's bundle up and go for an arctic trek."

"Cool." Noah shouted and bounced.

His cousins cheered and clapped.

"You said it, buddy. We'll definitely be cool out there." Mitch rolled Luc and Anna onto the floor.

Jake and Sam rushed in, poked them with wet noses, and licked their faces with sloppy tongues.

"Me, too. Me, too." Noah dove to the floor and joined the giggling pile of cousins and panting dogs.

"Sounds like fun." Brian stretched out his legs and rubbed his thighs. "Good idea, but I'll wait inside in the warmth to hear all about your big adventure."

"I always say you can't beat an arctic trek." Erin smirked at Claire and Gayle.

"Yeah, I could use a cold blast. Mind if I join you?" Drew stood, ready to join the action.

Erin's pulse skittered, and she bit her bottom lip. "I'll come, too." She really had no other choice. She needed to keep Drew and Noah apart, where they belonged.

Erin, Mitch, Drew, and the kids all piled on warm clothes.

"You dogs can come, too." Erin ran a hand along Sam's side. "Hey, should we call these hairy creatures reindeer or polar bears?" She opened the door and ushered the kids and dogs outside.

"They're polar bears." Noah hollered and leaned to avoid touching them.

His cousins clapped their mittens.

"Be careful. They eat people, you know." Uncle Mitch swiped his ski gloves like bear paws ready to pounce.

The kids squealed and giggled.

Erin stepped outside and spotted the gate for the first time in two days. The wind gusted with less force, and snow swirled off the roof and tree branches but not from the sky. Her relief exploded. "Woohoo, the storm blew away." She thrust both hands high in the air, and if her parka and chunky boots had allowed, she would have cartwheeled. Instead, she tromped through thigh-high snow. "Woohoo, woohoo, woohoo."

Noah, Luc, and Anna imitated her cheer and waved their arms.

Drew cleared his throat. "I guess I should throw in a woohoo, too."

"Woohoo," Mitch shouted, waved his arms, and jumped into a snowbank.

Erin's houseguest would soon depart. Her worries would end, and she could enjoy the rest of the weekend. She could say goodbye to the irritating outsider, airplane talk, and her frazzled nerves. Under her scarf, she grinned.

"Follow me, everybody." Mitch led the way and stomped loops around the yard.

The rest of the group followed, huffing and puffing as they followed his tracks.

All the while, Jake and Sam zigzagged, romped, and snatched at their mittens.

Erin trooped through the snowdrifts, and her breath whooshed frosty clouds. "Whatever you do, watch out for bears." She wedged herself between Noah and Drew. So far, so good with Noah focused on his uncle, the leader of the arctic expedition.

The group passed imaginary whales, seals, and reindeer. They crawled on ice floes and dodged polar bears. Finally, they arrived at the North Pole and plunked themselves in the snow.

Uncle Mitch scanned the area. "I don't see Santa. I guess he stayed back to watch over the busy elves in his workshop."

He had a great imagination and kept the kids amused. Erin wanted to hug him on the spot. Even Drew cooperated. He stayed in the background, not interfering or grabbing Noah's attention.

Then he stood and fell back into an untouched patch of snow. "Hey, watch me make a snow angel." He lay in the snow and flapped his arms up and down along his sides and spread his legs apart and together. He rocked upright and stepped aside to show off his snow art. Sure enough, he left an outline of a snow angel.

"I want to make a snow angel." Noah tugged on Drew's hand. "Please, will you help?"

Drew glanced at Erin and back at Noah.

She squinted through icy slits. Even though she stood right beside her son, she didn't matter. He sought Drew's assistance with a snow angel. Despite the cold, her temperature rose. She needed to stop Drew's game this instant.

"Come to this clean patch of snow. Now lie back." Drew held Noah's hands until he leaned nearly horizontal and then released. "Now flap your arms." He demonstrated the right technique.

Noah flapped and jumped before Drew finished instructions. "Hey, I made an airplane," he shouted, flinging up his arms.

His exuberance stabbed Erin. She forced a fist against her achy stomach.

Drew stared at the snow and shrugged. "Yeah, I see an airplane."

Noah's eyes glittered between his hat and his scarf.

She needed to stop this foolish talk. Until this

weekend, Noah had never paid much attention to planes, and she hadn't encouraged any interest. Since he'd met Drew, he played airplane games, talked about flying, and made snow airplanes. Maybe he inherited his newfound obsession from Eric, and the presence of another pilot awakened the magic gene. No doubt, Drew caused the problem.

The sudden changes in Noah made no sense. Growing up, she had created hundreds of snow angels with Mitch, and never once did she ever create anything remotely similar to an airplane. Her face radiated hot and cold, and she scowled, hidden by her scarf. "Luc and Anna, let's see you make snow angels."

They fell back, flapped their arms and legs, and jumped to admire their angels.

Mitch fell to his hands and knees and flopped sideways. "How about a snow dog?"

Erin peered at the outline of a four-legged critter. The shape could be a dog or a horse. Thank goodness, it resembled nothing like an airplane. "Try again, Noah. Slide your legs apart this time and make an angel."

"But I like my plane. Hey, stop, Sam." Noah waved away his dog.

Sam crouched with his front paws on the tail of Noah's plane, rolled, and wiggled his back like a giant eraser. By the time he rolled back onto his four paws, he smudged the picture into an uneven patch of snow.

"Hey, you ruined my plane." Noah stomped and flailed at Sam.

The dog just wagged his tail, shook, and sprayed him with snow.

Noah's shouts faded to a wail.

"Good pup." Erin's muttered praise blew away,

camouflaged by the wind. Sam never failed to ease her tension.

"Don't worry, Noah." Drew stepped closer. "I'll save you from the crazy bear." He clapped but didn't succeed.

Instead of running away, Sam bounced sideways and grabbed Noah's mitt.

"No, I'll save you from the pretend bear." Erin stepped in, her protective mothering instinct growling to the surface. "Go away, Sam. Go chase Jake." No way would she stand by while Drew jumped to the rescue. Noah should depend on her, not Drew.

"Hey, team, nothing stops explorers." Mitch pointed toward the house. "Let's head back to civilization to warm up."

Noah poked Drew's arm. "I wish we could fly home."

Erin gritted her teeth and grabbed Noah's hand. She needed to try harder to rein in Drew's poor influence. He couldn't leave soon enough.

****

Drew stepped back. With her face mostly covered, Erin hid her expression, but she straightened and stiffened. She detested Noah's continual references to flying. No doubt about it. She probably blamed him, but what could he do? At Noah's age, he had been similarly obsessed with everything aerial. "Hey, bud, we're stuck in the Arctic. The only way out is to hike. Let's go." Drew motioned for Noah to follow him.

"C'mon. Let's run." Erin dashed ahead. "Follow me."

The cousins pranced, bumped into each other, and collapsed into the snow.

Whenever the kids fell, Jake and Sam barked and licked their faces.

Close to the house, Drew paused and waved on the others. "You finish the trek. I'll check my car and the road."

"I want to come." Noah caught up to Drew.

No way would Erin allow the idea. He waited for her to rein in Noah's determination.

"Not now, Noah. Come with your cousins and me." She waved him back.

Noah didn't argue. Escaping her tone, prodding with icicles, Drew veered toward the gate.

The dogs played and wagged around him.

Soon, he would head for home, back to his quiet, orderly existence. He would be alone again with no one to talk to and burdened with the ever-present worry about making the grade. Beads of sweat trickled down his sides.

He had never spent much time around kids, but these past two days, he'd grown sort of fond of Noah. He was a smart little guy, curious, and full of energy. His appealing qualities would have made his dad proud.

Drew trudged along, squeezed his mitts into fists, and whacked at the sting in his chest. He'd missed so much because of an absentee father. Now, another loss loomed if his position with the SnoWings didn't work out. On the rest of the way to his car, he stomped an angry path.

He found the road and his car in the same state as two days ago—totally covered. But at least, he didn't have falling snow to contend with and could shovel and make progress. Soon, he'd escape this wintery prison. He should celebrate his freedom. To his surprise, behind his scarf, his quick grin slid into a frown. Instead, burdens and loneliness swallowed any joy.

Drew headed to the shed to find a shovel and maybe even a snow blower to clear the driveway. Suddenly, he didn't care if he dug out his car today or not. He didn't want to say goodbye to Erin, Noah, and the rest. He wanted to see Erin again, and if he travelled the airshow circuit this summer, hire her to take care of Jake. He wanted to play games with Noah, even if airplane games were off limits. He wanted to listen to Brian tell Air Force stories. He would even play charades again. Most of all, he wanted Erin to tilt her head and laugh at something he said.

When Drew returned to the house, he encountered Erin standing, hands on hips, giving instructions. "We'll form three teams. Team One is Team Fun. Mom and Claire, you get to play with the kids and answer calls. Seeing the weather clearing, clients will want to make arrangements to pick up their dogs. Team Two, Mitch and I, will dig out the dog runs. Team Three is Dad and Drew. You get to clear the driveway, so Drew can leave."

Obviously, she could hardly wait. His stay dragged long enough.

Brian and Drew forced shovels down the driveway, through the gate, and toward Drew's buried car. The wind dropped, and snow glinted off snowbanks. At first, they worked in silence, scooped, and threw heavy loads of snow. Shoveling steadily, they took an occasional break to catch their breath. In the distance, the yellow outline and blue flashing lights of snow removal equipment crawled along the country road.

"Gayle and I enjoyed sharing your company this

weekend." Brian raised a gloved hand and swiped the moisture under his nose. "Maybe you and Erin will stay in touch."

"I'd like to…uh, if she's interested." The wish drummed his heart into extra beats.

"She might need to be convinced." Brian blew out a cloud of frosty air and leaned on his shovel. "Sometimes Mom and Dad still know best. But don't tell her I said so."

"Of course not, sir." Drew scooped another shovelful of snow. Two days ago, he'd been desperate to leave this place. Now, he craved a continuing connection with the family, especially Erin.

"Call me Brian, not sir. We're friends."

The kind words soothed like salve. Drew needed a good friend. He didn't like talking about himself, but bit by bit, he let his history trickle out. "I bounced between my parents like a game of dodge ball. Basically, I felt like an outsider in two homes." His chest and eyes stung with thorny memories.

"That life sounds rough." Brian put a foot on his shovel and grunted reassurance.

Drew stabbed the snow, and with each scoop, he threw out another detail. "I don't have a family I can count on." Then he paused to catch his breath and survey snowbanks as high as his waist. "I hoped Dad and I could work out a few issues from the past and maybe start fresh. Now, I don't know when we'll get together."

After a couple of hours of steady work, they uncovered Drew's car and cleared a path to the main gate.

"Sorry you missed the weekend with your dad."

Brian rested an elbow on the shovel handle, puffed, and squinted. "But every cloud has a silver lining. The storm gave our family the chance to adopt you."

"Thank you for your warm welcome." Exhaustion pulled at his body, and Drew blotted any worries about trusting Brian with so many, painful details. He massaged his forearms, and as he blinked, moisture slipped out and froze onto his eyelashes. Maybe Brian didn't notice or blamed the cold. He wiped his cheeks with the back of his gloves and fought to keep his emotions in check. One way or another, he needed to resolve his unsettled past.

Chapter 7

The weekend with Drew stretched forever, yet the time with family skated by. Erin would soon happily say goodbye and remind him to find another kennel. He redeemed himself from first impressions, and with any other career, he might even be pleasant company. But she refused to befriend a pilot. His presence near Noah caused nothing but trouble.

Late in the afternoon, after hot chocolate and cookies, the family gathered by the front door.

Erin hung back and let the rest of the family handle the fond farewell.

Except for her, the group circled Drew and Jake like they were sending off a favorite family member.

"Nice to meet you." Mitch shook Drew's hand and slapped him on the back. "I'll stay tuned for SnoWings news."

Gayle and Claire took turns hugging him.

Erin avoided eye contact and bent to pat Jake. She couldn't resist saying a proper goodbye to the eager, black-and-white dog. He wasn't to blame for the weekend's events.

"I cook dinner for the family almost every Sunday, and you're always welcome." Gayle nodded and smiled. "I'll email our address."

"Yes, come and join us." Claire touched Mitch's arm.

"Come anytime." He reinforced the invitation with a firm nod.

Erin straightened and kneaded her nervous stomach. She swallowed, not saying a word. No one cared how she felt, and she definitely didn't want to include him in the next family gathering.

The children knelt to give Jake hugs.

Finally, Erin coaxed them to let go of the poor dog and pet Sam, too. The quicker Drew stepped out the door, the better. Her family's warm words swarmed like bees, and she folded her stiff arms and bit her lip. They had no business inviting Drew to keep in touch because she wanted him to stay as far away as possible.

Brian hugged Drew and murmured something into his ear.

Erin glared and strained but couldn't hear. Her dad's extreme friendliness, while not uncommon, stung.

Drew's expression lifted, and he nodded.

"Bye, Drew. Please, will you take me flying sometime?" Noah threaded between him and the door.

"Uh, oh, I don't know." Drew shot a glance at Erin.

She swept away her gaze and ignored him. "No, Noah. Only grownups ride in Drew's jet." Erin stepped in, hands on hips. "You can give Jake one more hug."

Instead of bending to hug Jake, Noah dove at Drew, threw his arms around his hips, and squeezed hard.

Distress burned in Erin's stomach, and she shook her head. She took Noah's hand firmly while staring at the painful truth. He adored the guy.

Drew returned a quick squeeze and held up his hand. "Each of you give me a high five...Noah...Luc...Anna. Okay, Jake and I better go

before the sky turns dark. I enjoyed the weekend here."
He glanced from Brian to Gayle, to Mitch, to Claire,
and back to Erin.

"Now, go to the window and wave." Brian herded
the kids from the door, followed by the other adults.

Drew faced Erin. "Thank you for everything. I'll,
uh, never forget this weekend."

"The weekend has been memorable, for sure." Erin
would leave him to decide whether she considered the
memories pleasant. She stuck out her hand and ended
the weekend the same way they met, with a handshake.
But this time, his hand radiated warmth. Savoring the
pleasant surprise, she parted her tingling lips.

Drew put on his gloves and paused. "If you don't
mind, next time I go away, I'll book Jake here."

She lifted a hand to her chest and stepped back.
She considered saying yes, but she couldn't. His
passion for flying signaled trouble. She needed to focus
on business and steer clear of any man, especially a
pilot. She owed her commitment to Noah and his dad's
memory. No, Drew would need to find another kennel
for Jake. "I wanted to discuss future plans. I hope you
can…at least, I suggest you find another kennel." Erin
bit her lip. She needed to stand firm.

Drew wrinkled his forehead and shifted. "Oh, I
see." He paused, and he dropped his gaze. "I'm
disappointed. If you change your mind, please, let me
know."

Glancing at his eyes, shadowed as dark as raisins,
Erin crossed her arms. "I'm sure you can easily find
another place. Jake's a good dog, and other kennels in
the area offer similar services."

"Okay, if you prefer." He cleared his throat. "I

better go. Thank you again." He headed toward the gate with Jake, stopped partway, and waved.

As he disappeared down the road, Erin seesawed. She couldn't afford to refuse a client, even a pilot and dangerous influence. Since she took over, business had been okay, but she could accommodate more dogs and needed to grow. Maybe she'd made a big mistake in declining his business. Biting her lip, she sighed and joined her family. She could deal with business logistics later. No way would she waste valuable family time second-guessing her decision.

As she prepared dinner and reunited happy owners and dogs, she popped in and out of the house. Just as she lifted from the oven a warm, cinnamon-spiced apple crisp, she welcomed her evening assistant to take over the next shift. Oliver was a local college student, who sandwiched work between classes and sports.

The cousins ran off for a little more playtime, leaving the adults with a few minutes to relax.

"I liked Drew." Claire took a bite of apple crisp. "He played well with the kids."

"He appreciated time with family." Gayle sipped her coffee, hugging the mug with both hands. "He's all alone with his dad so far away and no close siblings."

"Flying's a sensitive issue with you, sis." Mitch held up his hands, shielding her protest. "But he must be an expert. The SnoWings are top of the class."

"I told him you two should keep in touch." Brian raised his eyebrows and tossed her a pointed glance.

"Okay, dear family, you need to stop. I agree he's nicer than my first impression, but I'm not interested." Her stubborn streak rushed to the surface. Apprehension twisted her stomach, and she pressed a palm on her middle. They needed to understand her legitimate concerns and drop the subject. She stared at her dessert.

"Of course, you're not interested." Mitch waved his spoon.

"Mitchell." Erin spat her brother's name. He knew how to irritate with a mock straight face, and her patience snapped.

"Ooh, she only calls me by my full name if she means business." Mitch grinned.

"I do mean stop." Erin clanked her spoon.

"Okay, you two." Gayle gathered empty plates. "Mitch, quit teasing your sister." She grimaced at Claire. "As kids, they argued this way."

"Anyway," continued Brian, "whether or not you want to see him, I intend to keep in touch. He hopes to address some issues, and I told him I'd be happy to be a sounding board." He passed his plate to his wife. "Do what you want, Erin. I can't force you to get together. But you might enjoy a little male company besides Noah once in a while."

Heat burned Erin's face. She expected family loyalty and didn't appreciate interference. Maybe they meant well, but she didn't need their advice. Without saying a word, she stood and grabbed a stack of dishes. Their comments didn't help at all. If they truly cared, they wouldn't match her with a pilot of all people. She sighed, and her hands shook until a coffee cup toppled off the pile of dishes and shattered on the floor.

Her mom and Claire hurried to clean up the pieces.

No one mentioned Drew for the rest of the visit. Maybe they finally understood he didn't belong anywhere near her life.

****

The quiet emptiness of Drew's house shouted and amplified his aloneness. He called his dad again, and the phone rang five times before he answered. "I finally caught you, Dad." Drew's throat squeezed.

"Well, hello, Drewzer. Major bummer the storm hit." His dad chuckled.

At the nickname, Drew bristled. As a kid, he soon learned the breezy twist usually preceded an excuse for a broken commitment or something left undone. "Yeah, the weather dealt a bit of an adventure." Images of Erin and her family rushed in, and he half smiled.

"I wouldn't mind hearing your story, but can we talk another time? A few of the neighbors came to play cards, so I can't really take time to talk right now." His dad covered the phone, and his muffled voice said, "I'll be right back."

"Oh, sure." The way his dad slammed shut the conversation, he didn't have a choice. "When you're free sometime, why don't you give me a call?"

"Sure thing. You take care, Drewzer. Make sure you don't get stuck in a snowbank…ha."

Drew ended the call, tipped his head into his hands, and rubbed his aching temples. Some things never changed. Like always, his dad probably wouldn't call, and if they talked at all, Drew would lead the effort. He sighed. Chasing his dad all these years drained dry his energy.

Would he ever connect with his dad and sort out their wobbly past? Would he ever learn to trust people and regain the confidence to soar with the SnoWings? Intense pressure stalked him everywhere, and he'd hoped getting far from the base this weekend would set him free. But no, weather buried his plans.

To escape the empty house, Drew and Jake hiked to the park down the block. Drew trudged through the snow and exhaled a haze of frosty air.

Jake spotted a rabbit and took off across the snowbanks.

The exertion comforted Drew's soul. Surprisingly, so had the stormy weekend. Brimming with tension at the outset, the weekend morphed into an unexpected gift even though Erin might not agree. She and her family were everything he'd missed. His chest ached with envy and gratitude. Would he ever experience a similar circle of comfort and warmth? He thumped his torso. They obviously loved and supported each other, led by a dad they respected and trusted.

"Jake, come." Drew called and slowed his pace. Flashes of black and white darted through the snow into view. "Time to go."

He'd keep Monday as a vacation day. The day off would give him time to reflect and get his head focused on the mammoth challenges ahead. This evening and tomorrow he would relax, except for one important errand. Brian encouraged him to keep in touch with Erin, and he intended to follow the advice. He needed to properly thank his hostess, catch her dark eyes glinting, and savor her outdoorsy glow. Maybe he would even call and test Brian's sincerity about getting together.

****

Erin's helper, Ted, handled the evening kennel check while she tucked in Noah, lit the fireplace, and curled up with a blanket and a novel. After reading the same page three times, she slammed shut the book. The image of Drew's downturned face prickled like burrs. He wasn't the abrasive man who showed up on Friday afternoon, and besides, she needed clients. If she had agreed to care for Jake next time Drew travelled, his eyes would have brightened. But refusing his request still made sense. As a pilot, his life intertwined with too much risk and danger.

She threw aside the blanket and jumped to get a head start on tomorrow's morning chores because stickiness lingered on the kitchen floor. Kneeling beside a bucket of soapy water, she scrubbed. Opening her heart to a new relationship scared her almost as much as flying. Three years ago, Eric's horrific crash changed her world in an instant. A mistake in the air ripped apart her life, and she'd never again risk her feelings. Her throat clenched and burned with pain she struggled to contain.

She sat back on her heels, shuddered, and relived the fateful day. Eric had stretched his limits to satisfy one more farmer and spray another field. Probably exhausted, he lost concentration for a few seconds. No one would ever know for sure. His small plane plunged, burst into flames, and had burned him beyond recognition. She shuddered, wrung out her sponge, and squeezed her eyes against the horrific image. Just then the phone rang and jolted her upright. She tossed her sponge in the bucket and wiped her hands on her flannel pajamas.

"We arrived home safe and sound. I just wanted to let you know." Gayle greeted her.

Bright as ever, her mom always showed she cared. "Thanks for letting me know, and thank you again for helping this weekend. I don't know how I would have handled everything on my own. Noah and I are lucky you all live close by." Erin's voice caught. Even if she didn't need their advice, she counted on their support.

"You can rely on us, and your dad likes to keep busy, so he and Mitch didn't mind at all working in the kennel." Gayle paused then sighed. "You don't have to follow our suggestions, dear. Listen to your own heart. On the way home, I told your dad and Mitch to leave you alone."

"Thanks, Mom." Erin wiped a tear off her cheek and swallowed through her tight throat. Her mom's quiet, gentle tone and words hugged her close. She always said the right, comforting thing.

After the call, Erin knelt and continued scrubbing and reflecting on the weekend. Drew contradicted her first impressions. At first, his natural reserve appeared clipped, cool, and arrogant, but he had made the effort to fit in and be a pleasant houseguest. Still, his positive qualities didn't change anything. He was a pilot, not a friend. She scrubbed harder. Noah and the business demanded her full attention.

She wiped away the weekend grit, and happy memories flowed. Because of Eric, she grew deep roots in Moose Jaw. When they met, everyone teased them about how similar they were in so many ways, even down to a one-letter difference in their names. She couldn't possibly let in another man. She shivered, stood, and admired her work. The floor gleamed except for several large paw prints outlined in the dampness. Sam left his mark. She shook her head and threw her arms around his shaggy neck. Maybe now she could relax, tuck her feet under his warm belly, and read her book.

Her family only wanted to help, and she couldn't stay upset. If she decided keeping Drew as a client made sense, she would. He left open the door and would welcome a change of heart. She'd give the decision more thought and might consider taking him back but only for business reasons.

On Monday morning at breakfast, Noah chattered between bites of cereal. "When will we see Grandma and Grandpa again?" Milk dribbled down his chin.

"Probably on Sunday we'll go to their place." Erin smiled and dabbed his face with a napkin.

"When will we see Uncle Mitch and Auntie Claire and Luc and Anna again?" Noah stirred his cereal.

"They'll come to Grandma and Grandpa's house." Erin glanced at the clock, conscious of the school bus schedule.

"When will we see Drew and Jake again?" Noah's eyes glistened.

"I don't know." Her pulse jumped. Her son would never see them, unless…unless she decided to keep Drew as a client for the sake of revenue.

"I want to ride in Drew's plane." Noah clattered the spoon on his dish.

His wish pierced Erin, and she sipped her coffee's soothing warmth. How could she distract her son from this new-found obsession?

"You need to finish your cereal and get ready for school." She pointed at his bowl and fought to ignore the internal game of hopscotch unsettling her. Surely, after a few days, Noah's memory of Drew would fade, and he would forget airplane questions and ideas. She would keep him busy with other things. Something new would soon grab his interest.

Ted handled the early morning shift, alleviating some of the pressure.

After she waved Noah onto the school bus, she finished the rest of the kennel chores. Most of the dogs left the previous evening, and only a few remained today which gave her extra time to clear more snow.

Sam followed her around the yard, sticking his muzzle into snow banks and sneezing wet, snowy sprays.

As she shoveled the heavy snow, she huffed and paused every few minutes to watch Sam and the other dogs frolicking in the shimmery whiteness. She savored the air, gently cupping her cheeks with no hint of the weekend's extreme temperatures. The breeze and exercise boosted her energy. She spent much of the morning outside, clearing pathways and play areas for the next wave of dogs booked for the coming weekend. Near lunchtime, she scooped a final shovel of snow and tossed it aside, along with the last of the weekend stresses. She inhaled her fresh, peaceful surroundings, stretched wide her arms and tipped her face to the sun. She welcomed back her normal life, free of complications. Taking another deep breath, she smothered a hint of apprehension. Her challenging roles as single parent and business owner still loomed.

****

First thing in the morning, Drew headed to the toy store to choose Noah's surprise. He browsed for a long time, strolled up and down the aisles, and hunted for just the right thing. He considered games, puzzles, and cars.

Picking up an item, he shook his head and set it down. He examined it again, and his spirits soared. Erin might not be very happy with his choice, but Noah would be thrilled, guaranteed.

A toy airplane couldn't harm anything, keeping Noah entertained for hours. He could practically hear the little guy's squeals of delight at the way the side of the plane flipped up to reveal the interior filled with pilot and passengers. A real plane ride remained out of the question, but Erin didn't officially ban toy airplanes. Drew spun and hurried to the cashier.

Then he browsed several stores on Main Street to find the right gift for Erin. He avoided anything too big, too small, or too personal. Should he choose flowers or chocolates? He opted for a colorful bouquet, and as he paid, another inspiration hit. He hurried to the car to keep the flowers from freezing and drove straight home, envisioning a creative project. The extra gift would cost only time which he could spare. Whether Erin acknowledged the fact or not, she could fill a gap with his offer.

At home, he worked methodically to create neat, hand lettering with a decorative border and paused to admire his work. He wrapped Noah's surprise in colored flyers and set aside everything to deliver after lunch.

Drew tossed Jake's tennis ball and weighed whether to call his new friend, Brian. He paused, ball in hand, to reflect.

Impatient as ever, the dog jolted him with three, sharp barks.

"Okay, Jake. I'll play." He threw the ball down the hallway, glanced at the clock, and paced. Then he flipped the TV on and off. Filled with mundane activities, the rest of the morning dragged.

That afternoon, armed with gifts, Drew set off with Jake for Canine Corner, their weekend refuge. He gripped the steering wheel with both hands and took jagged breaths against the tightness lodged in his chest. Blood surged through his arms and legs like the adrenaline rush he experienced in the cockpit. "We'll surprise them, Jake. I hope they don't mind the drop-in visit."

Jake wagged his tail and paced back and forth on the back seat.

Surely, Erin would realize he meant well. Could a short, drop-in visit bearing gifts cause any harm?

****

Erin settled Noah with his action figures and tackled some housework.

"The good guys beat the bad guys," Noah called from the living room.

"Oh, I'm glad the right guys won. I'll see you in a minute. I just washed the bathroom floor." Crawling on hands and knees, Erin backed out of the bathroom and bumped into Sam. She wiped several sloppy, dog licks off her cheek and forehead and calmed him with pats. "Good dog, Sam." She hugged him and nestled her face next to his soft ears.

"Mom, somebody's here." Noah shouted and banged on the window.

"Are you sure? I don't expect any dog drop-offs today." Erin dumped the bucket of lemony water, dried her hands, and joined Noah in peering out the living room window. "I wonder who's here."

Noah bounced, waved, and hollered. "Drew came back."

Biting her lip, she cringed.

She didn't want to see him again, yet she had no choice. He'd arrived unannounced, complicating her life.

Chapter 8

"Drew? You're right, Drew's here." Why had he returned? Did he forget something? Erin glanced at her well-worn sweatshirt and jeans. If she'd expected him, she'd have freshened her appearance. She raised a hand and poked her stomach where butterflies fluttered.

"I'm so happy. I knew Drew would come see me." Noah bobbed and waved.

Sam wagged so vigorously his whole body shook along with his tail.

Jake jumped out of the car and bounded ahead.

Drew juggled a wrapped package along with a couple of smaller items.

Warmth invaded Erin's cheeks, and she ran her fingers through her hair and moistened her lips. She shouldn't care how she looked.

Noah ran to the front door and swung it open. "Hi, Drew. We can play. Hi, Jake."

Erin shivered. She needed to avoid him and keep him away from Noah, and now, she couldn't. Standing on the doorstep, he apparently didn't need an invitation. "Hi, Drew. I'm surprised to see you."

"Don't worry. The road's clear, so this time I won't overstay my welcome." Drew laughed and stepped aside.

Sam burst out the door to wrestle with Jake.

"Did you forget something?" He didn't belong

here. Why on earth had he returned unannounced today? The butterflies inside her morphed into a hyperactive frog. Apprehension jumping, she fought to stay calm.

Drew cleared his throat and paused. "No. I didn't forget anything. I just wanted to say a proper thank-you for everything."

"Can Drew come in, Mommy?" Noah fidgeted and tugged her sleeve.

Erin shivered and weighed the surprise complication. She wanted to shout, no, never. But Noah's enthusiasm overpowered, forcing her to reconsider. She bit her lip. "I guess so. Do you want to come in?"

He stepped into the entranceway and shut the door against the cold air. "I won't stay long. I just need to drop off these things." He extended the triangular package. "I hope you like flowers. They could probably use some water."

"Oh, thank you. You didn't need to deliver anything." Erin tore off the paper, and the sweet fragrance of a multi-colored bouquet floated. "They're beautiful."

"I can't show enough appreciation for all your hospitality. And now...buddy, I chose something to thank you for letting me stay here." Drew held out another package.

Erin inhaled the swirling, floral aroma. Drew shouldn't have spent so much, and he certainly shouldn't have included her son in the gifts.

Noah ripped off the paper, and his eyes lit. "Oh, cool." He paused, examined his gift, and shouted. "I got my own airplane. I love it. Thank you, Drew. You're the best." He bounced and spun in a circle.

Drew grinned and glanced at Erin.

The lump of pressure in her chest burned and spread. She lowered her gaze and swallowed. Drew didn't comprehend airplanes were off limits. Maybe she hadn't been clear enough, or maybe he just didn't care. Drew's gift confirmed her instincts. He meant trouble.

She smiled at Noah with dry, tight lips. "Lucky you, son. You got a pretty special present." Any polite words to thank Drew lodged in her throat.

Drew shifted and coughed.

She should second the invitation, but she barely resisted her urge to shove him out the door.

"Hey, now we can play with my new plane." Noah zoomed the plane in front of Drew.

"I'm glad you like it, but sorry, I can't stay today, Noah." He shook his head and reached for the doorknob.

Noah crinkled his face for a moment and ran off, swooping the plane in all directions.

Drew tipped his head toward the action. "I hope you don't mind."

Erin opened and closed her mouth. Distress twisted her insides into a burning mass. "Maybe I need to make my feelings more clear. Airplanes…" She shook her head, swallowed, and calmed her wavery voice. "Airplanes do not belong in this home."

Drew furrowed his brow. "I'm sorry I bought the toy. I, uh, couldn't stop myself. I knew Noah would appreciate it, but I shouldn't…"

Erin shook her head, blinked, and dabbed her eyes. She needed to regroup. He didn't fully grasp the terror she fought. "You've made Noah a very happy boy."

"I'll leave in a minute. I just have one more thing to give you before I go." He rocked from side to side.

"Not something else." Erin raised her eyebrows and blinked hard. "These flowers are enough."

"I wanted to repay you for all you did. Here you go." He held out an envelope.

Erin smiled and jiggled her knees. A man hadn't brought her gifts in a very long time. She cradled the flowers and tore open the envelope. "I can't guess."

Inside, she found a hand-drawn certificate with precise lettering.

This coupon entitles Erin Humphrey to twenty hours of free labor. Redeemable evenings and weekends for miscellaneous kennel duties or spring home and business improvements. Expiry date: Must be used within thirty days (before my busy season). Signed: Drew Dixon.

Throat squeezing, Erin swam through a swirl of feelings. He deserved marks for creativity and thoughtfulness. He had observed first-hand her labor-intensive business in action and remembered she had ideas for business improvements. His gift generously packaged his time and expertise. Still, she couldn't accept his charity. She couldn't let him hang around and influence Noah, and she certainly couldn't get closer to a pilot of all people.

"You're very generous. Nice artwork, by the way. But really, you've given me too much." She held out the certificate. "Thank you, though."

Drew raised both hands and backed away. "No, the free labor is yours, and I won't take back my offer. Call me for help…whatever you need."

"Oh, I couldn't possibly." She would never redeem

the certificate. "But thank you, again. I appreciate the gesture."

Drew lowered his gaze and shifted.

Then Noah zigzagged around the corner and braked abruptly.

"I better call Jake and get on my way. High five, Noah?" He held up his hand.

Noah slapped Drew's palm. "Come again soon," he urged. He clutched the airplane to his chest.

Noah sounded surprisingly mature, issuing an invitation. Erin smiled and squeezed his shoulder.

"Bye. Take care." Drew turned, raising his hand in a half wave as he opened the door.

The cool air rushed in along with Sam, and Erin folded her arms. The sooner Drew left, the better.

"I'll wait for your call." Drew stepped outside and swung the door shut.

Sam whined and ran to the window.

Noah peered out and waved.

In case Drew glanced back, Erin stood back from the window out of sight. If she had doubted, even for a moment, how much he appreciated the family weekend, she now understood. His gifts screamed gratitude. He selected personalized items and delivered them himself. But a toy airplane? How could he?

She fisted her hands and took shaky breaths. Drew meant well. His judgment might be a little off, but he intended to be kind. If he wasn't a pilot, he might be attractive. If she had been even remotely interested in dating, she might consider him a decent prospect. But they couldn't possibly spend more time together.

"I love my plane." Noah whizzed by.

"You're a lucky boy."

"Will you play airplane with me?" He swooped in a circle.

"You and Sam fly around the house while I finish a bit of cleaning. Then we can have story time." She bit her lip. Stories would be a calming reprieve and a welcome distraction.

Long after Drew's car disappeared through the gate and down the road, Erin stared out the window. She still hugged the bouquet, and the flowers' sweet perfume overwhelmed. She wrinkled her nose and set the flowers in water. Drew's lingering presence forced heat through her. Desperate to air out every trace of his alluring, masculine aura, she raced to open windows. If she could possibly prevent another visit, she would. He shouldn't return.

She bent and inhaled the perfume of roses and daisies. No doubt, the oversize bouquet cost a bundle. She picked up the handmade certificate and examined the details. He designed it by hand, instead of using a computer template. She propped her elbows on the countertop and cradled her head. She didn't need this complication at all.

"Zoom." Noah, with Sam chasing, darted through the kitchen. "Watch, Mommy." Noah swooped and twirled.

"Yes, that move is pretty cool." Erin shifted her gaze from the bouquet to the certificate.

"Mommy, you're not watching." Noah tugged her sleeve.

Erin blinked and refocused. "Wow." She mustered little enthusiasm. "Take a few more loops, and find three stories you'd like to read."

The gifts sat on the coffee table like bright beacons

signaling trouble. She appreciated the gesture but didn't need constant Drew reminders. Noah's toy plane irritated her enough. She snatched the certificate, read the message one last time, tore it in four pieces, and threw it in the recycle bin.

Dealing with the flowers presented a tougher challenge. She didn't have the heart to throw away a beautiful bouquet, but she knew someone who would enjoy them. She'd give them to Ted's wife, Vera, her neighbor on the next acreage over. Eventually, Drew would realize she refused to redeem the gift certificate, but he would never know she gave away the flowers. At least, his gesture would transform into something positive instead of an unwelcome reminder.

****

Drew bumped along the rural road. He steered with one hand and rubbed his throbbing temple with the other. He shouldn't have arrived unannounced, and he definitely shouldn't have chosen a toy airplane. He cringed the moment Erin's eyes clouded, and her face flushed crimson. He knew she banned actual flying, but he underestimated her aversion to a harmless toy.

"I made a giant mistake, Jake." He gripped the steering wheel with both hands to avoid icy patches and tall ridges of snow. Without a doubt, his gift choices delighted Noah and offended Erin. A belt of tension notched tighter around his head.

Erin responded with courtesy but no enthusiasm, and she didn't even pretend to like the toy airplane. She smiled a pale imitation of the real thing, nothing like the beaming face she showed her family on the weekend. She noticed his artwork on the gift certificate, but she likely wouldn't redeem his labor. He pounded the steering wheel with one hand and rotated his cramped shoulders. How could he have presumed she would welcome him back? How could he have risked offending her with a toy airplane? He took a deep breath but couldn't rid the persistent stiffness. He'd do anything to redeem himself and see her again.

In the last year, he focused so intently on the SnoWings, he temporarily put dating on hold. Then the *incident* confirmed nothing should interfere with training. A woman could be a big distraction, so he really should forget her and direct his energy where it counted. Still, even if she despised airplanes, she gave his heart a zing he couldn't resist.

Jake paced and then rested his furry chin on Drew's shoulder and scanned the road ahead.

As Drew approached the city limits, he braked. His errand completed, he faced the rest of the day, stretching like a gaping hole with nothing to fill it. Normally, work kept him busy enough that he hardly noticed his sparse social life. Today, the unplanned, open time shone a light on his aloneness. Worse, a swirl of issues nagged—his tenuous position on the SnoWings team, missed time with his dad, and Erin's disapproval. He sighed and rubbed his temple.

Should he call Brian? If he contacted his new friend this soon, would he surprise him?

Brian said they should keep in touch, and he sounded sincere. He understood military life and listened well while Drew shared personal revelations. If they weren't so cold yesterday, on a mission to clear snow so Drew could finally leave, they might have talked longer. Brian's encouraging grunts and nods unlocked a cache of memories and feelings Drew sealed inside far too long. Still, he really didn't know Brian very well. He shouldn't assume the rapport they shared over a stormy weekend marked the start of a lasting friendship.

When he arrived home, he accepted Jake's persistent invitation to play and threw the ball down the hallway seventeen times. Then before he changed his mind, he grabbed the phone and called.

"Hello." Brian answered on the first ring.

"Drew here. Drew Dixon." Waiting for Brian's reaction, he held his breath.

"Glad you called. I didn't know if you travelled safely home yesterday, but I gather you did." He laughed.

"Yes, sir, Jake and I are home." Drew held the phone farther away to adjust the volume of Brian's booming voice.

At his name, Jake barked once.

Drew tossed another ball. "Thank you for welcoming me this past weekend and especially for listening."

"Hey, I might be tough to shut up, but I'm happy to listen." Brian chuckled again.

"Like I told you, I had hoped to talk with my dad about a few things. Now, I don't know when we'll see each other. So…I…" Drew cleared his throat and wiped the moisture off his upper lip.

"Do you need a fill-in dad? I'm more than willing. My offer stands."

"I'd really appreciate your time, sir." Drew coughed, causing the pressure in his head to intensify. Asking for help wasn't easy.

"Remember, my name is Brian. Call me Brian. I

mean it. You can save the sir stuff for the base."

"Okay, Brian." Drew smiled and contained a sigh of relief. His new friend lived up to his word.

They decided to meet for hot chocolate at the coffee shop in Belle Plaine on Tuesday evening. The small town located between Regina and Moose Jaw would give them both an easy, twenty-five-minute drive.

Drew ended the call, stood, stretched, and jumped lighter and freer. Nothing had really changed with his uncertain pilot status, latest faux pas with Erin, or tenuous family relationships. But his spirits lifted, easing the throb in his temples. Despite everything, maybe life could improve.

****

Erin read three stories and then took Noah outside to play fetch with the dogs. She needed to keep his mind off airplanes.

After playtime, Ted arrived in his red truck.

"You're early for the late shift." Erin greeted her helper with open arms.

"I cleared my snow and figured you could use some extra help."

A retired farmer, Ted and his wife, Vera, lived just down the road. He wore a knit hat over his bald head. Leathery wrinkles from years of working in the sun and wind covered his kind face.

"Come here, mister." He grabbed Noah in a bear hug and pretended to toss him into a snow bank.

Noah squealed and flailed. "Stop. Put me down." He giggled and twisted.

Ted set him right side up on his feet.

Erin laughed at their antics. "Aw thanks, Ted.

You're the best. Earlier today, I made progress, but I should clear the foundation area, in case we get a quick thaw. Oh, and before you go, I want you to take something to Vera."

"Why don't you take a break and deliver it in person? She told me to send you over for some fresh cookies." He patted Sam's head.

"Yum, I like her cookies. Let's go get some." Noah jumped in a cheer.

"Just make sure you save some for me, mister." Ted rubbed the top of his head.

"Sure, I could use a cup of tea and some of her wisdom." Vera always welcomed her, Noah, and even Sam. Erin wrapped the flowers and put them in the car for the short drive.

A few minutes later, Vera swung open the door with a flourish. "Does that intriguing package contain flowers? But what's the occasion? I didn't hear anything about a good neighbor day." She wiped her hands on her apron and flicked flour off her spiky, gray hair. "Come in. I'm happy to see you." She waved them inside.

"The flowers come with a bit of a story." Erin inhaled a whoosh of rich, chocolatey air and extended the bouquet. She followed Vera to the cheery, yellow kitchen.

"The cookies are ready, so your timing is perfect." She put the kettle on for tea, switched on some cartoons for Noah, and sent Sam to chase the cat. "Now, Erin, sit here and tell me why I deserve a lavish bouquet for no reason at all." She bit a cookie and waited.

Erin wrinkled her nose and described the weekend and the reason for the bouquet. "So, I can't enjoy the flowers." She shook her head and clunked a palm on the table. "But you can."

Vera listened silently, nodded, and chewed. Then she shook her head. "They're lovely, but I can't accept them."

"But I want you to enjoy them. I would appreciate the favor." Erin's spirits dove. Her neighbor should agree, not reject the idea.

"Giving away the flowers wouldn't solve the problem, would it?" She patted Erin's hand.

Erin swallowed and shook her head. She hadn't at all expected this reaction. Normally, Vera showed kindness and understanding.

"A nice young man made a kind gesture. My accepting the flowers wouldn't change anything. He wants to thank or impress you...or both. I can't take them. Every time I admired them, they would remind me of that poor, young man pining away." She refilled their cups.

"But..." Erin blushed. Vera should understand, not refuse to help. She clutched her napkin to still her trembling hands.

"No buts." Vera blinked and slid away the package. "Take the flowers home, and enjoy them as a beautiful, thank-you gift. Sometimes, we just have to accept the nice things people do."

She signaled no arguing through intense, blue eyes and firm, pursed lips. Erin swallowed her tea and nodded. She gripped her cookie, crumbling it through her fingers.

"Oh, speaking of doing nice things, thank you for giving Ted the weekend off. We're lucky we left before the storm hit." Vera crinkled her face and raised her eyebrows.

"He works hard, and he deserves time away." Erin shrugged and brushed cookie crumbs into a neat pile.

"I tell him the same thing every day. After all, we're supposed to be semi-retired. Anyway, I plan to surprise him for our anniversary, and I found a last-minute deal to Las Vegas."

"Sounds like fun." Erin smiled and clapped her hands into a clasp on the table.

"The only thing is…" Vera moistened her lips. "I have a small problem. Our anniversary and the trip happen next week."

"You mean, Ted would need more time off already?" Erin bit her bottom lip and squelched a groan.

Experience told her Oliver's busy schedule left no room for extra work hours. Again, she would be shorthanded and couldn't ask her family for backup. Next weekend loomed way too soon. They'd assume they were correct the kennel business demanded too much.

She'd have to find help elsewhere. No way would she cause them worry.

"I hope you can get Oliver or someone else to fill in on short notice. I'm sorry I didn't give you more warning." Vera bowed her head and shredded her napkin.

The agitated lump inside Erin churned. "I'll figure out a plan, but yes, next time I'll need more lead time."

"Oh thank you, Erin." Vera jumped out of the chair, bent, and hugged her tight. "I promise you I'll return him refreshed and ready to buckle down."

Erin counted on Ted. She'd manage somehow for a few days but not for long. Without his reliable, ongoing help, she'd barely survive the coming weekend, let alone the exhausting days ahead.

Chapter 9

The next morning, Erin watered her flowers, took a deep breath of the fragrant blooms, and chased Drew out of her daydreams. She inhaled the scents of roses and daisies, a soothing, indoor garden in late March.

With morning kennel chores finished, she called her mom and spilled an update on Drew's latest visit. Then she described the flowers and how Vera made her keep them. She paused and waited for her mom to fill the silence.

"How do you feel about Vera's reaction?"

"I don't know, Mom. I feel so confused." A river of feelings rushed up and down her spine. She battled a murky combination of appreciation, frustration, pleasure, and guilt.

"Don't worry. Everything will work out," her mom said. "Vera is a pretty wise neighbor. Just enjoy the bouquet if you can."

"Easier said than done, but you're probably right. Thanks, Mom." She rubbed her forehead and slid her hand down to her warm cheek.

"Speaking of Drew," her mom continued, "your dad plans to meet him this evening in Belle Plaine."

"Really? Drew didn't mention anything yesterday." Pleasant warmth sizzled into hot indignation. "Why? What is Dad doing? Is he playing matchmaker?" She planted a firm hand on her hip.

"Maybe I shouldn't have said anything. He might want to keep their meeting between the men."

"But they just met this weekend. What are they now, best friends?" Erin paced and bumped Sam's nose.

"Try not to worry. Your dad offered to be a confidante and found Drew took him up on the offer. I get the feeling he needs a father to talk to and has no one but yours to turn to right now."

After making plans to join her parents for Sunday brunch at their place in Regina, Erin ended the call and set down the phone with a satisfying clunk. Hard as she tried to avoid Drew, she couldn't quash the constant reminders. She ducked and dodged, but she couldn't escape. Now, her dad even agreed to mentor the guy.

Frustration twisting and tangling deep inside, she paced around the house swinging her arms and squeezing her hands into fists. What burning issue did Drew need to discuss? Her dad could befriend a guy who needed a sympathetic ear if he wanted, but she didn't like the idea one bit. She couldn't stop the visit tonight, but she'd discourage future meetings. Her dad's first loyalty should be to his daughter.

She dropped to the office chair, swished her ponytail, and twisted the tendrils wriggling free. So far, she didn't know who could fill in for Ted's looming vacation. He had some big shoes to fill. Oliver declined extra hours because his college exams approached, and the list of substitute workers Ray recommended appeared sadly outdated. Definitely, she couldn't burden her parents with regular kennel chores. Struggling to identify a quick solution, she bit her lip and pounded the desk. She didn't know another student she could hire and train on short notice.

Staring at her computer screen, she reviewed her bookings for the next week and wrinkled her nose. Ray's projections showed the kennel should be at or near capacity most of the year, but next week's bookings dipped like this week. Fewer bookings eased her immediate staffing dilemma but hinted at a decline in overall business demand. Erin twisted her ponytail into a bun, let it fall, and propped her head in her hands. She needed to analyze booking patterns and amp up her marketing, but first, she needed a plan for next week. While she sliced cheese for sandwiches and waited for Noah to arrive home from school, the phone rang.

"Mrs. Humphrey?" A woman's voice greeted her.

"Yes?" She didn't recognize the voice. No one called her Mrs. Humphrey.

"This is Noah's teacher calling, Paula Jansen."

Erin took a sharp breath. "Is Noah okay?"

"Noah's fine. He's riding the bus. I wanted to ask you about a guest for our class. We're learning about different careers, and some of the children have invited a parent. So far, we'll hear from a fireman, a policeman, and a radio announcer."

"Would you like me to speak about operating a kennel?" Erin peered out the kitchen window at the kennel building and stood tall. Her face flushed with pride. She waited for a response and pictured the teacher's sculpted, brunette hairstyle and pert face.

"Oh, I'm not sure. Noah didn't mention your business," said Mrs. Jansen. "He said he has a friend who is a jet pilot, someone who stayed with you last weekend."

Erin clenched her teeth and grimaced. Worded in

that manner, her relationship with Drew probably didn't sound innocent.

"I know Noah's dad was a pilot," she continued, "perhaps your friend might come in his place and speak to the students."

Erin opened and closed her mouth. Drew followed her everywhere these days. "Noah is referring to one of my clients—someone I just met recently. He happened to get storm-stayed with my family over the weekend. I'm not really in a position to ask him to visit Noah's class." Irritation simmered, and she twisted the tap and filled a glass with cool water. Before sipping, she pressed the glass to her cheek.

"Oh, I understand. Okay then..." Mrs. Jansen clicked her tongue.

The teacher's displeasure hung like a dark curtain. "If you want the students to learn about running a kennel, I'd be glad to come." She lightened her tone but gritted her teeth. Mrs. Jansen had her own agenda, and she wasn't part of it.

"Hmmm...you have an interesting idea." Mrs. Jansen made another clicking sound. "Thank you for the offer. I'll check my schedule and let you know."

Erin plunked down the phone, knelt, encircled Sam in a hug, and buried her face in his soft fur. "Now, the teacher wants Drew. Everyone hypes him. Give me a break. Of course, my business doesn't rank up there with his glamorous profession."

Sam thumped his tail.

The crunch of gravel outside alerted her a vehicle approached. She jumped and peered out the front window.

The school bus slowed at the gate, and Noah

stepped off. But instead of meandering to the house as usual, he trotted in a straight line.

She smiled at his brisk pace. He must have an exciting school story to share. She opened the front door and waited.

Sam brushed by and lumbered out to greet him with wet kisses, toppling him sideways.

"No, Sam." Noah rolled to his knees and struggled in his snowsuit and backpack to stand.

"Come, Sam. Leave him alone." Erin called from the doorway. "Hi, Noah. Did you have a good day at school?"

"Yes, and I have something exciting to tell you." Noah puffed and wriggled into the house.

Erin helped remove his outer layers. "Okay, tell me your news." She squatted to eye level.

"Mrs. Jansen says Drew can come to school to talk about jets and stuff." He beamed and bounced.

Erin hated to disappoint him, but she would not grant his wish. Suddenly, the creamy aroma of grilled cheese sandwiches, ready for lunch, sickened her. Drew definitely spoiled everything.

****

Back at work, Drew fought seesawing emotions. His pulse beat in his temples, tapping a constant reminder of his anxious state. His uncertain position on the SnoWings team still hung over him like a stuck umbrella. On the bright side, he anticipated time with Brian this evening, although Erin might not be too impressed.

At the base, Drew ignored his mixed feelings and focused on the immediate task. He needed to perfect his precision, aerial manoeuvers, prove his skills, and regain the team's confidence. The size of the challenge shook him right to his queasy core.

He'd prove he could meet the team's standards. If the sun glinted a distraction, it couldn't interfere. He'd use the center jet as his reference point and never, ever even glance sideways. Multiple times a day, he drilled into his brain the same instructions through the rigorous tryouts for the SnoWings and every time he prepared for a flight. After the *incident*, his pep talk intensified to a stern lecture.

Drew joined the team of nine standing clustered in the centre of the sparsely furnished, crew room. The grayish green walls matched his subdued mood. He listened to the Team Lead's instructions and participated in the pre-flight briefing to review the day's missions. He flexed his shoulders up and down to ease the knot in his neck. Tight muscles made dull pain creep right to his temples.

"Questions? Is everything crystal clear?" The lead pilot scanned the group and lingered for a second. "No questions? Let's go."

Drew caught the lead pilot's forced eye contact and pointed message like a slap, making sweat trickle inside his uniform. As he strode to the tarmac, he stared ahead, his arms and hands prickling.

As they prepared to board their individual jets, the teammates joked and teased.

From the outer rim of the circle, Drew laughed but never led the relaxed banter and camaraderie. He'd never connected easily with the other guys or joined smoothly in the casual humor. Now, shame about his serious error magnified his awkwardness.

"I heard Regina Airport closed because of the

weather. Did the storm shut down your travel plans?" Kyle, one of the other new SnoWings, caught up and bumped his shoulder.

"Yeah, unfortunately, I couldn't get away." Drew flicked his arms to boost the blood flow.

Kyle ran a hand over his bristly, ginger hair. "So, you didn't get a sunburn." He fell in time with Drew's pace. Glancing over, Kyle bunched his freckled cheeks into a grin.

"Maybe a touch of frostbite. I got stranded at Canine Corner and suffered my share of the cold like everybody else." Drew chuckled, never breaking stride. "I worked in the kennels, cleared snow, and played with dogs."

"Sounds like a doggone good time." Kyle laughed and punched his shoulder.

Drew grinned. Joking around with Kyle transformed him from hesitant outsider to tentative insider for a few, playful seconds. He could have elaborated about the family he met, Noah's fascination with airplanes, and the fun they shared, but the serious business of flight demanded his full attention. The day passed quickly. He performed to the team's high standards and completed a series of complex formations. In just a few weeks, they would perform a spectacular airshow at locations across North America. One day at a time, he would make the grade.

After work, Drew and Jake ran and played in the park. The dog never ran out of energy, even though the teenager next door tossed balls for him at noon and after school for a few dollars a day.

Drew finished dinner and set off to meet Brian in Belle Plaine, hardly more than a truck stop along the

Trans-Canada Highway. He invited Jake to join him for company. With his thick, fur coat, the dog could wait in the car for an hour. He'd be far more content riding along than staying home alone.

The highway crews had cleared the roads, leaving only the sparkling white ditches as evidence a blizzard recently struck.

At the diner, Drew slid into a booth opposite Brian and scanned the retro décor. Black-and-white tiles checkered the floor, and record albums dotted the walls. The red vinyl benches in the booth matched stools lining a lunch counter. "Hello. Thanks for coming."

"Good evening." Brian nodded, set his mug on the table, and smiled. "The hot chocolate's good. How are you? Long time no see."

"Seems like ages." Drew chuckled and inhaled the diner air, heavy with the scent of burgers and fries. "I had a pretty good day." He motioned to the server to bring him the same beverage. The jukebox in the corner spun out a fifties rock tune and bounced in time with the clatter of dishes and hum of conversation.

"Prairie weather always surprises us. Funny the difference a couple of days can make." Brian swished his mug. "True to form, Saskatchewan blasts us with a blizzard and then moderates to just below freezing— mild, by prairie-winter standards. But hey, you didn't invite me here to talk climate."

"Yesterday, I visited Erin and Noah." Drew wiped his damp upper lip with a napkin.

"You liked my suggestion and didn't waste any time. Glad to hear." Brian grinned and raised his mug in a mock toast.

"I just dropped in for a few minutes." Drew

shrugged, uncertainty stiffening his shoulders. Maybe he returned too soon.

"Why did you only stay a few minutes? Did she toss you out?" Brian chuckled and gulped his drink.

"Nah. I just delivered some small gifts. You know, to thank them for the hospitality." A rush of adrenaline thumped his heart faster. More than anything, he longed to replenish his memories and absorb Erin's striking, almond eyes and velvet cheeks.

Brian used a teaspoon to scoop the melted marshmallow floating on top. "You're very generous. I'm sure they appreciated the gifts."

"Noah definitely did. Erin…I'm not so sure." He shrugged and lowered his gaze. Maybe the hairline crack in his voice slipped by before Brian noticed.

"Keep charming her. All the armor she wears protects a soft heart." Brian winked and grinned.

The neon light in the window lit his face with a flickering orange reflection.

With a steady hand, the server set a steaming cup in front of Drew.

Glancing up, he nodded thanks. "If you say so." Drew swirled his drink and lifted it to his lips. He savored the sweet, creamy beverage.

"I do." Brian hit the table with an open palm. "Now, let's get down to business. You wanted to talk about something else?" He wrinkled his forehead and stared.

"I'm not quite sure where to begin." Drew unclenched his jaw, opened his mouth, and closed it again. He cleared his throat.

"Pick up where you left off. Describe more family details." Brian leaned an elbow on the table and rubbed his chin.

Again, Drew cleared his throat. "I nearly told you everything...except my dad is a recovering alcoholic." Did he really want to rehash the turmoil? Why had he wanted to share his past? Now, he couldn't change his mind and rewind his words.

"Alcoholism is not an easy condition for a family to handle." Brian frowned, sipped his drink, and waited.

Drew lifted his mug and set it down. He raised a hand and massaged his temple while he spilled the painful story. For many years, alcohol ruled his dad and left a trail of broken promises. "After a while, I was a bit suspicious of almost everyone and everything. When you're part of a team like the SnoWings, you can cause major damage with a lack of trust." He clutched his mug. "For the last year, Dad has abstained from alcohol, so I hope we can start fresh. Maybe we can finally support each other and build a stronger relationship." After a long monologue, Drew paused to hear Brian's words of wisdom.

"You won't regret making an effort to see your dad." He stroked his chin. "You can't change him or the past, but you can change your outlook."

"I know. I need to make strong connections and trust people." Drew took a deep breath. Should he reveal his personal challenge? Maybe he could risk talking to Brian. "The weekend with your family zapped me into realizing what I want in life, in addition to my pilot career, of course."

The server appeared at their table. "Would you fellows like refills?"

"No, thanks." Brian checked his watch. "Little did I know our crazy clan could inspire." He raised his eyebrows and rolled his lips together. "You mean you want a family? Tell me more."

"I mean…" Drew fingered his napkin. "Your family shows so much respect and trust gluing you together. You're always there for each other." He stared at the chocolate puddle in the mug and rotated it.

"Sometimes we take our relationships for granted. I'm no expert, but I'd say with trust, the more you give, the more you get." Brian rubbed his chin.

Staring at Brian's hand absorbing the orangey hue from the neon sign, Drew soaked in the wisdom and drained the final traces of hot chocolate. "You've given me lots to consider. Thank you for your advice." His headache eased. Brian had no idea how his steady presence helped.

They headed outside toward their cars.

"Like I said before, I'm happy to listen or talk, whichever you prefer." Brian shook his hand, hugged him, and slapped his back a couple of times. "I hope things get better with your dad." As they parted, he snapped his fingers. "Hey, we invited all the kids and grandkids for Sunday brunch at our place. Why don't you join us?"

"Uh…" Drew hesitated, heartbeats tripping. "I guess I could. Sure, if Gayle, Erin, and the rest of the family don't mind, I'd like to join you."

"Hey, same as Erin's place on the weekend, the more the merrier in our home. Maybe you, Erin, and Noah could ride together."

"Maybe." Drew inhaled the cool, evening air and jingled his car keys in time with his racing pulse. Making travel arrangements would be a good excuse to call Erin. But how would she react? He raised a hand in a quick wave and got in the car.

As he drove toward Moose Jaw, he sucked in his cheeks. Talking to Brian, he avoided the most pressing issue of all—his tenuous future with the SnoWings. He never forgot for an instant where he stood with the team, but no one outside the team had any idea what happened and the possible repercussions.

He had yet to work up the courage to confide his career threat. The whole stressful situation tensed his shoulders, neck, and temples. Even though the car heater blasted so much hot air Jake panted in the back seat, it didn't stop Drew from shivering while he sweated. Maybe with an ounce of fatherly support, he could rebuild his confidence and forget the *incident*. But right now, he ran on the same treadmill, stuck reliving the moment over and over.

Drew switched radio stations and found easy listening melting into country music. He tapped on the steering wheel to a mournful, hurting song. If he joined the family brunch, he might offend Erin, so maybe he should change his mind and bow out. Brian would understand. Still, he had accepted the invitation and welcomed more time with the family, especially Erin. Hope jumped in his chest. With any luck at all, her feelings would grow and turn the attraction mutual.

Chapter 10

Should he call Erin today to offer her a ride to Sunday brunch or wait another day?

Drew stopped at the grocery store on the way home from work and zigzagged up and down crowded, colorful aisles grabbing several items. With his newfound flipping skills, he'd whip up pancakes for an easy dinner that would satisfy his sweet tooth. He planned to take Jake out for a run, eat, and then call Erin.

As he drove the short distance home, he carried Brian's advice like an invisible passenger. Give trust, and receive it in return. Without exception, he needed to rely unequivocally on himself and his teammates. He needed to believe he would stay on course. He needed to count on every teammate to fly every formation safely within his own four feet of airspace. Trust echoed everywhere.

He parked and chuckled at Jake's eager, panting face in the front window. If he could believe in his skills, maybe he could stay calm every time the commanding officer strode by and avoid soaking the armpits of his shirt. Maybe someday he'd feel so confident, he could make normal conversation with the man. Right now, he had doubts, but at least, he executed today's training missions according to plan.

The SnoWings didn't waste words on positive

feedback. His lead pilot and teammates said nothing about the way he performed today's manoeuvers, and silence translated to no concerns. If they noticed even the slightest error, they pounced.

In the cockpit, the familiar adrenaline rush sharpened his senses. He focused without fail. He could prove his skillset. But now, the burning question of the moment nagged. Could he strike up the courage to call Erin?

The phone rang, and Drew set down groceries with one hand, patting Jake with the other. His heart pumped an extra beat. Had his dad actually kept his promise and called? He shouldn't get his hopes up for what would likely never happen, but he wished all the same. On the third ring, he answered.

"This is Erin calling from Canine Corner." She paused. "Is this a convenient time to talk?"

Her cool, professional tone suggested official business. He took a sharp breath and cleared his throat. "Erin, oh, hi. You were on my mind." Heat rushed to his face, and he bit his tongue. True, but his greeting sounded too personal. She'd wonder why.

"Oh? Well, what a surprising coincidence," said Erin.

Her voice held a question, but she didn't ask. Why had she called? He waited.

"I wanted to discuss the gift certificate for free labour. I didn't intend to redeem it, but I'm really stuck." She emphasized the last word.

"Stuck in a snow bank?" He laughed, and the warmth in his cheekbones intensified. His humor attempt might be weak, but it worked. When he heard her laughter, a hint of pride puffed his chest.

"No, I'm stuck for help at the kennel." She sighed. "Usually my helper, Ted, takes over for a few hours on Sunday. Then Noah and I go to Regina to visit our family. But Ted's wife booked a trip to celebrate their anniversary, and I haven't found anyone to fill in. So, I'd like to accept your offer of free labour."

"I, uh, yes, of course. I'd be glad to help." The heat in his face cooled, and his elation plunged into disappointment. He would miss the family brunch. Obviously, she didn't know her dad invited him. Moisture beaded on his upper lip, and he brushed it away with the back of a hand. He would bow out and let Erin enjoy the family get-together. "Name the time, and I'll be there."

****

Erin ended the call, ran her fingers through her hair, and stared out the window across the snowy blanket. She didn't understand herself anymore. Two days ago, she tore up the gift certificate, determined never to use it. Yet now, she enlisted his help. She needed him here for the dogs, of course. She wanted to avoid him, and yet, for some strange reason, she pictured teasing him and making his serious face crack into a cautious smile.

She returned to the kitchen and laid dishes on the table. "Dinner's ready, Noah. No toy at the table, please."

He groaned but landed the plane and washed his hands before he hopped onto his chair.

She served plates of beef stew and breathed in the savory aroma of beef and vegetables.

Sam crowded under the table, drooling, and occasionally nudging her leg.

"Sit straight and eat nicely." She chewed her first bite, and the phone interrupted.

"Hi, Erin." Her dad chuckled. "Your mom told me I better confess."

"Don't keep me in suspense." She motioned for Noah to eat.

"You know I had a visit with Drew a couple of nights ago?" Brian coughed.

"Yes, so I heard." She stiffened and cleared her throat. "I wanted to talk with you about your new friend." She didn't mind if her dad noticed her clipped tone.

"Oh, you do?" Brian paused. "Hmm."

His feigned innocence didn't fool Erin for a minute. She pictured his twinkly eyes and crooked smile. "Yes, we can talk more in person," she said. "I'll see you Sunday at your place."

"About Sunday…" He chuckled again. "I invited Drew to join us for brunch. You might even want to ride together."

"Oh, Dad, no." Heat shot to her cheeks. She didn't even attempt to hide her exasperation. She dropped her fork and gave Noah an encouraging nod.

He promptly filled his mouth with another bite of stew.

"You sound concerned," said Brian. "But he really appreciated the invitation."

Her dad showed no sign of remorse. Suddenly, a startling realization sent a hot flush to her cheeks. Drew doubled booked himself to help her. Her parents expected him for brunch, and she needed him to oversee the dogs. She bit her lip and took a deep breath before she answered. "But why?"

"I consider him a friend. He doesn't have any family close. He's kind of lonely," Brian observed.

His voice did nothing to soothe her. She tightened a fist around the napkin scrunched on her lap even though her dad's assessment rang true. Drew didn't have much family, and he treated his dog like his best friend. She couldn't really argue.

"Your association doesn't have to be anything more than friendship." He sucked a mouthful of air and paused. "You might have fun."

The hand holding the phone trembled. With the other, she flashed Noah a thumbs-up for continuing to eat politely without her coaching. But how would plans work? With their current arrangements, they couldn't both attend the brunch. She paused and concentrated on keeping a calm tone. "Try to understand, Dad. I don't want him there. We made the best of the storm situation, but he's not really part of the family. He's…he's a pilot."

"Aw, Erin." He sighed.

She anticipated his familiar speech encouraging her to socialize more. "Besides, we can't both attend on Sunday." She explained the situation relating to the kennel.

"Hang on." Brian chuckled, covered the receiver, and in a muffled voice, briefed Gayle.

"I won't uninvite Drew just because you don't want him here. But he needs to work out an interesting dilemma." He chuckled. "After you sort out the plans, let us know how many to expect."

While listening to Noah tell school stories, she finished dinner and mulled over the possibilities. If she gave Drew an out, he would join her family for brunch, and she'd resent him even more. If he cancelled brunch plans to monitor the kennel, he would disappoint her dad and leave her feeling a little selfish.

Even though some kennel owners left the premises unattended for brief stretches, they took a risk she wanted to avoid. She racked her brain for someone to replace Drew. How irritating that he created the immediate scheduling conflict, and yet, she was stuck sweating over a solution.

As she cleaned the dishes, a quiet revelation filled her like water in the sink. Since she met Drew, she thought of Eric less often. He faded into the background with his face in her memories blurring around the edges like an old photograph.

Her startling observation tripped her heartbeat. She needed to raise her energetic son and build a strong business. She didn't need a man, especially not a pilot. Shuddering, she bit her lip. How would she solve the brunch dilemma? The absence of a workable solution for dog care still tormented her.

The next morning, Erin woke focused on two priorities—Noah and business. After she sent her son to school, she would analyze the downward booking trend. Following playtime with Sam and the other dogs, she made a soothing, fragrant cup of orange-spice tea. Then she gathered all the paperwork and financial records for Canine Corner.

First, she reviewed bookings since she took over in January. Fleeing the prairie winter, clients had booked enough dog-care spaces to fill the kennel to near capacity. Advance bookings, arranged by Ray, produced strong February results. Bookings slowed in early March, and now, business trickled in. She sipped her steaming beverage and searched for clues in the financial statements and client files. Summarizing her findings, she confirmed with a jolt that overall revenue dipped slightly from the same time last year. Her pulse sped. Bookings for the spring and summer months trended twenty-five percent lower than projections. What made business drop? She needed quick answers. Maybe others were skeptical of a new owner like Drew's initial reaction.

She'd sunk a big slice of Eric's life insurance into this business and needed to build success, no matter what. Reality struck her in the face and boosted her heart rate into a sprint. Instead of thriving, her business slumped. She twisted a lock of hair and pored over the information until Noah banged his arrival. The morning's work had flown by without revealing any answers.

Opening the door, Erin inhaled the soft, fresh air and discovered spring hurried in while she worked. The sun shone, and the snow glistened and softened into sticky mounds. "How was school?" She swept Noah into a hug and hung up his jacket.

"I did a lot of work and stuff." He thumped Sam's side and wiped the sloppy, dog lick off his cheek.

She tousled his wavy hair. "After lunch, we'll have fun."

"Is Drew coming to play?" Noah's face broke into a grin.

"No. Guess again." No, not today. She fought to calm her pulse from beating as erratically as a tap dance. Why didn't her gullible heart listen to her rationale brain? She needed to keep him away.

"I don't know." He tilted his head.

136

"Let's build a snowman. The sticky snow is perfect to roll and shape big balls." Playing outside in the fresh air would be fun and therapeutic. She'd clear her mind, and for a while, forget the nasty complications looming.

****

Trust your teammates, Drew, every single one. Watch the lead jet and focus. In the air, he coached himself and accomplished his goals for the mission. But the moment he landed, his dilemma flew to mind.

As he strode from the tarmac to the training depot, he squinted in the sun glinting off snow banks lining the runway. The simplest answer would be to explain the situation, apologize, and decline to attend the brunch. Brian and Gayle planned to host their family anyway, so they wouldn't miss him. But his heart beat a reminder of how much he wanted to be there.

He'd sampled a taste of normal family life, and now, he craved it like candy. He wanted to join in the teasing and glimpse Erin's perfect, white smile. He wanted to surround himself with people who not only loved one another but genuinely liked and trusted each other. If he spent more time around them, maybe he'd absorb their magic and find a place he truly belonged.

The team's quips and laughter filled the crowded crew room but didn't pull him away from his solitary reflection. How could he help Erin with the kennel and still join the family brunch? If he found a fill-in helper who met her approval, maybe he could offer a rain check on his free labour and let someone else take over. He would gladly honor his debt any other time.

He gathered his belongings and headed outside. Where could he turn for help? His teammate, Kyle, once mentioned he liked dogs. Maybe he would do him a favor. "See you tomorrow." He raised a hand to a cluster of team members who stood joking and sauntered next to Kyle toward his car.

"I wish we had great days like today more often." Kyle jingled his car keys and tossed them in the air.

"You mean the team's work? Oh, yeah, the weather." Drew breathed the fresh air and put on sunglasses. A mild breeze nudged, hinting of warmer days to come. He slipped and sidestepped another icy patch in the parking lot. "Yeah, my dog and I will enjoy our outing."

"I wouldn't mind owning a pet, but I've avoided getting one because of moving around so much." Kyle formed a handful of snow into a ball and threw it at a light stand.

"Jake and I've been together for a while. Most things change, but he's one of the constants in my life." He paused by his car, and his upper lip moistened. "Hey, if you really like dogs, I'll make a proposition." In the cockpit, he ignored a little perspiration, but on the ground, he hated showing his discomfort. He swiped a finger across his lip.

Kyle laughed. "Sounds interesting." He tossed his keys high and caught them. "Go ahead. Shoot."

"The situation is a bit complicated..." Drew explained his double booking. "So, Erin needs help to oversee the kennel. You wouldn't have to work hard. You'd just hang out and keep the dogs company for a few hours."

Kyle's freckled face broadened into a grin. "Oh, I get your drift. I would be a dog sitter on a large scale."

"The only catch is, you won't get paid." Drew leaned on his car. "At least, not cash. I'd buy you dinner next week."

"I could handle a free meal. But only if you treat me to an expensive steak dinner." Kyle laughed and punched his shoulder. "Nah, just kidding. I'd be glad to do you and your girlfriend a favor."

"She's only a friend." Heat like burning embers sizzled in his face, and he raised a hand to shade his eyes as much from Kyle's scrutiny as from the sun. "She's not actually my girlfriend."

"Sure, I can help you and your prospective girlfriend." Kyle grinned and jingled his keys. "You're on. I'm happy to help."

"Really? I can't thank you enough." He pumped a fist. "You just made my day." He got in his car, shut the door, and pounded the steering wheel. "Yes, I found a solution," he hollered. He glanced in the rear-view mirror at his beaming smile. Now, he just had to tell Erin what he'd done.

As he drove home weighing options, Drew steered through sunbeams reflecting off puddles. Should he call her to tell her he found a willing substitute, or should he tell her in person? Talking in person made sense, so he could read her reaction in her flashing eyes, firm cheeks, and full mouth.

To be honest, he just plain wanted to see her and Noah. They'd talk, laugh, play with the toy airplane, and enjoy some fun together. If he dropped in yet again, would he annoy her? He might as well take the chance, and depending on how he found her mood, he might float an idea.

He stopped at home to pick up Jake and continued to Canine Corner. When they arrived, sun glinted off a snow family in the front yard. Erin and Noah had been busy. A snow dad, mom, and two children sported hats and scarves, waved branch arms, and beamed button smiles under carrot noses.

"Did you see what we made?" Noah beat Erin to the front door and jumped in place while he pointed out their snow creations.

Sam trundled past him to meet Jake.

"I saw your nice work." He smacked Noah's hand in a high five. "Why doesn't your snow family include a snow dog?"

"They need a dog. Mommy, can Drew and I make one?" Noah beamed and bounced in a circle.

"Hi, again." Erin leaned against the entrance wall, raised an eyebrow, and crossed her arms. "You're a regular here."

She wore a patterned sweater with jeans, and her cheeks glowed pink like a sunrise. A flush rose in his face, and desire coursed through his veins. Someday, maybe he'd hug her close.

She tilted her head. "Why the surprise visit?"

Her half smile did little to soften her prickly tone. Instantly, Drew hunched his shoulders. He shouldn't have dropped in. "Sorry, I should have called first." He cleared his throat.

Noah tapped his mom's arm.

Erin squeezed Noah's shoulder. "Drew didn't come to play."

"Please, Mommy." He squiggled free.

"I didn't exactly come to play, but if you don't mind, I could stay and build a snow dog." Drew met Erin's gaze and shifted.

She tilted her head from side to side and wrinkled her forehead. "Dinner's almost ready, but I guess so.

I'll join you for a few minutes." She grabbed jackets.

Noah jumped and hollered. "Oh, thank you, Mommy."

In the yard, Drew helped Noah roll and pat smooth balls of snow, sculpting them into a roly-poly dog.

Erin joined them in scooping and patting sticky globs of snow to form a canine nose.

Finally, they stood back to admire their work.

"He's funny." Noah clapped his mittens together, giggled, and pointed.

"Way to go, guys." Erin knocked the snow off her mittens. "Your creation is almost as cute as Sam."

At the sound of his buddy's name, the black-and-white dog woofed.

"Oh, sorry, Jake." She petted his head. "You're pretty cute, too."

"Yep, we did excellent work." Drew still held a small snowball in his hand, and suddenly, he took a chance and lobbed it. He held his breath, waiting for Erin's reaction.

Erin dodged but couldn't avoid the snow that splatted her shoulder.

"Hey, you got Mommy." Noah laughed and pointed.

"He sure did." Erin's face wavered between a smile and a frown. She bent and scooped a handful of snow into a ball and faked a toss. As Drew lunged left, she flung the snowball and thwacked his temple.

Drew burst out laughing, echoed by the others. He hadn't played in snow since he was a kid. Warmed by the fun, he savored the joy that tingled in his chest.

Smiling, Erin raised both arms. "Touché. I played softball, so watch out."

"Get me. See if you can hit me." Noah tugged on Drew's arm.

Drew grinned, tossed a snowball at the eager boy, and then dodged an onslaught from Erin and him. Ducking and flinging snowballs in all directions, he laughed at the delighted reactions to their snowy competition.

The dogs frolicked, barked, and grabbed mouthfuls of snow.

Finally, they all collapsed in a white-sprinkled collection next to the snow family and dog.

"Okay, you guys, we need to stop. I'm cold, wet, and hungry." Erin put up her hands.

"Can Drew and Jake eat supper here?" Noah threw one last snowball.

Erin paused and knocked snow off her sleeves.

Drew shook his head. "Not today, Noah. We better go home." He wished he could stay, but he didn't want to wear out his welcome.

"We could have so much fun." Noah tugged on his mom's arm.

Erin pursed her lips and mimicked her son's saucer-like eyes. She glanced at Drew. "I guess if you like, you can stay." She bent and brushed snow off her legs. "Dinner's nothing fancy—just a chicken casserole—but I made plenty."

"If you're sure..." A combination of hunger and anticipation rumbled in Drew's stomach. He savored the idea of her company even more than the food. Her invitation must mean she wasn't too upset anymore over the toy airplane.

"Yes, you can stay. Stay. Stay." Noah grabbed Drew's sleeve.

Erin raised a finger and hushed Noah's chant. "He's sure anyway." She smiled and motioned toward the house. "No, really, I don't mind. You're welcome to join us."

Heartbeat jumping, Drew grinned. She must not totally dislike his company. Maybe she secretly enjoyed it. Could the dinner invitation possibly mean a turning point?

Chapter 11

Now, what had Erin done? Drew and Noah chatted like old friends, leaving her the odd person out at the dinner table. She should never have invited him to stay.

"How's school?" Drew buttered a bun and handed it to Noah.

"My teacher said you can come to school." Noah reached and nearly spilled his milk.

Just in time, Erin caught and steadied the glass.

"She did?" Eyebrows raised, Drew threw her a questioning glance.

Irritated, she leaned forward and plunked both palms on the table. "Noah, I already told Mrs. Jansen I wouldn't ask Drew to take time off work to come to school." She wanted to keep him away, not arrange another chance to influence her son.

"But the kids want to learn about pilot stuff." Noah scrunched his face.

"Noah, eat your dinner this minute." Erin fixed her gaze until he put a spoonful of noodles into his mouth. His attraction to Drew had to stop. Noah absolutely could not use him as his role model. She picked up her fork and stabbed her salad. She set the example now, and no outsider could possibly take his father's place.

"The SnoWings do sometimes visit schools." Drew swiped his face with his napkin.

Stiffening, Erin passed the casserole to offer a

second helping. As a guest, he shouldn't interfere with her decision.

"I really want Drew to come to school." Noah set his fist on the table with his fork pointed upward.

Erin paused. Her feelings were so conflicted. How could she help a five-year-old boy understand why she needed to keep him away? Maybe Drew would make the same offer to anyone. As Canadian military representatives, the SnoWings probably served the community with various activities, but she did not like the idea one bit.

She sighed and bit her lower lip. "I don't feel right asking you to visit the class as a personal favor, but I'll pass on the information to the teacher. She can make a request through the normal channels."

"Tell her to mention my name. I'd love to talk to the kids." Drew's eyes shone.

"Okay, I guess so." She raised her napkin to cover her flushed cheeks and regain control. She had met this man less than a week ago, and now, like the sticky, white stuff outside, their connection snowballed. He repeatedly appeared on the doorstep, and today, he shared another family dinner. She stood, clattered together the plates and cutlery, and dropped them into the sink. He didn't belong anywhere near her home or her life.

For dessert, she served fruit and frozen yogurt and waited for Drew to explain the reason for his latest drop-in visit.

Finally, as he finished the last bite and sipped tea, he shifted in his chair, and rosy color splotched his cheekbones.

"Noah, you may be excused." Erin wiped a fleck of

sauce off his cheek. "Take Sam and Jake downstairs to play ball."

Drew rested his forearms on the table and cleared his throat. "I, uh, I need to tell you what I did."

"You sound slightly ominous." She took a deep breath, gritted her teeth, and cradled her mug.

His eyes flashed. "I double-booked myself for Sunday, but don't worry because I found a solution." He vouched for Kyle's reliability, how he loved dogs, and didn't mind filling in. "So, we can all go for brunch together."

Erin crossed her arms, sat back, and bit her lip. He had a lot of nerve delegating her business to someone else's care. She wanted to stop him cold, but she took a deep breath and let him finish.

"I arranged a substitute worker, but I could just decline your parents' invitation instead. You decide."

He rubbed his chin and shifted in his chair.

She studied his pinched face, blinked, and swallowed her dismay. He had overstepped his bounds to arrange a fill-in helper, but he just intended to help. "Do you really want to join our family for brunch?"

"Yes, I'd really like the chance to get together." He curved his lips into a half smile. A twitch flickered in the corner of his left eye, and he blinked and rubbed it.

Erin uncrossed her arms and sat forward. Kyle would be on duty for just a few hours. He would keep an eye on the dogs and if an emergency struck, alert her. Honestly, any willing person could handle the job. Drew would accept her answer without argument. If she approved, she'd probably make his day. Brightness would enliven his dark eyes and handsome face. But if she agreed, she would again allow him near Noah. An

146

intense tug-of-war jostled until her words trickled. "I guess I can accept Kyle's offer...just this once."

Flushing, he relaxed his jaw and straightened in his chair. "Whew, I'm glad you approve. Kyle will take good care of things." He smiled and nodded. "Thank you for giving me the chance to join you."

"Thank you for making the arrangements." She covered her smile behind her coffee mug. He wanted to please.

"Now, do you mind if I help with dishes and then play for a few minutes before I leave?" He raised his eyebrows and smiled.

Pleasantly surprised by his cleanup offer, she widened her eyes then tilted her head and bit her lip. A short playtime couldn't hurt too much. But after today, she would never again allow him to visit her home. She needed to protect her familiar world.

"Thanks for offering, but I can handle cleanup." Erin picked up the serving dishes from the center of the table. "Noah needs some time to unwind before bedtime on a school night, so he may not play long."

Drew shifted from one foot to the other and cleared his throat. "I understand. I promise I won't overstay my welcome."

She rattled the load of dishes. Maybe he already had.

After he joined in several loops and dips with Noah, he kept his word and soon departed.

Then Ted arrived to handle the evening chores, leaving Erin free of kennel duties. Thoughts spinning, she got Noah ready for bed and tucked him in. She needed to talk to someone about the internal tornado Drew's latest drop-in visit prompted. Who could help her sort out her complicated feelings? Should she use her mom, Claire, or Vera as a sounding board? With both hands, she clutched and massaged the sides of her head. Her family and friends might believe she needed another man, but they didn't live with sorrow deep in their bones. They hadn't walked in her shoes, so they didn't qualify to dole out unwelcome advice.

She plopped on the carpet beside Sam and ran her hand down his furry back. No one else realized the business pressures closing in, either. For now, she'd keep the challenges private. If revenue proved lower than expected, she didn't need anyone saying, "I told you so." She flipped on the TV weather and caught the forecast for more mild days ahead. Last weekend's freak storm marked the end of winter, and the snow would soon disappear. She couldn't wait to see Canine Corner without a blanket of snow. She'd viewed pictures of the summer landscaping and flowers, but she wanted to experience the yard in full bloom. Before she could decide on a confidante, the phone rang.

"How are you? I called to check in."

Vera's cheerful voice greeted her. "Hi, Vera. I'm fine, maybe." She swallowed through a narrowed throat and leaned into a fist. Her neighbor's greeting probed deep. She pictured her intense, blue eyes peering below the gray fringe, spiked in all directions.

"You don't sound convinced," Vera said gently.

"I'm..." Erin's voice cracked, and a small sob slipped out. "Sorry, I just have a lot on my mind."

"Aw, you carry a big load, dear," Vera said. "Do you want to talk about your worries?"

Her friend clucked soothing noises, and her sympathy warmed like tea. "I can't right now. Maybe we can get together tomorrow." Her voice shook, and she swiped at the tears wetting her cheeks. The murky mix of challenges she faced combined in an overwhelming heap.

"I understand. Go to bed early tonight and get a good rest. Everything always looks brighter in the morning," Vera said.

"You're right. All my challenges hit at once today." Erin wiped her eyes.

"I'll come tomorrow morning and help you hash over the details then. How does that plan sound?"

"Perfect, thank you." Erin ended the call and wrung her hands. She couldn't begin to explain everything plaguing her or map possible solutions. Even advice from no-nonsense Vera probably wouldn't help anything.

****

Halfway home, Drew realized the question he wanted to ask Erin would have to wait for the drive to Regina. He looked forward to Sunday more than he anticipated anything in a long time. When he arrived, he found the message light blinking on his phone.

"Hello, Drewzer." His dad's voice crackled. "I promised to call. Sorry, I took a few days. If you want to talk, call me this evening."

Drew dropped his jaw and listened to the message a second time. Hearing his dad's voice topped off an already great day. He scored flawless aerial execution, a teammate's big favor, and Erin's hospitality. He couldn't have asked for more.

He gave Jake a rawhide bone to keep him quiet and, with quivery hands, returned the call. "Hey, Dad, I got your message."

"You called me first, so tell me what's on your mind."

Frank always got straight to the point. "I, uh…" Drew fumbled for words. He needed to face his dad to have a serious conversation, meet his gaze, read his body language, and gauge his reactions. "I hope we can get together in person sometime like we planned."

"Yeah, the weather threw us a bit of a curve ball, or should I say a snowball?" He chortled. "Bummer the way the weekend worked out."

Drew ignored his dad's cheesy, weather pun. Noise and laughter, likely a TV sitcom, jangled in the background. He competed for his dad's full attention. "Can you hear me okay?"

"Hang on a sec. I'll turn off the TV." Frank paused and returned. "Okay, now, where were we?"

"I'd like to see you in person to give us the chance to really talk." Drew paced back and forth.

Frank grunted, sighed, and paused. "Something on your mind?"

"Yes, I'd like to discuss several things, actually." Drew spun and retraced his steps. "I'd like to visit, but I can't take off another day. Heading into air show season, training gets pretty intense."

"Maybe I ought to come there? I've never been to the thriving metropolis of Moose Jaw, Sask-at-chew-wan." As he exaggerated every syllable of the province's name, he laughed.

Drew forced a chuckle. "You don't know what you're missing." He glanced out the living room window at the shrinking snow banks and growing puddles. The weather didn't match balmy, Phoenix weather, but spring would soon be here.

"Why do they call the city Moose Jaw?"

"You're a little off topic, Dad." Drew laughed. "But since you asked, most locals say the name comes from a Cree word, *Moosegaw,* which means warm breezes."

"You have warm breezes there?" Frank raised his voice. "Now you're talking."

His dad never changed. His raspy voice scratched Drew's eardrum. "I guess so. Sometimes, the weather turns very pleasant." Drew paced up and down the hallway with Jake trailing.

"Because if I leave the sun in Phoenix, I don't want to freeze off my buns." Frank ended with a holler.

The news warmed like a hot shower, and Drew's pulse strummed quicker. "You mean you'll come?"

"How's next weekend?"

Frank's gravelly voice boomed. Heart thudding, Drew pumped a fist. For the first time in his grown-up life, he'd host his dad. Finally, they would have a chance to really connect. "Yes, next weekend works. I'll keep it clear."

After the call, Drew dropped to his hands and knees and wrestled with extra vigour to grab Jake's toy. For a few minutes, he celebrated the good news before the stiffness settled back into his shoulders. His dad broke promises all the time, and just because he returned a call didn't mean he had totally reformed. Drew took deep breaths, forcing himself to relax. He better calm down until his dad actually showed up. If he didn't get too excited, he wouldn't be too let down if the visit didn't happen.

Chapter 12

Vera predicted right. Erin felt better in the morning, but she still carried some heavy burdens. Interacting with Sam and the other dogs never failed to lift her spirits, so she headed for the kennel as soon as Noah hopped onto the school bus. Breathing in the soft, spring air scented with mud, she tossed balls and patted dogs in the outside exercise area until a car hummed into the yard.

"I'll be right back, pups. You amuse yourself for a few minutes." She headed around front, greeted Vera with a wave, and then herded the dogs into their individual runs.

Vera hurried to the kennel and gave her a big hug.

Together, they doubled back toward the house until Erin suggested they stay outside and enjoy the pleasant temperature rising steadily above the freezing point. The melting snow softened the path into a slushy mess around the edge of the property, so they hiked through the gate and up the road, breathing the green and earthy hints of spring. "Are you and Ted ready for your trip?" Erin's busy schedule loomed in a messy lump.

"We're close. We still have a couple of days to get ready. I'm sorry Ted's absence adds to your pressures." Vera folded her gloved hands.

"Yeah, staffing concerns me." Erin avoided a puddle. Of course, she fretted about juggling the workload. "But don't worry about it. Ted's entitled to vacation time." At the moment, business volumes concerned her even more than the lack of an assistant.

"You undertook a big job here." Vera swung her arms wide.

"Yes, but I love the kennel. I really do." Erin refused to believe she couldn't manage the load. "I'm just a little overwhelmed right now. In the last week, everything changed." Eyes welling with tears, she stared across the swirl of white and brown prairie. Uncertainty clutched her middle, and she pressed both hands against the tension. Drew's presence interrupted her predicable routine in a very unsettling way.

"Everything?" Vera stared ahead and quickened her steps.

"Well, a few, new things cause concern." She adjusted her pace to match her neighbor's spunky stride in red, rubber boots.

"Do the flowers you almost gave me explain your feelings?" Keeping her gaze forward, Vera swung her arms high.

Sam bounded in circles with the constant motion flapping his golden ears.

Erin smiled at his doggy joy and sighed. "I didn't want the flowers. I can't handle Drew in my life."

"Should I tell you a story?" Vera stared into the distance.

"Sure." Her lip quivered. Maybe if she absorbed mature wisdom for a while, she would know where to begin.

"Ted is not my first husband." Vera stopped and faced her.

"He's not?" Erin squinted and shook her head.

"But you've been married thirty-five years."

"Yes, and I love him dearly. But he wasn't my first love. I was only thirty when my first husband died in a car accident." Vera strolled a few steps and then accelerated.

Erin sucked a mouthful of air. A person never knew someone else's pain. She kept pace and waited to hear more.

"I almost wished I had gone, too. But I had two little children, and in the early weeks and months, they kept me going." Vera stared at the path ahead.

"I'm sorry." Erin coughed and sputtered. Her heart ached with a rush of painful memories, and she strode faster.

"Don't be sorry. My story has a happy ending." Vera put a hand on her arm. "At the time, I couldn't imagine marrying another man, but my friend introduced me to Ted and convinced me to give him a chance. At first, I resisted, but eventually, I agreed to date him. Of course, I made the right choice, and I'm very thankful. We built a beautiful life together. We had two more children, and now, we cherish our grandchildren. Life carries on in a wonderful way."

"I had no idea." The words caught in Erin's throat, and she sniffed. She couldn't reject her advice. Vera had experienced similar pain.

"Of course, you didn't know our history." Vera smiled and squeezed her hand.

They crunched in unison for a while.

"Thanks for sharing." Erin cleared her throat and digested the shocking revelation.

"Trust me. Ted and I prove second chances count, and love grows."

"I haven't even gone on a date with Drew, but I feel like I'm unfaithful to Eric." She stared across the field to a rural road. A car cut across the prairie in the distance, probably transporting people just going about their normal routines.

"Eric will always live in your heart. He'll always live in Noah. Nobody's asking you to erase your past." Vera puffed and slowed.

Her neighbor radiated quiet wisdom. When Erin's family broached the topic, they didn't base their advice on personal experience. She could always say, "You have no idea how I feel." But she couldn't shut out Vera. She had survived a devastating loss, too, and understood.

"I have no idea if this Drew fellow is the right partner." Vera sloshed her boots through mud. "But I know you're too young to live the rest of your life on your own. Maybe Noah could even have a brother or sister someday…"

Hope surged in Erin's heart and then plummeted. She paused and switched directions toward the house. In the melting sunshine, she sank with each step. "Sometimes single motherhood exhausts my energy," she confessed. "When I see Noah thriving on Drew's attention, I feel so…so crushed. No matter what, my job is to protect him."

Vera stopped and wrapped her in a hug. "I understand, and I also believe people come into our lives for a reason. Could he possibly make you both happy?"

Erin took a deep, shuddery breath. Thank goodness Vera didn't expect a response, because she didn't know the answer. "I'm ready for tea. What about you?"

They trudged the rest of the way in silence.

Sam padded beside them in a straight line, imitating their somber moods.

Seated at the kitchen table with a mug of steaming lemon tea, Erin bowed her head to Vera's intense gaze.

"Okay, dear. What else?" Vera leaned across the table and rubbed her arm.

She yearned to ignore the words of wisdom and stay within her comfort zone, but she couldn't argue with someone who understood her situation better than anyone. Sipping her tea, she braced herself. "My other problem concerns the business, but I don't know if I understand the issue well enough to even explain…"

"Are you worried about something besides staffing?" Vera cupped her mug in both hands.

Erin breathed lemony steam. "I can work out a staffing plan, but I discovered a bigger problem. Bookings are not as strong as I expected. Business has declined. I need to analyze trends to find a solution."

"I understand your concern." Vera blinked several times.

"I'm sure I can rebuild the business. But first, I need to figure out the problem." She tapped a finger on the table and bit her lip. Vera set down her mug. "I do know some of the old-timers in the area have quit travelling as much. Some don't even have a dog anymore."

"Could I have possibly bought a dying business?" She set down her mug and rubbed her forehead with both hands. She had a lot of investigation and work ahead, because no matter what, she would build her business into a success.

Long after Vera departed, her presence lingered.

After she lost her first husband, she had built a new life. But Erin needed to find her own path. Opening her heart to another man would be risky and scary. As for business, at least she had a clue to explore.

She spent the rest of the morning reviewing her client files and making a list to call, targeting customers who hadn't boarded a dog in the past six months. Using her marketing skills, she designed the calls with a dual purpose. She could promote her services to drum up more business and at the same time, do market research on clients' needs. A follow-up survey would gather feedback from the clients who had already used her services.

As she made lunch and waited for Noah to arrive home, she answered the phone and recognized Noah's teacher's voice. A trace of irritation flitted by as she visualized Noah's teacher with perfect hair and smiling, pink lips.

"I wanted to thank you for sending the note today." Mrs. Jansen spoke quickly.

"You're welcome. No problem. If possible, my client will arrange to visit the class." Whenever she mentioned Drew, her heart fluttered. She placed a calming hand on her chest, moistened her lips, and stared out the window.

"He's not just willing to help out. He's already committed." Mrs. Jansen stretched her words and laughed. "I talked to the SnoWings' contact at recess and booked your friend for Monday."

"Oh, already?" Erin stirred and inhaled the scent of sage floating from chicken noodle soup. Noting the slight inflection on the friend label, she stiffened. Catching her own defensiveness, she reminded herself she had nothing to hide. Besides, the teacher's perky approach fit perfectly with Noah's lively personality.

"If you'd like to join the class on Monday and hear your friend speak, you're very welcome," said Mrs. Jansen.

Heat rushed through Erin. Sitting in a classroom while Drew described his flying adventures would be torture. Noah would bubble over with more stories and dreams of flying, reminding her of aerial adventures she'd rather avoid. Queasiness struck, and she opened the window and gulped fresh air. Of course, she wanted Mrs. Jansen to realize she excelled as a caring, supportive parent, so she thanked her for the invitation. "If I can find a fill-in helper for the kennel, I might come." She leaned toward the window, swept her hands through her hair, and breathed deeply. Apparently, she would see him, whether she wanted to or not.

****

Drew counted down the days until his dad's visit the following weekend. An internal motor sped the whole time he exercised Jake and drove to the base. To make up for lost time, he'd plan a mix of conversation, reflection, and action.

What did his dad expect? Did he have any inkling of Drew's hopes? He never gave any sign he thought their relationship missed anything. He never hinted he sensed the hurt inside his son. Drew tested the words he would say and the best way to share his feelings. He couldn't change the past, but he could clear the air and start rebuilding a relationship.

Water pooled on the roads where snow piled only a few days ago. He slowed, lowered the window, and heard a bird chirping. The promise of warmer weather boosted his mood. His newfound optimism reflected a different, milder eagerness than his former enthusiasm. He never forgot one more mistake could cost him his SnoWings career. Someday, he'd fly free of the grip of fear, and maybe, his former intensity would return.

Would his dad want to tour the base? He would have to arrange security clearance for a family member. The weekend might quickly fill. Moose Jaw had its share of tourist attractions, so they could easily spend a few hours sightseeing. Anticipation and apprehension tingled up and down his spine. He would find a way to talk to his dad about growing closer and planting the seeds of trust. He wouldn't find the experience easy, but he longed to make the weekend both fun and meaningful.

At the base, he switched to pilot mode. As he strode toward the building, he took deep breaths of crisp, morning air. He could make the grade. His familiar mantra accompanied his footsteps. *One day at a time, you can trust yourself and your teammates. Stay focused. You can do it.*

He practiced the same intricate manoeuvers repeatedly until the Team Lead approved. The day exhausted him. After he completed the drills, he didn't even notice Kyle waiting by the door until they nearly collided.

"Hey, what's for dinner?" Kyle stretched his eyes wide.

Drew laughed and rotated a stiff shoulder. "I'll probably cook something gourmet from whatever instant package I find in my cupboard."

"No, seriously. My wife's hosting book club tonight, so I'm on my own. I'd suggest we dine out, but you probably have to get home to your dog." He matched Drew's stride.

Occasionally, in the crew room, he'd heard Kyle mention his wife. Lucky him to have a partner at home.

"Yeah, you're right. Jake waits by the window. But I do owe you a dinner, and I don't mind paying in advance." He laughed and willed his shoulders to relax. "Be warned, though, you have no idea what you requested. I'm no cook." For the first time, a teammate wanted to share a meal together outside work. He rarely hosted guests, and the idea slightly unnerved him. "But sure, why don't you come over to my place, and we'll order in."

He took pride in his small, tidy home, furnished with brown, leather sofa and chairs and a swirly-patterned, earth-toned carpet to cozy the living room. To a newcomer, the surroundings would likely appear comfortable and inviting.

Kyle followed him there. "Let's order food from the Thai place on Main Street. The food is delicious, spicy, and authentic, guaranteed. You'd never guess the quality by the storefront or the décor, but you won't find a better, casual meal anywhere."

Over a feast of spring rolls, chicken satay, and pad Thai spread in cardboard containers on the kitchen table, they rehashed the day and toasted the coming weekend.

As he refilled his plate, Kyle bantered good-naturedly.

By the time Drew finished his second helping, he dissolved the rocks in his jaw and shoulders.

"So, what's your story, man?" Kyle tipped back and rested his hands on his belly. "I'm stuffed, by the way."

"You want to hear my background?" Drew crossed his arms. Holding personal details private kept things simple. Kyle's question might be innocent enough, but he didn't need to know the details of Drew's broken family.

"Yeah, even after all these months training together, you stick to yourself so much the other guys and I hardly know you. Like I only found out yesterday, you have a girlfriend."

Drew raised an eyebrow and tossed Jake's ball. "She's not my girlfriend." Oh, how he wished. The spark in his heart intensified, and warmth jumped to his face.

"Oh, right. Your potential girlfriend. So…?" Kyle tapped his hands on his middle.

Drew cleared his throat. "I don't have much to tell. I graduated from the Military College in Ontario. My family's not close." He made the understatement of the year. His half-siblings remained practically strangers, because his parents chased other relationships and passed him back and forth like a football. "Although, I just heard my dad will arrive next weekend." He shifted in his chair. "I've never met anybody I wanted to marry. So far, relationships haven't worked out, so here I am in Moose Jaw, single and uh, fighting to keep my place on the team." Moisture beaded on his upper lip, and he wiped it with a finger.

"You've been doing fine lately. You made one mistake. Forget the past." Kyle lobbed an imaginary ball over his shoulder.

"Makes sense, but I'm under a microscope." Drew lifted his napkin and wiped his lips. These days, his confidence would fit in his back pocket.

"I know. But as long as you beat yourself up, you can't recover." Kyle rubbed his cropped, ginger hair and shrugged. "We've all made mistakes." He peered at Drew.

"Some errors wreak more havoc than others." The *incident* rushed to attack Drew's equilibrium. As he sensed the room tilting, he gripped the chair arms. Inhaling sharply, he released his hold and then gulped his soda. He rubbed Jake's thick coat until his view of the room steadied. His teammate had no idea the anxiety he suffered.

Kyle nodded. "We all know what happened, but have you figured out why?"

Drew shrugged and flinched at the tension grabbing his temples. "I go over and over the situation in my mind. It happened so fast…" He stood to clear the table and put away the leftover food. "But thanks. I appreciate the vote of confidence."

Why had he made the near-deadly mistake? He couldn't count the times he asked himself the same question, and the answer always pointed to one word— trust. He failed to trust every single teammate to be in the precise, correct position. Distrust, plain and simple, sent him off course, but he didn't need to reveal his disturbing secret.

Kyle followed him to the living room. "Getting together has been great, but I better go and charm the book club women. Not having a wife, see what you're missing. You, too, could make a guest appearance in a roomful of women dissecting books." He laughed and gave him a playful punch on his shoulder. "Thanks, man. I appreciate the meal. See you Sunday morning at

Canine Corner. I'll finally get to meet your girlfriend."

"She's not…" Drew shook his head.

"Oh, right. She's not your girlfriend." Kyle smirked and stretched.

"Right. Well, bye. Thanks for coming." Drew bent his arm in a single wave and muttered, "Hey, Jake, I actually had fun."

From the front sidewalk, Kyle called over his shoulder. "Maybe you should ask her on a real date."

Drew pulled back his shoulders. He liked Kyle's idea. Energized by the company and ribbing, he darted from room to room, chased Jake, and tossed the ball. With a peer, he had shared some laughs and delicious food. The satisfied lump he carried wasn't just the large portion of Thai food in his belly. He belonged.

Fitting in with the rest of the team started somewhere, maybe even tonight. Kyle believed in his ability as a pilot. Drew could salvage his SnoWings dream. A lightness buoyed in him, and the new sensation could only be…newfound hope. For the first time in ages, his whole life glowed brighter. He glanced at the clock and judged he had time to make a call before bedtime. Why hesitate any longer?

Chapter 13

Erin stepped out of a long soak in a hot, vanilla-scented bath, wrapped a towel around her hair, threw on a robe over her tingling skin, and dashed for the phone. On the fourth ring, she answered the call.

"Am I, uh, calling too late?"

Drew's deep, hesitant voice greeted her. "No, almost but not quite." She paused, mouth slightly open, and toweled her hair with one hand. "Another ten minutes and you might have caught me in bed, but you called just under the wire."

"I just had dinner with Kyle, the guy who'll take care of the dogs."

"Did you have fun? You enjoyed dinner?" Had he called just to chat? She cinched her robe and trailed a foot over Sam's furry coat.

Sam panted and thumped his tail.

"The food and the company were both great. Did you have a good day?"

Maybe he called just to talk. "My day consisted of the usual full schedule with Noah and the dogs. I also did some business analysis." She shook her damp hair. She didn't mind talking, but why had he called?

He cleared his throat. "You have a lot going on there. Don't forget your gift certificate. You can put me to work next week."

"I'm not sure." Asking him for help would just

complicate her life. Her persistent, internal butterflies fluttered a warning.

"I'm counting on working there. Now, you must wonder why I called."

"Yes, because you usually just show up on my doorstep." She flushed. She shouldn't flirt.

He laughed. "I wanted to mix up my approach a bit and not be too predictable. Anyway, I had planned to talk in the car on Sunday. But I realized Noah might hear, and I didn't want to make the situation…uh, I didn't want to make you uncomfortable."

Knees slightly weak, she sank cross-legged to the kitchen floor beside Sam.

The dog licked her hand with his smooth, moist tongue.

Drew stumbled over his words more than usual, so he must be working up the courage to ask her on a date. Her butterflies zigzagged like they would burst right through her skin.

Vera would tell her to accept his invitation, relax, and enjoy a real, one-on-one date. He didn't faintly resemble fair, muscular Eric, but his lean body and smooth, olive complexion were attractive. If she desired a man and wasn't terrified of flying, she would find his status as military pilot alluring. If…she faced so many ifs…and above all, she needed to shield her wounded heart.

"But I wondered…since Noah is so interested in airplanes…"

His words snatched her back to reality. He mentioned Noah and not a date at all. Noah grabbed his attention, not her. She bit her lip and waited.

"Has he ever visited the flight display at the

museum? Could I possibly take him to see it sometime?" He took an audible breath. "The gallery features a whole section on the SnoWings."

She tensed her entire body.

"He loves planes, and you'd probably rather avoid them." Drew paused and then rushed on. "But you could come, too...if you don't want us guys to go alone."

Erin rubbed her head and clenched the damp towel. She did not expect this invitation at all, and her mind spun, angry and confused. He tripped over his words, not to invite her on a date, but to seek permission to get Noah even more hooked on airplanes. Drew couldn't set aside his passion. He embraced flying so fully, he still didn't grasp that she shunned airplanes in any form. Of course, her son would jump at the opportunity, but she couldn't allow it.

"I'm sorry, but the answer is no." His request set off fireworks. She thrust away the damp towel. "I definitely need to decline." She would do almost anything for Noah, but she would not allow Drew to encourage his newfound fascination with flying. Sure, Noah could use another male role model besides his grandpa and uncle, but not now. She wasn't ready to let go yet.

"I figured you might not like the idea."

Hot embers burned her chest, and sparks sizzled her tongue. His lowered voice didn't smooth the idea into anything near palatable. "I appreciate the offer, but honestly, I detest flying, and I don't want Noah to become any more airplane crazy."

"Oh, okay then. You're his mom, and you know what's best. I figured I could at least ask."

His voice faded to a low murmur. "Thank you, anyway. We'll see you Sunday unless you pay us a surprise visit tomorrow." As they said goodbye, her peace offering earned a soft chuckle. Then she sprawled on the floor for a long time, patting Sam, and analyzing her jumbled feelings.

At all cost, she had to keep Noah safe, and she absolutely did not want him growing up to be a pilot like his dad. She strived to give him stability and prevent him from getting attached to a man who would eventually transfer with the military and say a permanent goodbye. Her logic made perfect sense, but a single question jabbed her in the chest, and she cringed. Why did Drew's invitation to Noah, not her, leave her a little deflated?

Her brain buzzed too alert for sleep, so she worked on diagnosing Canine Corner's challenges. Getting her business back on track warranted much more attention than Drew. She swept aside her daydreams and stared at her balance sheet. She needed answers, and she required them now.

Erin stayed awake late, reviewed her original business plan, and scribbled questions to explore. Even so, on Saturday morning, she still rose early as usual. In the yard, winter retreated quickly like an apology for last weekend's storm.

Noah joined her outside in the sunshine to clean stalls and play with the dogs. "I'm almost six." He tossed a ball and laughed as a Springer spaniel jumped and chased it.

"You're getting so big. How many days until your birthday?" Another loss squeezed Erin's heart, remembering another occasion Eric would never celebrate. Noah had been so young when his dad died, he still didn't fully realize what he lacked.

Noah counted on his fingers and ran out. "Twelve?"

"You're pretty close. In fifteen more days, you'll turn six." Erin squatted to rub a poodle and a terrier. Some dogs needed more pats than playtime.

"For my birthday present..." Noah tugged a ball from a beagle.

"What's on your birthday wish list?" Erin sat on her heels.

"Maybe a plane ride?"

His innocent, hopeful expression swept upward and tugged at her heart. "Oh, Noah, I don't think so." She stood and touched his arm. "What about a toy or a game?"

"I have a lot of stuff like that, but I've never had a real plane ride." He bounced and flapped his arms like wings. "Drew could take me."

Just then, she spotted Ted driving through the gate and lost her chance to reinforce a definite no.

Waving, Noah ran to greet him.

Erin rounded up the dogs and ushered them back into their stalls. Since she'd soon lose Ted's help while he and Vera vacationed, she planned to fill her free time with errands in town while he handled the kennel chores.

"Don't rush. I'll work for a few hours." Ted scratched Sam behind his left ear while he held up his free hand to give Noah a high-five. "Bye for now, mister."

"Can I stay and help Ted?" Noah splashed in a puddle.

"If your mom lets you stay, I don't mind. But I'll put you to work, mister." Ted winked and adjusted his ball cap.

"Are you sure?" She swept her gaze swept from Ted to Noah. The offer tempted so she could enjoy an efficient afternoon without a small companion.

"I'm sure." Ted nodded and reached to tickle him.

At the same time, Noah wriggled out of the way and piped in. "I'm sure."

Erin laughed at their unison. "Okay, thank you, Ted. Be good, Noah." She hugged him.

On the way to Moose Jaw, Erin blared the radio and sang. Usually, singing lifted her spirits, but not today. She switched radio stations and belted out a different song. Stopping at a light, she glanced at to her right and froze, mouth wide open. Her daydream had morphed into reality.

Drew sat in the driver's seat in the next car.

She closed her mouth and blinked.

Then the man in the other car transformed into an aged imitation of Drew but definitely not the real Drew. He smiled and flicked his eyebrows.

Flipping her gaze forward, she smothered a giggle as heat like a sunburn burned her face. She stopped first at the bank to meet her financial consultant, Parker Brown.

In his glass-walled office, he confirmed her business plan remained sound, with cash flow still close to projections. "You're smart to monitor the situation early, though. You can take steps now to stabilize the business before any declines cause serious trouble."

Erin asked several questions and made notes. Biting her lip, she hurried away, more determined than ever to rejuvenate Canine Corner. Back in the car, she drove past her old high school and favorite pizza place. Some things changed, but Moose Jaw stayed familiar and comforting, even down to the historical murals painted on the sides of buildings throughout the downtown area. She bought groceries and bulk dog food then browsed for ideas for Noah's birthday present. He already had plenty of toys and games, and she left empty-handed. He deserved a special surprise, anything but a plane ride.

Back in the car, she checked the clock. If she could force herself to stop, she had time for one more task. Drew's idea to take Noah to the aviation display at the museum had been an unpleasant surprise. But she could only discourage her son's newfound interest in airplanes and camouflage her fears for so long. Much as she wanted to, she couldn't banish airplanes forever.

Her decision would make Drew happy, but his opinion didn't matter. She needed to support Noah's interests and show him she wasn't afraid of an everyday thing like airplanes. Maybe if she could desensitize herself to the sight of airplanes, she could put the crippling fear behind her once and for all.

Encouraging healing, her gentle, caring mom had suggested a therapist more than once. On a pleasant summer afternoon, she and Erin watched Noah dart from the slide to monkey bars at a playground.

"I'd love to see you smile more often." She sidled closer and rubbed one hand up and down her daughter's back. "Many people seek help to overcome phobias, dear."

"Please stop. I don't need professional counselling." Her mother's concern only magnified the problem. A lump rose in Erin's throat. "I'm not crazy. I have a valid reason to be afraid, and my fear will probably lessen in time."

"But you can't live this way." Gayle shook her head.

At the gentle but unwelcome encouragement, Erin stiffened. Blinking back tears, she bit her lip. The foreboding ache in her heart twisted and burned. She couldn't possibly accept her mom's advice, wise and logical as it sounded.

"Erin, I…"

"Please stop, Mom." Motioning to her son, she had shot to her feet and dashed across the gravel. "Noah, we need to walk home now."

Three years later, her fear hadn't lessened and might have even grown. She drove toward the museum, slowed for puddles, and marveled at how quickly winter melted away. Determined to face her fear and finally overcome it, she gritted her teeth.

Years ago, she had loved to join Eric for a Sunday afternoon flight over the fields in the area. They cruised above the patchwork quilt of crops and drank in the vivid greens, yellows, and golds spotlighted in the sun. Back then, she stepped onto commercial flights without a care, excited to explore the destination ahead. Now, everything had changed.

The radio blasted an upbeat song, but the closer she got to the museum, the more her body screamed disapproval. Heart pounding, she rushed her breath in short shaky spurts. She forced a slow, steady pattern of inhaling and exhaling, reminding herself she wasn't boarding a plane, just observing. But her logical and reasonable brain couldn't calm her pulse, racing like she had just run a marathon.

Erin slowed and steered the car into the parking lot. Dread pumped her heart into overdrive and made her alarmingly lightheaded. She parked at the far end of the row of cars, switched off the ignition, and forced herself to step out. She took a deep breath of fresh, cool air and dragged herself toward the door.

A couple of families chatted and laughed, and their relaxed state only magnified her discomfort. At the entrance, she nearly turned and ran.

Then a man opened the door and motioned her in. "After you." He stepped aside and waited.

She could still change her mind. Her arms and legs weighed like heavy stumps of timber, and she glanced over her shoulder at the door. A few strides and she could get outside to safety. But instead of escaping, she paid her admission, opened the guide map, and forced herself in slow motion to head directly where she did not want to go. She chose the aviation gallery first and circled it a couple of times, skirting the displays and willing her heart rate to return to normal. Finally, as she breathed slowly and counted to ten, she paused and forced herself to study a small plane.

Parents talked in quiet voices to their children, pointing out details and answering their questions.

Drew understood her son well. Noah would love exploring real planes up close. Heat radiated from her face, and her pulse jarred her temples. Shivering, she wrapped her arms around her middle. She shuffled to the next display and the next and forced herself to stop and examine each. She concentrated on breathing slowly and steadily, until she couldn't feel her chest thudding. Every second tortured her to the core.

After a few minutes, she explored the SnoWings gallery and stood in front of the diamond formation modelling one of the team's signature, aerial stunts. Her heart rate skyrocketed again, and she paused. She stepped closer and read the posted information. Drew flew with this elite team. Years ago, she had seen the SnoWings perform at the local air show. When they earned international accolades, the team made the news. She noted their history, long tradition of aerial excellence, and many accomplishments.

Drew must be an expert pilot to fly in such elite company. Eric had never aspired to do anything dramatic like the SnoWings. But as a pilot, he admired the skills demanded of those in more daring lines of work than spraying crops.

Knees shaking, she toured the gallery, beat back her anxiety, and learned more. She stepped inside the ground crew area and other behind-the-scenes spaces usually reserved for the pilots and crew. Pausing beside the Tutor jet, she fought a wave of nausea and stepped away. As long as she didn't linger long, she kept her emotions in check. If she didn't stop, she tricked her nerves into believing she could flee easily to safety at any moment.

After half an hour immersed in the world of aviation, she had tested herself long enough, and she gulped fresh air and sprinted to the car. She couldn't wait to embrace her familiar world with both feet planted firmly on the ground.

In the car, she collapsed into the seat, breathed, and waited while her shaky arms and legs stabilized. She opened the windows and let a giddy soup of giggles and sobs blow away with the breeze. After a long time, she inspected her pale face in the rear-view mirror, pinched her cheeks, and fluffed her hair. She calmed herself enough to drive and steered toward the edge of the city. With every block, her accomplishment lifted her, and by the time she hit the open prairie, only her seatbelt held her down. A sliver of pride edged out fear. She forced herself to explore air travel, and she survived.

Near her turnoff, she waved as a neighbor passed. Today beamed bright. In the yard, the snow family and snow dog shrunk and slouched in the sun. But she could celebrate more than spring.

Noah and Ted waved, following Sam to welcome her home.

Relief rippled through her entire body. She'd never change her mind and allow Drew to take Noah to the museum, but someday, she just might gather the strength to treat her son to a visit. Perhaps eventually, she could even tolerate flying again. Today, she passed her own grueling test, and maybe, just maybe, she rounded a corner toward healing. Drew would be impressed. Of course, his opinion shouldn't matter a bit. Suddenly, she recoiled from a startling realization. She cared what he thought.

****

Would he never learn? The next evening, Drew still berated his impulsive action. He flopped on the sofa, stared at the ceiling, and pounded the cushions. He couldn't resist sharing his passion, but of course, his offer to take Noah to the flight museum did nothing to endear him to Erin.

Jake barked and grabbed his pant leg.

With nothing better to do, Drew accepted the invitation for a late-night tour around the neighborhood.

174

The streetlights lit icy patches on the pavement, and he crunched and slipped at a steady pace. Passing homes where people settled in for the evening, he caught light dancing from TV screens. Through a large, front window, he spotted a couple sitting beside each other on the sofa. Their smiling profiles and obvious closeness punched him right in the gut.

Last evening, he should have never rushed to call Erin. After he socialized with Kyle, his old confidence kicked in and got him in trouble. As he hiked around the park, he dragged the weight of his poor judgment. He rotated his stiff shoulders. The memory of Erin's sharp reaction shot tension up and down his arms.

He would go to the family brunch, and then he'd give her space. He had bigger issues than a woman. Still, the attraction tugged and teased his heart. His yearning welled and ached, and he strode faster and faster until he broke into a run.

Jake jumped and nipped his heels.

Even though he couldn't imagine life with someone who shunned flying, he hungered to see her smiling face. He craved a spark to light his path. They could have fun together, a relaxing break from the stressful, SnoWings challenges. Would she ever relent and welcome his company?

Chapter 14

Just outside Moose Jaw, Drew glanced in the rearview mirror and spotted a familiar car. He waved, thankful his teammate followed toward Canine Corner. Surely, Kyle wouldn't make any embarrassing girlfriend comments. Warmth flooded his face like a fifth grader's, not at all like a fully qualified Captain in the Air Force. Drew arrived, greeted Noah, and introduced Kyle. "We work together."

"Oh, are you a pilot?" Noah squinted and bounced.

"Yes, I am. Do you like jets?" Kyle bent to Noah's level.

Noah clapped and raised his voice and arms in a cheer. "I love airplanes."

"Me, too." Kyle grinned and high-fived Noah.

"Hi. I'm Erin." She extended her arm and shook his hand. "I can't thank you enough for helping."

Her fluffy pink sweater enticed Drew like cotton candy, and her fitted jeans outlined her toned shape. He couldn't resist her natural beauty, and heat rushed to his chest.

"I'll show you the kennel, but really, you don't have to do anything other than monitor the place." Erin swept her arms wide. "Make yourself at home."

"I never sit still, so you better assign a job." Hands in his pockets, Kyle surveyed the surroundings.

Muddy patches dotted the driveway and grass.

"Hmmm...let's see. You could wash the car, paint the living room, and tackle the laundry. Take your pick." Erin kept a straight face and shrugged.

Both men laughed.

Drew soaked up her humor. If only she enjoyed him half as much.

Erin smiled. "Seriously, if you don't want to just relax, feel free to give the dogs some attention. They thrive on extra pats and playtime." She gave a quick tour of the facility.

"Don't worry about a thing."

Kyle flashed a smile and thumbs-up. He sauntered with them to the car.

Then Drew opened the passenger door with a flourish.

Erin smiled and slid inside.

Noah settled in his booster seat in the middle of the back between Sam and Jake. "What should we sing first?" He bumped the front seats with his feet.

"Sing?" Drew raised his eyebrows. Riding with a child demanded a whole new skillset.

"We always sing in the car." Erin switched off the radio.

"Okay, I can sing, too." Drew tapped on the steering wheel. He had no idea what song to suggest.

"Okay." Noah clapped. "What song do you like?"

"Hmm... let's sing 'You Are My Sunshine'." Drew scanned the road and hummed.

"You named one of our favorites." Erin led off with the first line.

The trio belted out the lyrics with the dogs panting accompaniment. They took turns choosing their favorite songs.

Drew smiled and listened to Erin's rich, soprano voice. He didn't mind singing. Her harmonizing added fun. He tapped his free foot, and the forty-five minute drive to Regina zipped by. The cozy atmosphere hugged him all the way. For a brief interlude, they formed a family, enjoying a closeness he never knew.

Before long, the highway merged into south Regina.

Erin pointed out directions. "Nice voice." She glanced his way and lowered the window.

"Average at best, but thanks." Drew shrugged. Her sweet voice tempted like caramel sauce, and he craved more. "You sing well." He liked her singing and her other qualities. "The guy behind us is pretty talented, too." He tipped his head toward the back seat.

"We're almost at Grandma and Grandpa's." Noah raised his voice and clapped.

Glancing at the rear-view mirror, Drew caught a quick glimpse of him stretching and peering out the window. He shifted and scanned ahead. Noah's excitement was contagious.

"I see the mall. Hey, Drew, I'm almost six." He tapped the seat.

"Do you have a birthday soon?" Drew twisted and glanced over his shoulder.

"In only fourteen more days on April eleventh." He clapped his hands.

"You're kidding me, right?" Drew slipped his arm between the seats and tickled the small knees behind him. An unexpected burst of affection rushed to his chest. Erin's son must flood her life with endless joy.

"Nope." Noah giggled and shook his head.

"Can you guess my birthday?" Drew kept one hand

on the steering wheel and used his free hand to point at his own head. His fingers vibrated slightly. The coincidence surprised and amused him, but how would Erin feel?

"I don't know," said Noah.

Drew tapped a one-handed drum roll on the steering wheel. "April eleventh."

"We have the same birthday." Noah shouted. "You can come to my party and have a party, too." He bounced as much as his snug car seat allowed.

Drew glanced at Erin.

She stared out the passenger window. "How amazing."

Her flat tone sent a clear message. He clenched his jaw so hard it ached. Obviously, he irritated her without trying. Now, his birth date caused trouble. What next?

At his grandparents' place, Noah jumped out of the car. He ran with Sam and Jake to his waiting cousins.

The kids and dogs all collapsed in a happy heap on the patches of snow and grass.

Brian beamed at the door and waved in everyone.

Mitch stepped outside to shake hands. "Good to see you."

Carrying a box of candy decorated with a gold ribbon, Drew followed Erin inside and melted into the background, unsure if the camaraderie from last weekend would continue. Brian gripped his hand like a hammer.

"Welcome to our home. Glad you could join us."

"Hi, everyone." Gayle gave hugs all round. "Last but not least, welcome, Drew."

He smiled and extended his hostess gift.

She clasped her hands together. "Oh, you're very

kind to give me chocolates. You shouldn't have, but I'm glad you did. Thank you so much."

"Hey, are you sure they're yours? Drew knows I can't resist chocolate." Brian pretended to tug them out of her hand.

Drew chuckled. He scanned the living room, rimmed with overstuffed, floral furniture. The home radiated warmth and laughter, and the spicy scent of cinnamon buns lured. He basked in the flurry of enthusiastic greetings.

"I'm sure you're hungry, and Gayle has everything ready. Drew, sit there between Erin and Claire, so they can keep you in line."

"Whew, you just took off the pressure. They'll leave me alone." Mitch wiped his brow.

"Aw, I want to sit beside Drew." Noah squeezed in.

Erin hesitated, frowned, and shifted over one spot.

Within minutes, Drew's apprehension dissolved, and he settled into the familiar, warm circle. Only a week ago, he was stranded in the storm, but he would have guessed longer because so much in his heart had changed.

Gayle passed a casserole of eggs and heaping platters of ham, fruit, and cinnamon buns. "We're happy you're here."

"Thank you for the invitation." Drew surveyed his loaded plate and inhaled the savory blend. "Everything smells delicious." Gratitude welling, he cleared his throat. This time, he was invited to their family event by choice, not because of the weather. He almost belonged.

Everyone talked at once, teased each other, and

laughed between mouthfuls of food.

"How did your week go?" Mitch popped a grape into his mouth and passed the fruit plate.

"Busy, thanks, but good. I heard my dad will visit next weekend." Drew gripped his fork.

"You must be happy." Brian beamed, nodded, and gave a thumbs-up. "When he's here, maybe we can meet." He speared a bite of ham.

"I, uh, I'm not sure of our plans, but maybe." He wiped his upper lip. His erratic dad might not blend with a normal family. Concern rose and lodged in his stiff shoulders. His dad didn't compare to solid, jovial Brian, but maybe he could learn from a model of good, fatherly behavior.

Drew cleared his throat and searched for a new topic. The tension in his back shouted he shouldn't have mentioned his dad's visit in case plans changed. He couldn't pin down unpredictable Frank, the opposite of solid, consistent Brian. Oh well, he could worry later. Right now, he'd just absorb the warmth as though he was a genuine member of this happy, normal family.

"Come on, everyone. Please, eat more, or you'll leave a pile of leftovers." Gayle passed the platters and squeezed Noah's hand. "Grandpa and I want to get you a special birthday surprise."

"Oh, I don't know, Grandma. Does Noah deserve a present?" Brian reached an arm over Erin and tickled his grandson.

"Stop, Grandpa." Noah giggled. "For my birthday present, I hope Drew takes me on a plane ride. Drew has the same birthday."

"Really?" Gayle widened her eyes and glanced at Erin.

Erin nodded and bit her lip.

"Yes, we share a birthday. In the car on the way here, we just realized we're twins." Even though he had never once suggested he would take Noah on a plane ride, he glanced at Erin and caught her quick frown. She probably thought he encouraged the idea. "Sorry, Noah, I can only fly grownups in my jet."

"Remember, you need to dream up some other birthday wishes." Erin rubbed his back. "We'll plan something fun, and you'll have a special day."

"Speaking of fun, maybe the guys should take the kids outside. Would you munchkins like to go to the park?" Mitch drained his coffee.

"Excellent idea." Brian patted his girth. "I need to burn off a few calories. Want to come, Drew?"

"Sure...I mean...maybe first, we should wash dishes." He scanned the array of plates and serving platters. He would gladly stay to help Erin.

She waved him away. "Feel free to go. Mom and Claire don't waste time. We'll be a speedy, cleanup team." Erin hugged Noah goodbye and headed for the kitchen.

"We can use the peace." Claire pursed her lips.

Mitch grinned, kissed her, and wrapped her in a hug.

The affectionate exchange drove a pang into Drew's heart. He squeezed his fists and turned. Their obvious happiness shone and stirred his loneliness. Maybe, someday he'd know how they felt.

****

Gayle, Claire, and Erin loaded the dishwasher and put away food.

Erin kept her business booking challenges private,

182

but she mentioned Ted's impromptu vacation and her struggle to find backup staffing.

"You have your hands full." Gayle wiped the countertop.

"Nothing I can't handle. I'll figure out a plan." Her mom didn't have to hint the kennel demanded too much. She scrunched a tea towel and clunked a pile of plates into the cupboard.

"What about backup while Ted's away?" Gayle paused and exchanged a glance with Claire.

"Don't worry." Erin grabbed the broom and attacked the crumbs on the floor. "Noah's teacher invited Drew to speak on Monday morning about his pilot career. Part of me wants to be there, and part of me wants to stay as far away as possible. I told her if I could get away from the kennel, I'd come. But now, I'm not sure…"

"I'll dog sit." Gayle rinsed her cloth. "You should go, so I'll handle kennel duties."

"You will? Oh, thank you." Erin relaxed her grip on the broom for an instant and then stiffened and clenched it tight. Her mom's kindness dissolved any chance to use work as the perfect excuse to avoid the school visit.

"Gayle's right. For Noah's sake, you need to participate." Claire refilled their cups. "Now, let's sit and relax before the park team gets back."

Erin flopped beside her mom on the sofa. She never tired of the understated earth tones surrounding her.

"Ah, I need this chance to relax." Claire sighed and sank into a comfortable chair. "I feel like a busy chauffeur delivering Luc to soccer games and Anna to dance classes."

Erin curled her legs sideways and soaked up the soothing balm. In their own ways, her mom, sister-in-law, and the room's hushed tones all soothed.

"How do you feel about Noah's birthday wish?" Claire sipped her tea.

Fear did a small flip inside Erin. "I'm annoyed Drew and Noah have another thing in common besides their obsession with airplanes. He's not going on a plane ride." She would deal with his wish for a combined celebration later, but first, she'd sort out her prickly feelings. Even if he was a nice guy, she didn't need a pilot in her life.

"Are you sure the answer's no?" Claire peeked over her mug and raised her eyebrows.

"I'm certain." Erin fisted a hand and thumped the sofa. "When Noah met Drew, he turned airplane crazy." She took a deep breath. "What would you do?" She floated the question out for either her mom or Claire to answer.

Gayle and Claire exchanged glances.

While awkward silence hung in the air, Erin studied her hands.

Finally, Gayle put a hand on Erin's arm. "I remember a little girl who fell in love with dogs and pestered us daily until we got one."

Erin laughed. "I might have hounded you just a little, but owning a dog is a normal, everyday thing."

"To some people, so is flying." Gayle squeezed her daughter's arm. "I'm not saying you should go out and charter a plane for Noah's birthday, but I doubt you'll ever totally quash his interest."

"His recent obsession surfaces daily." Erin wrung

her hands. She crumbled inside. Much as she wished, she couldn't redirect her son's enthusiasm.

"Maybe his extreme interest in planes came with his genes." Claire twirled a blonde tendril around a forefinger. "You know…the way Luc inherited Mitch's soccer skills."

"You're lucky. Mitch passed on healthy, down-to-earth interests." Her heartbeat ricocheted, and she took a deep breath. Voice quivering, she forced a half smile. "Yesterday, I immersed myself in the world of aviation, and I survived."

"Oh, Erin, I'm so proud." Gayle smiled and rubbed her arm.

"For my next challenge, I'll force myself to board a plane." Erin shuddered. She couldn't imagine how or when she'd muster the courage.

"One step at a time." Gayle patted her hand.

"Would you…I don't know if I should ask this question…" Claire shifted and scanned out the window.

"Go ahead." Erin sat straighter.

"Would you ever consider asking Drew to take you and Noah on a flight? Just a short, trial run?"

Claire curved up her light eyebrows and parted her lips.

"Never. I couldn't possibly." Erin twisted and tugged a lock of hair. No way would she consider Claire's idea. She bit her lip. "I just want to get to the point where I can stand hearing Noah chatter about airplanes, or I might consider flying somewhere for a holiday. Maybe, eventually, I could tolerate a big commercial flight—the kind with safety announcements and two pilots."

"Mitch always tells the kids, never say never, so

possibly?" Claire shrugged and sipped her tea.

"I learned a long time ago, I shouldn't always listen to Mitch. He's the same guy who, when I was Noah's age, talked me into eating an earthworm." Erin scrunched her face and stuck out her tongue. A wave of affection overtook her, and she giggled.

"Ew." Claire wrinkled her nose.

"Ew." Gayle echoed, tipped back her head, and laughed.

At the same moment, Brian jostled in the front door along with the other men, kids, and dogs.

"A sound of disgust is the welcome we get?" He groaned and winked. "You sure know how to hurt a guy."

"I won't take your reaction personally." Drew took off his jacket. "Hey, I liked the park. I haven't been on a swing or a slide in years."

"I bet you had fun, too." Erin swept her son, niece, and nephew into a group hug.

"We had the best time." Noah wriggled free and bounced. "We flew as high as the sky, all the way to the moon."

Erin gritted her teeth and forced a half smile. "Your adventure sounds awesome." Of course, the park expedition included air travel. To her dismay, flying permeated everything these days. For a few more minutes, Erin enjoyed the casual banter. Then she stretched and stood. "Thank you for the great food and visit, Mom and Dad. We should head home. I promised Drew's friend we wouldn't stay all day." In the car, Erin smothered a yawn.

Noah sat quietly in the back.

"No singing on the way home?" Drew glanced in

the rearview mirror.

Erin turned her gaze toward the back seat.

Head drooping, Noah slumped fast asleep with Jake and Sam curled on either side.

Erin stared out the window. For a moment, she discounted Drew's career. He had many good qualities. "Can I tell you something?" She glanced sideways and swallowed a gasp at the sight of his handsome profile. How could she resist her growing attraction?

****

"Of course." Drew scanned the road ahead and surveyed the high, blue canopy of sky. Patches of brown and gold overtook the snowy fields and held the promise of warmer days. His dad would arrive to springtime in Moose Jaw.

He glanced at Erin as she stared out the window, teeth resting on her bottom lip. A rush of admiration struck every time he witnessed her quiet strength. She expertly juggled a busy life as a single mom. She entertained family and handled kennel chores. Did she want to share something personal? Her serious tone suggested something important. He squeezed and flexed his fingers on the steering wheel, stared at the road, and waited.

"Only a couple of people know my challenge. I'm not really sure why I want to confide details, but you're so...calm and down-to-earth. You show integrity and common sense." She glanced over her shoulder to make sure Noah still slept.

Drew concentrated on the road ahead. "You just gave me a pretty big compliment. Are you sure you described the right guy?" He tilted his head and sucked in his cheeks. She rewarded his quip with a smile, and pleasant warmth crept into his chest. "So now, you've buttered me up…" He relaxed his hands on the wheel.

"I want to consult you about my business."

She tossed her thick, dark hair. Erin trusted him enough to ask for business advice? Savoring the surprising praise, he shifted and sat a little taller.

She explained the recent booking challenges and asked for his perspective on the booking decline. "Are other clients possibly skeptical of a new owner? I know someone who acted leery." She smirked and wrinkled her nose.

"After I saw you in action, I totally changed my opinion. Nobody could take better care of the dogs." The swell of peace in his chest confirmed his opinion.

"Caring for the dogs is the easy part." She shifted and twirled a lock of hair. "Does Vera's theory hold any truth…aging clients with reduced need for kennel service?"

"What about business image? Maybe you need a bigger social media presence to attract a younger, mobile clientele." He drummed his fingers on the steering wheel. Brainstorming led to creativity, and she valued his ideas.

"What about a new name?" She jumped in. "The front gate and kennel building need a fresh coat of paint."

Energy flowing, he helped her list ideas and design a plan to rejuvenate her business. Excitement hummed in his limbs. With a project to tackle, he could spend all kinds of time at her place.

"My family said the kennel demanded too much at this stage. They wanted me to take an office job or even live closer in Regina. But, I know in my heart Moose

Jaw is where I belong, and running this business is my dream." Erin flattened her lips into a firm line. "I need to build success." She squeezed the armrest.

"You will. I know you can." Pulse accelerating, Drew glanced over. Her jaw jutted, and she could do anything she set her mind to. Could she possibly be his perfect woman, even if his passion was her poison? He couldn't live without flight.

Earlier today at the playground, Mitch had flagged Erin's feelings as the three men pushed swings.

Noah urged them to send him higher and higher on his imaginary airplane.

Next, Drew pretended, along with the other men, that he was a big, ugly troll who hid under the play structure and tagged the kids while they ran and squealed.

While Brian roared and chased the kids, Mitch leaned on the slide beside Drew and caught his breath. "Noah's pretty stuck on flying these days, and Erin's not too keen on the idea."

"So I gathered." Drew clamped his jaw. Did they all blame him for Noah's recent fixation?

"Flying's in his blood." Mitch shook his head.

"I can relate. I've always loved jets." For a moment, Drew had savored the pleasant memory.

"Almost home." Erin snapped her fingers. "Thanks for the creative session."

"No problem." He'd make time for whatever she needed. Arriving at the acreage, he spotted Kyle striding between the kennel and the house.

Kyle waved, veered toward the car, and bent to pat Sam and Jake, who ran to greet him.

Swatting the travelers with their tails, the dogs

wagged in circles.

"Welcome back." Grinning, Kyle stood, hands on hips. "Since you left, I've played almost nonstop. The dogs don't tire easily, but they wore me out."

"Welcome to my life." Erin held open the car door.

Noah popped awake and jumped out.

"You have a pretty nice life here." Kyle rested a hand on Sam's golden head and scanned the yard.

"Do you want to come in for ginger ale and cookies? After the big favor, I owe you some hospitality." Erin waved them inside.

"Do you want to play?" Noah bounced in a circle.

Kyle glanced at his watch.

Drew hesitated and scanned the little guy's bright face. He didn't want to tire or irritate Erin. For sure, Noah would entice him into playtime.

"Sure, sounds good." Kyle lowered his wrist and grinned. His friend didn't consult him, but Drew didn't mind. He'd stay all evening if he could.

In the kitchen, Erin served snacks and answered Kyle's questions. As Drew zoomed the toy plane with Noah, he caught enough of the conversation to satisfy his curiosity. When Erin married Eric, she grew to love rural life on another acreage just outside Moose Jaw. No doubt, she was entrenched here.

"After Eric...after he died," she said, "while I regrouped, Noah and I lived in town for a couple of years. Then I decided to tackle a new challenge."

"So, you shopped one day and threw in a kennel next to the groceries?"

Kyle kept a straight face, but humor reflected in his pale, blue eyes. His friend pulled out information Drew yearned to hear.

"Not quite." Erin laughed. "I had always wanted a business of my own, and I researched options. I love dogs, so when I bought Canine Corner, I intertwined all my plans and interests."

As she described her business and the life she loved on the acreage, she sparkled with enthusiasm. Listening captivated, Drew wanted more than ever to help her in any way he could. Her passion for the kennel mirrored his passion for the SnoWings before the *incident*. He could see clearly she had found her true calling.

Drew glanced at the clock and then Kyle. "Think it's time to depart?" He'd rather stay but hated to wear out his welcome.

"Thanks for the refreshments." Kyle stood and carried his glass to the sink.

"I appreciate the huge favor." Erin smiled and followed the two men to the door.

"Aww," Noah whined. "I want to play more."

"I'll see you tomorrow at school. We'll have fun." He cinched the promise with a high five.

As he headed to his car, Kyle jingled his keys. "Hey, Dixon," he called. "Nice girlfriend."

Drew spun and scrunched his forehead. "She's not my—"

Kyle laughed. "How'd a guy like you get a girl like her, anyway?"

Drew only wished he could call her his girlfriend. He grinned, shook his head, and drove away. He belted tunes all the way. Perfect, aerial formations jetted through his head and looped around images of Erin's glowing face. Still, as beautiful as he found her, he faced a major hurdle before he could truly call her his ideal woman. Would he ever entice her into an airplane?

Chapter 15

The next morning, Gayle arrived while Erin and Noah finished breakfast.

Erin savored the comforting aroma of oatmeal, toast, and coffee that wafted through the cozy kitchen. Smiling with peanut butter trim, her son munched on toast.

"Hi, Grandma. Mommy gets to come to school today."

After welcoming Gayle, Sam sat, stared at the table, and drooled.

"We get a visitor at school today." Noah slipped the dog a bite. "Guess who."

"Who?" Gayle poured herself a cup of coffee and joined them at the table.

"Drew will come. He'll teach us pilot stuff. When I grow up, I want to be a pilot." Noah chewed and widened his eyes.

"You'll be a great pilot." Gayle nodded and patted his hand.

"Time to catch the bus." Erin raised her eyebrows. Her mom shouldn't encourage his pilot dreams. Drew influenced him more than enough already.

Gayle wiped Noah's sticky face, helped him load his backpack, and stood with Erin, waving as he caught the school bus.

"Of course." Erin crossed her arms. "Other

children want to be doctors and police officers, but not my son. My son wants to be a pilot like…" She bit her tongue. At Noah's young age, he didn't remember his dad. If he hadn't heard from his mom, he wouldn't even know his dad had been a pilot. But now, Noah found a real, live pilot to emulate.

"Maybe he's just going through a phase he'll outgrow." Gayle shrugged and patted Erin's arm.

"The same way I outgrew my dog-loving phase?" Erin threw wide her arms toward the property's outreaches.

Sam wagged and bumped Erin's legs.

"Let's hope he switches to a different goal." Gayle hugged her.

"Thanks for your help, Mom." Sighing, Erin soaked up her reassurance but wasn't convinced. In the car on the way to school, she planned her day. After the session with Noah's class, she would go home and work. A partially vacant kennel meant chores wouldn't be too demanding. Between caring for the dogs and playing with Noah, she needed to call her client list. She'd also make a list of improvements and repairs to refresh Canine Corner.

Drew's insightful ideas were important in the mix. Hints of excitement and apprehension tickled her spine. Drew stood handsome enough in his jeans and plaid shirt, but a military flight uniform would highlight his trim, muscular body in a new way. Suddenly, warmth jumped to her cheeks. She needed to stop her daydream this minute. She shouldn't be picturing any man, let alone a pilot. Still, she couldn't ignore totally Vera's advice. Eric lived in her heart, but he could no longer share her life. Drew knocked and waited, ready for more. Squeezing and releasing her fingers, she considered the possibility. If she mustered the courage and desire, she could unlock the door and swing it wide open. But allowing Drew into her life would only mean complications she didn't need. Staying single was predictable and safe. Why risk a change now?

****

As he glimpsed the back of Erin's flowing hair and red coat disappearing into the sprawling, brick school, Drew stepped out of his car. If only he arrived a few minutes earlier, he could reach her in time to exchange a few words before the class started. Anticipation slid up his neck and tickled his scalp. The break in his Monday routine, teaching Noah and the rest of the kids, would be fun. Erin would make the visit even better, like the butter on the popcorn.

He sprinted down the hall, decorated with colorful artwork, and caught up outside the classroom door. "Good morning, Ms. Humphrey." He held his breath.

She tucked her hair behind an ear and smiled. "Good morning, Captain Dixon." She clicked her heels together and mock-saluted.

At that moment, the teacher swung open the door and caught them laughing. "Oh, hello." She raised her eyebrows. "Thank you for coming."

Drew scanned her face and precise hair and instantly dropped his expression into line. She probably assumed they rode together. Color bloomed in Erin's cheeks, but he could do nothing to ease her discomfort. She probably didn't want the teacher making any false assumptions about their relationship. Of course, if he had his way, he would fulfill the teacher's notion of romance.

195

Mrs. Jansen waved them in then pointed out coat hooks and places to sit.

Crayons, running shoes, and a large hamster cage scented the classroom and bombarded him with childhood memories.

Sitting at tables in small groupings, children wiggled in their chairs.

"Hi, Mom. Hi, Drew." Arms spread wide, Noah zigzagged between the tables and chairs and hugged them.

"Listen, boys and girls." Mrs. Jansen raised a finger to her lips. "Noah, you may introduce our guests."

Face flushed pale pink, he nodded and led them to the front. "This lady is my mom. Her name is Erin Humphrey. She takes care of me and the dogs at our kennel. This man is my friend, Drew. He's a jet pilot."

"Thank you, Noah, and welcome to both of our visitors." Mrs. Jansen smiled and raised a hand to hush the children's murmurs. "Captain Dixon is a pilot with the SnoWings, and he will teach you how jet pilots work, but first, Noah's mom will describe her dog kennel."

Glancing at Erin's lush hair and pink cheeks, Drew inhaled a sharp breath. He fought to calm his heartrate, accelerating in her presence. Everything she said and did enthralled him, and he absolutely had to find a way to experience more.

****

"I didn't know you wanted me to speak today, but sure." Erin hesitated and shifted to the center of the room. Clearly, the teacher considered Drew the feature presentation. She served the role of movie trailer, but she'd prove she had an unusual and interesting job. "If you have a dog, put up your hand."

Half the class raised a hand. "Canine Corner is like a camp for dogs. When dog owners go away, we babysit."

Looking at their friends, a few kids murmured comments.

"If your family travels, maybe you leave your dog at a kennel. I feed the dogs, give them water, take them outside to play, and keep their spaces clean." Scanning the children's nods, she strolled across the front of the room.

"Do the dogs get lonely?" A girl at Noah's table squinted and tilted her head.

"Sometimes, maybe a little." Erin held up her fingers to show a small amount. "But most of the time, they're happy because I give them lots of attention."

A boy with eyes like two green marbles waved a hand. "Who's taking care of the dogs right now?"

Erin smiled. "Noah's grandma offered to work at the kennel."

"Those questions are excellent, boys and girls." Mrs. Jansen stepped beside Erin and clapped. "Now, let's welcome Captain Dixon." She applauded again.

Erin's hunch proved correct. From the back of the room, she had an excellent view of Drew in his fitted, red, flight uniform. He cut a striking figure in a one-piece jumpsuit with a zipper up the front. Crested gold bars sat on his shoulders and marked his rank like beacons.

"Good morning, everyone." Drew scanned the class. "When I was about your age, I decided I wanted to become a pilot. Who has flown in an airplane?"

Several children raised a hand.

"Flying is fun, isn't it? Would you like to ride in a plane?" He scanned the room.

As he quizzed the kids, his animated face and gestures captured their attention. Clearly, he loved his work. Erin cringed when everyone in the room, including Mrs. Jansen, nodded vigorously—everyone, except her. Of course, her son had to be the keenest kid, flailing both arms. Flitting her gaze across the room, Erin clasped her trembling hands on her lap. She could daydream and float miles away from the risky world of planes and aerial stunts, or she could torture herself and listen to every detail. Suddenly, her fear spun her out of control and caused a light-headed sensation that rotated the room's vivid, art projects. Until the motion stopped, she squeezed her eyes tight. Gulping air, she struggled to concentrate on deep, even breathing.

She forced herself to listen to his description of flying school, smooth take-offs, bumpy landings, and fancy loops in the sky. Her attention diverted to her pounding heart, and she tugged it back to his glowing face and steady voice. His voice lilted, free of the pauses that sometimes dotted his speech. Much as the topic repelled her, it fascinated the kids. No doubt, Noah wasn't the only child in the room who aspired to become a jet pilot.

"Now, what questions do you have?" Drew scanned the room. When several students shot up their hands, he grinned and nodded.

"How fast do you fly?"

A boy with carroty hair rose onto his knees.

"We fly really fast. We can travel almost eight hundred kilometers per hour." Drew swooped a hand.

"When you fly upside down, what does it feel like?" Noah tipped sideways.

"The motion feels like a giant hand ripping you out of the seat." Drew made a big sweeping gesture. "To stay safe, you need to strap your seat belt on very tight. Even your face stretches." He pinched his cheeks upward. "Try it."

"Good job." At the squashed faces, he grinned and nodded.

"How do you fly close together and not bump into each other?" A boy leaned as far as he could across the table.

"We have instruments in the plane to tell us where to fly." Drew smiled and paced.

"If you fly crooked, what happens?" A girl bobbed her head and swished her ponytail.

"We practice lots and watch the lead jet, so we stay straight." Drew pointed ahead with both hands.

"Have you ever crashed?" A boy splatted his hands together.

Instantly, her jangled nerves blurred his freckled face. Erin gasped, and her eyes filled with tears. Fighting to gain control, she glanced at Drew's blurred face. He paled as white as the chalk on the board.

"No, I've never had an accident. Planes almost never crash." He shook his head and crossed his arms.

Erin blinked until her vision cleared, and his hard jaw emerged through the mist.

He caught her glance, and his pale face tinged pink. Did she imagine his apparent discomfort or did something cause him concern? Finally, the questions ended, and the class applauded.

Erin forced her eyes open wide, flexed her tingly

fingers, and took several deep breaths. She rose, and her legs vibrated slightly but held her. "Thank you for inviting me." She nodded at Mrs. Jansen and blew Noah a kiss.

"Bye, Mom. Bye, Drew." Noah bounced and waved as they headed out the door. "When I grow up, I want to be a pilot just like Drew."

Sudden dread clenched her stomach. Of course, he did. She waved and shuddered. Dissuading him from his goal would be next to impossible.

Erin and Drew strolled to their cars side by side.

She angled her face to the sunshine and breathed air infused with the fresh scent of a new season. Anticipation swirled her nearly off balance. "The kids loved you." Her lips trembled.

"Not too hard to listen to?" Drew arched his eyebrows.

His confident pilot persona disappeared, and he wanted reassurance. She shook her head. "You didn't bore anyone for an instant." The presentation proved difficult to endure but definitely wasn't boring. "The teacher booked you to star as the main attraction and, at the last minute, added me as the warm-up act."

Drew chuckled. "I'm glad she asked you to speak. You're a strong role model, and now, the kids all know you're more than Noah's mom."

"I agree." Her breathing and heart rate settled, and a trace of pride glimmered. Determined and capable, she didn't have to…no, she refused to live forever as Noah's terrified mom.

Beside her car, they paused and locked their gazes on each other.

"Thank you for coming. You didn't have to." He

moistened his lips. "You didn't even know the teacher intended to invite you to present."

"I wouldn't have missed the opportunity." She wanted to support Noah, but her other motive niggled. Drew added a welcome spark to the morning.

"I'll see you this evening." Drew nearly touched her arm but dropped his hand to his side.

"Tonight?" She would be extremely busy working and playing with Noah.

"You need help to replace Ted this week, so you can use your labor credit."

Drew's firm jaw and half smile said she shouldn't argue. "But...I'm sure you have other more important things to do." She ran fingers through her hair.

"No buts. I insist." Drew thrust forward a hand.

"Thank you." She didn't argue with his signal to stop her protest. She met his gaze and blinked. His generous offer tempted. She needed help, and she didn't even mind his company. She'd just keep Noah busy and distracted, so he didn't follow him like a lost puppy. "I guess I'll see you later." Erin arrived home and faced a busy afternoon.

"Can I borrow Noah after lunch?" Gayle cracked eggs for an omelet. "I could take him swimming and give you some extra time for chores or whatever you need to do."

"He'd love to go. Thanks, Mom." Erin hugged her. She'd get more work done without her active son.

"I'm happy to help and get Noah all to myself." Gayle flashed a wide smile. "Special time with a grandchild is a grandma's dream."

"I'll use the time to call some of my clients...I should say, Ray's former clients. I want to promote bookings and ask for feedback to help grow the business." Erin glossed over the challenges. At this point, her mom only needed to know about the routine marketing activity.

Within minutes, Noah arrived home from school.

"Your dad had a birthday gift idea, but we can discuss it later." Gayle scooped Noah into her arms and squeezed tight. "We can't let this young man hear."

"Hi, Grandma." He squished his face into her middle. "I'm happy to see you."

Tilting her head, Erin smiled at the affectionate exchange. His muffled greeting couldn't smother his enthusiastic tone.

"I'm thrilled to see you, too." Gayle released her hold and examined his earnest expression. "Did Mommy behave at school?"

Noah wrinkled his brow and nodded. "Drew did, too. He told us jet stuff."

"I'm glad they both behaved, and I bet you learned a lot." Gayle crinkled her face into a smile and signaled a thumbs-up.

"What else did you learn at school?" Erin put her hands on his shoulders.

Noah wriggled free and danced in a circle. "I learned how fast jets fly. I want to be a pilot like Drew."

"You'll be an excellent pilot." Gayle smoothed his tousled hair.

Erin glared, took Noah's hand, and led him to the sink. Even if she overcame her fears, she didn't need anyone cheering on his pilot dreams. "Come and wash your hands for lunch. Guess what Grandma wants to do this afternoon?"

"I really, really want to go on a plane ride." He swished his hands under the tap.

"Let's talk about this afternoon." She squirted soap on his hands. "Now, rub hard."

He rinsed his hands and reached for the towel in Erin's hand.

"Grandma planned something very special to do with you today." She returned the towel to the hook under the sink. If only she could rinse away his new-found interest.

After the noon meal, Gayle headed to the pool with Noah.

Relishing the quiet, Erin filled a mug of tea, plunked onto her office chair, and called clients. The room, which doubled as a spare bedroom with a pullout sofa, contained a neat desk and filing cabinet. Her first call woke a man.

He snapped and hung up.

Then a woman agreed to talk, but after she described her health ailments in detail, she reported eventually, her dog had died. Erin jotted a note to remove the woman's name from her active client list and moved on. Finally, the third client held potential. The woman didn't travel at this time of year, but she would take a summer holiday and promised to book later.

After Erin called a few more people, she stood to stretch, refill her cup, and peer out the front window. The snow family and dog melted into a few lumps of snow strewn with hats and scarves. Puddles grew into ponds, signaling clearly rubber boot and muddy paw season had arrived. She loved spring except for the extra paw washing.

Ten minutes later, she resumed calls, and a pattern emerged. She couldn't ignore the harsh reality. Not that Ray deluded intentionally, but he shared a client list and financial history that camouflaged the trends. Most of the clients she contacted were elderly, didn't travel as much, and had less need for kennel services. Some no longer owned a dog. Almost no one admitted to switching to another service. Working steadily, she booked a few clients for the coming weeks and obtained a few promises to book later, but she determined revenue from the former clientele would decrease from projections.

Uneasiness swirled in her chest, and she shoved away her chair from the desk. Ready for a break, she stretched her tense back muscles and threw on a light jacket. A little fresh air and exercise with Sam and the other dogs might revive her tired brain and stimulate solutions. The financial road ahead appeared bumpy.

****

Drew returned to the base in time to finish some paperwork and review the afternoon's mission plan. Sharing his passion reminded him why he loved jets and had aspired to become a pilot.

"How'd school go?" Kyle popped into the office.

"Fun." Drew shuffled, organized, and stacked papers. "Nothing like a bunch of eager kindergartners to turn a guy into a rock star."

"Didn't anyone tell you? We SnoWings *are* rock stars." Kyle flipped his sunglasses off his head and struck an exaggerated pose.

"Speak for yourself." Drew laughed and stood, anxious to eat a quick lunch, head to the ramp, and channel the buzz in his limbs into high performance.

"Did you see your girlfriend there?" Kyle winked and punched Drew's shoulder.

"Why do you ask?" Drew lifted his eyebrows. He only wished she was his girlfriend.

"You're almost smiling." Kyle gave him a playful shove.

Drew laughed. "Am I?" At his teammate's teasing observation, he flushed. Kyle noticed the morning's positive effect. The time with Noah and his classmates boosted his spirits, and the prospect of seeing Erin not once but twice in one day produced an extra zing. "The weather helps...you know, milder."

"Sure, blame spring."

Kyle's droll tone and wink told Drew he didn't buy the explanation.

"Hey, maybe the four of us should go out together some evening." Kyle leaned on the edge of a work station. "Maybe we could bowl and eat pizza?"

"Uh..." Drew didn't know how to answer. Erin might not like the idea and refuse.

"C'mon. We'll have fun." Kyle flicked his eyebrows.

"Yeah, sounds great. Maybe I'll talk to Erin and let you know." He had no intention of inviting Erin to double-date with Kyle and his wife, but right now, he wasn't about to tell him. Erin wouldn't appreciate a bunch of pilot talk. Besides, he couldn't trust Kyle not to embarrass him, calling her his girlfriend, or worse, alluding to the *incident*. He shuddered. He needed to trust Kyle and the rest of the team in the air, no matter what. Did that absolute belief extend to the ground? Could he categorize types of trust? Could he separate it into compartments and apply it in the cockpit and return to his wary self on the ground? He pressed a hand to temple. His brain ached for answers.

"Okay, make sure to ask." Kyle slung his jacket over his shoulder. "Come on, let's grab some grub."

"Sure, I will." As he strode to the mess hall, he rotated his shoulders to ease his hard-as-rocks muscles. Kyle exuded good humor, and his invitation enticed. Maybe he could trust him.

"Are you ready for today's drills?" Kyle swung his arms and strode briskly.

"I hope so." Drew shrugged. No sense being over-confident. He only aspired to his teammate's obvious self-assurance.

"You hope so?" Kyle broke stride and jostled his shoulder.

Adrenaline buzzed in his ears, and he jumped clear. "I mean, yes. I'm ready." He straightened and doubled his pace.

After a successful afternoon in the air, he picked up a fast-food burger on the way home. He ate in front of the television news and took Jake for a long outing. Then he tidied his kitchen, opened mail, and paid a bill. Finally, he could leave for Erin's place without appearing again to be an inconsiderate, drop-in dinner guest. Drumming his fingers on the steering wheel, he hummed all the way to Canine Corner.

Noah must have caught sight of the car through the window. He opened the front door, beamed, and high-fived him.

Sam romped down the steps to greet Jake, and the two dogs sloshed through a massive puddle and rolled on the slushy lawn.

"Welcome back." Drying her hands on a kitchen

towel, Erin followed Noah to the entranceway and smiled.

"Hey, I had fun at school." Smiling, Drew dropped to squat at Noah's eye level.

"Yeah. Did you come to play?"

Noah's toothy smile lit up his face. "I want to help your mom, but maybe, if she doesn't mind, we can play for a few minutes." Drew raised an eyebrow. "What's my first job?"

"Seriously, do you plan to work?" She clutched the towel and widened her eyes.

"And play, please." Noah tugged Drew's sleeve.

"Yes, I plan to work. You have a credit in the bank." Drew used his fingers to count options. "I could do the evening rounds, clean kennels, fill water, and anything else you want." He shifted and cleared his throat.

"Hmmm." Erin twisted her mouth sideways and tilted her head. "I guess I'll let you off easy tonight."

"You're the boss."

Drew blushed and stuck both hands in his jeans pockets.

"Instead of playing, maybe I can help Drew?" Noah bounced and tapped Erin's arm.

A shadow flitted across Erin's face, and she took her time answering. Clearly, she had reservations about the idea.

"You can go outside for half an hour, but when I call you in for a bath, I don't want to hear any complaints. Is that arrangement a deal?"

"It's a deal." Noah scooted toward the back door.

Drew glanced at his eager helper and pumped a fist. "Okay, let's go." Outside, he jogged toward the kennel.

Beside him, Noah ran and leaped.

Drew stretched a leg forward and joined him in a celebratory jump. Erin allowed him to play for a short while and work in the kennel. Now, how could he persuade her to join him on a date?

Chapter 16

Thirty minutes later, Erin found the guys busy filling water bowls and chatting. Breathing calming gulps of musky air, she watched unnoticed.

Noah imitated Drew's movements and asked a string of questions.

The touching image, both bitter and sweet, squeezed her heart. Their expressions glowed like spotlights on the gaping hole in Noah's life where a father should reside. She swallowed to dissolve the lump in her throat and steadied her voice before she spoke. "Sorry to interrupt, but Noah needs a bath."

"Aw, not already." Noah fisted his small hands and thumped his legs.

Erin clicked her tongue and held up a finger. She wouldn't allow any bargaining for an extension.

"Remember the deal you made. Goodnight, Noah. Thanks for all your help. I'll see you soon." Drew raised his hand in a goodbye high-five, and his angular face softened.

Stirred at the sight, Erin pressed a hand to her chest. His gentleness with Noah and the dogs stirred an ache without a cure. His hug would feel strong and soft at the same time, but she blotted out the image. He made his living as a pilot. He lived a transient, military life. No, he didn't belong in her life.

"When will you come again?" Noah dragged his

feet.

Ignoring his resistance, Erin took his hand and led him away.

"I hope soon." Drew bent to fill a water bucket. "Maybe I'll see you tomorrow…if your mom agrees."

"Yes, please, come tomorrow. We can play." Noah shuffled and waved.

"I'm not so sure…" Erin turned and called over her shoulder. "Thank you, Drew. Filling the water dishes finishes the chores. Don't feel you need to work much longer."

"Before I leave, I'll let you know." Drew swung a bucket under the tap.

On the way to the house, Noah told her everything Drew had said and done.

She failed miserably at keeping them apart and diverting his attention to other activities. Even worse, hard as she tried, she couldn't unravel her own muddled feelings, which were as tangled as a ball of yarn.

Thirty minutes later, when she answered Drew's tap at the back door, she had tucked in Noah with the dogs snoozing beside him. "I finished tonight's jobs." He stood, hands on hips, and stretched back his shoulders.

She should let him head off into the night, but instead, she opened the door and allowed the chocolaty aroma of warm cookies to waft. "If you'd like, come in for tea."

"Are you sure you're not too tired?" He bent and scratched Sam and Jake, awake from their naps, behind the ears.

Even as Erin welcomed him, she questioned her judgment. She should head to bed and keep rested. Why had she invited in a tall, dark distraction? Doubt tingled in her chest, and butterflies fluttered. "I'll boil the kettle."

"I swept the floor to get rid of the stray kibble." Drew leaned his elbows on the kitchen table. "And I patted all the dogs to say goodnight." He chuckled.

As she handed him his cup of tea, she brushed his hand with her fingertips, and she jumped, jostling the hot liquid dangerously close to the rim. His electric touch accelerated her pulse and transported her back in time. Until now, only Eric had made her heart zing over practically nothing.

She set a plate of cookies beside pastel-patterned napkins in the centre of the table and breathed the comforting scent of chamomile tea. "My client calls today confirmed some bad news. Prospective business has shrunk."

Nodding, he chewed on a cookie.

"Unless I make changes, cash flow will dip lower."

He sipped tea and didn't interrupt or ask questions.

After several minutes, she paused and savored his chocolate eyes. "Well, what's your assessment?"

"You're one of the most intelligent and determined people I've ever known." His gaze never wavered.

Blushing, she covered her cheeks. "Oh?" She hadn't at all expected his reaction. She lowered her hands and clasped them on her lap. "You're one of the most intelligent, best listeners I've ever known." She trusted him and valued his advice.

"No, you give me too much credit." He shifted, bit a cookie, and barely shook his head. Raising his napkin, he wiped the crumbs from his lip.

"Yes, you are. I value your opinions. So tell me,

what's your reaction?" She lifted her cup.

"You already asked the right questions and know a lot of the answers." Drew straightened and adjusted his shoulders. "The brainstorming we did yesterday in the car is right on the mark. A few upgrades to the facilities, some paint and repairs, maybe a new name, and a marketing campaign on social media...all those improvements will make a difference. Set priorities to increase the client flow, firm up advance bookings, and reduce vacancy rates."

"I'll work those details into a written plan." Excitement danced through her, and she nodded and leaned forward.

"Your ideas all make perfect sense. You can turn around things." He wiped his fingers on a napkin.

"Thank you for the encouragement. More tea?" Erin picked up the teapot. Inside her, a warm hub radiated confidence. She could jump up and hug him for his steady, reassuring presence. Instead, she took a deep, calming breath and gathered her shaken composure.

"Thanks, but I really should leave. Sam wore out Jake, so at least, I don't have to play at the park tonight." He stood, shifted, and dropped back in his chair. "Oh...I wanted to ask..."

Erin set down the plate of crumbs and settled back.

"Kyle suggested we...uh, you and I might want to get together with his wife and him sometime for pizza and bowling. What do you think?"

Uncertainty flitted across his face. "I haven't bowled in probably ten years." Erin sighed, put a hand on each cheek, and considered the offer. Mulling the possibility, she slid her hands lower and pressed on her thighs.

"Your answer probably depends on whether you can get a babysitter and dog sitter." Drew stared at the table.

Bowling and pizza sounded casual, fun, and pretty low-pressure. She liked Kyle. He came across as a decent guy, and she'd probably like his wife, too. But could she handle a double date? She took a sharp breath. "Sure, maybe we can join them sometime." She let another surprise answer spill out, startling both her head and heart. A mix of pleasure and hesitation rose from within and burned her cheeks. "You're right. I'd need to find a sitter for Noah and the dogs." She was out of practice coordinating social plans.

"Sounds good. We'll work on a plan." Drew stood to leave.

Jake jumped to his side.

"Okay." Erin rubbed her middle. Maybe getting together wasn't such a wise idea. One thing might lead to another, and she still aimed to keep him and Noah apart.

"Of course, I host my dad this weekend." He tossed a crooked grin.

"Next weekend, I'll stay busy with Noah's birthday." She tilted her head. "And you'll need to celebrate your birthday, too."

"Then air show season hits, so I'll be away a lot." Drew stroked his chin.

"Well, maybe we can get together next fall." Erin kept a straight face.

When his quick reaction creased his eyes and darkened his face, she softened her expression into a smile. "Just kidding. Maybe tomorrow evening, we can figure out possibilities." Instantly, he brightened like she flicked a switch. "Sure thing. I'll see you tomorrow." As he turned, he flashed a grin.

Heart fluttering, Erin watched him stride to his car. She practically accepted a double date. Now, how could she keep him at a safe distance?

****

Drew slid into his car and bonked his temple with a palm. *Why did I mention a double date?* Of course, he wanted to invite her out. He'd love to do anything she liked. She was a thirst he couldn't quench. She'd worked her way under his skin, tempting him more each day. He daydreamed of ways he might broach the idea of going out together, but he didn't want their first date to involve bowling and pizza with another couple. He wanted to share a special, romantic evening alone.

He steered out of Erin's driveway onto the rural road. The sky hung like navy-blue drapery splashed with stars to wish upon. He swept his gaze from the road upward, his longing drifting into nothingness. He couldn't rewind the last few minutes and delete his words. Instead of the first date he imagined, he invited her to join a group activity with friends.

Peering into the dark countryside, he envisioned a date spiced with romance. They would start with a quiet dinner surrounded by antiques at a classic restaurant then stroll the treed pathways of Crescent Park. Maybe he'd brush her arm and hold her hand. His heartbeat sprinted. Maybe he would even touch his lips to hers in a gentle, goodnight kiss.

By the time he got home, he ached to fix his botched invitation. A casual group event couldn't substitute for a real date. He entered her number on the phone keypad and clicked end before the first ring.

The second he ended the call, his phone rang, and he answered immediately. "Hello."

"Hey there, Drewzer."

His dad's gravelly voice crackled. "Hi, Dad." A flash of annoyance pinching his temple, he waited for his dad's latest excuse.

"Drew, I got thinking. Maybe this weekend isn't the best time to come." Frank coughed.

"Oh, why?" Drew waited, a sinking weight in his chest. Some things never changed. His dad always promised things but never followed through. Disillusionment drenched him like his morning shower, and his pulse jabbed his temples.

"Yeah, because I realized the very next weekend is your birthday." His dad cackled a raspy laugh.

"You remembered." Frank wasn't known for marking special occasions.

"Why don't I time my visit to celebrate your birthday?"

"You mean, you'll still come, just a week later?" Drew clamped his teeth and hunched his stiff shoulders. He took a shaky breath and waited.

"Of course, I will." Frank emphasized each word.

His dad acted like he had never backed out of anything in his life. Drew leapt to his feet and paced.

"Same plan. I'll drive in Friday. Just a week later. Okay?" Frank hiccupped. "Whoops. Just guzzled soda."

"Okay." Drew slowed and tossed Jake's ball. "I'll see you then." Doubt still tapped in his temples, but he hoped for the best. This time, maybe his dad would make good on his promise. Surely, Frank hadn't postponed as the first step toward cancelling altogether.

"I'll see you then."

His dad's steady voice convinced him. "I'll hold you to the plan, Dad. I'm counting on you." Ending the call and setting aside the phone, he lobbed the ball again. Finally, Drew had told him what he expected. He trusted him to live up to his word.

Massaging his temples, Drew dropped to his knees and then grabbed Jake's tug-of-war rope. The back-and-forth and side-to-side motions mimicked his relationship with his dad. Just when Frank leaned one way, he veered somewhere else. After a while, Drew got worn down by the erratic behavior. He released his end of the toy.

Jake immediately dropped it.

Sometimes, Drew just had to stop struggling to get the results he wanted. He checked the time. Erin would still be awake, and he wouldn't sleep well with plans on his mind. Hesitating for an instant, he took a chance and called.

"Hello."

Her crisp voice suggested he didn't wake her. "I'm sorry to call so late. I made a mistake." Drew cleared his throat.

"Did you make a mistake involving Noah or the dogs?" She emphasized each word.

Drew hurried past her wary tone. "I want to invite you out but not bowling with another couple. I really bungled my plan." He sighed a loud whoosh of breath.

"Oh, I'm happy to hear you didn't make a serious error. Don't worry."

"No, I wanted our first date to be special." He stared out the window at the dark street. "I pictured us together with no one else and no interruptions. Then my

216

dad postponed his visit and freed this weekend. I just wanted to let you know…"

"Oh, I see."

She spoke quietly, and then he heard nothing but her rhythmic breathing. "I wanted to ask you…" As he formulated his explanation, he pictured her lovely face. She was probably biting her lower lip, puzzled by his comment. He pictured her running fingers through her lush hair, and he ached to touch her smooth cheek.

"What do you want to ask?"

"Could I possibly take you out for dinner this weekend?" Drew's heart pounded so wildly he could hardly breathe. He could practically hear the scales tipping back and forth.

"I'm not sure…"

Her voice trailed into silence. "I know you'll have to find a babysitter and a caregiver for the dogs." He forced a steadying breath.

"Well, yes, I do have those factors to consider. I promise clients that I never leave the premises unattended. I can't say for sure, but I'll ask my parents to babysit Noah on Friday or Saturday, on one condition."

"Okay, I can live with one stipulation." His heart beat an erratic rhythm, and he cleared his throat.

"I'll go for dinner, but I won't call it a date." Erin cut off a laugh.

"Of course, whatever you say." Privately, Drew could label the dinner event whatever he liked. "I still plan to come tomorrow evening to work in the kennel." He ended the call and breathed out with enough force to blow out a cake full of candles.

Maybe, just maybe, he would soon pull away Erin

with no son, no family, and no dogs—absolutely no distractions. But she didn't want to label their time together a date, so what did she mean? Had she agreed to the invitation as just a friend? Did she intend to hint they had no romantic future at all? He swallowed through his tight throat. Uncertainty trespassed into his mind and shook his confidence, but he straightened and pulled back his shoulders.

As he pictured her slim shape, brown, velvet eyes, and perfect, white smile, he breathed in hot bursts. If he had been asked two weeks ago, he couldn't have described his dream woman. Now, she lived, breathed, and tempted him, even if she despised flying. How could he convince her she needed him in her life?

****

The next morning, Erin kissed Noah good-bye and sent him out the door to catch the bus. Then she called her mom. "You had an idea for Noah's birthday gift. Can you share the details?" Multi-tasking as usual, she did squats and lunges. Sam circled and batted her with his enthusiastic tail.

"Please, don't ask. I told your dad you would never approve."

"Oh, Mom, you can tell." Erin bristled at Gayle's coating her words with a hint of teasing. A tingle racing down her arms, she held her bent position. "What's your idea?"

"Are you sure you want to know? You might get upset."

Her mom's lowered tone suggested a sensitive topic. "Don't keep me in suspense." Erin grimaced at an extra-vigorous stretch.

"Okay, okay, I'll tell you. But don't say I didn't

warn you. Your dad said Noah is so airplane-crazy that maybe we should pay for a plane rental from the flying club and let Drew take him on a flight over Regina and Moose Jaw."

"No, I would never allow that risky adventure." Wincing at the rush of pressure in her forehead, she straightened and stomped. Her tone didn't mask her exasperation.

"I figured you wouldn't agree." Gayle sighed.

"You're right. I hate the idea." Erin plunged to the floor to hug Sam.

He nuzzled her side and licked her forearm.

"Don't worry. We already bought him a new bike." Her mom's gentle tone reassured. "He will love a new bike." Erin stroked Sam's soft, wavy coat, and a sliver of anxiety dissolved. "Oh, Mom, Drew invited me out, and I just can't go on a real date." She rose and examined her reflection in the hall mirror. Her face, stiff as a wax sculpture, stared through eyes underlined with faint, blue semi-circles. "I have Noah and the business to keep me busy, and, of course, he's a pilot of all things." She sighed. "Besides, what would Eric say?"

"What do you think Eric would say?"

Her mom's voice held no edge of judgement. Erin sauntered to the living room window and drank in the wide, blue sky, patches of brown grass, and splotches of sticky mud.

"Erin, are you still there?"

"Yes, I'm still here. I'm thinking." Warm, caring Eric was a bear hug of a man. She took a deep breath. "He would say he wants me to be happy. He would never hold me back." His loving, generous spirit filled her heart. "He would say as long as Drew's a solid and kind man, go ahead."

"I agree with your assessment. Eric always wanted to make you happy."

Her mom's gentle tone enveloped Erin like a hug. "But he's a pilot..." She peered out the kitchen window to survey the backyard and kennel building. Bending over the sink, she twisted the tap, cupped one hand underneath, and splashed her face with cool water. They couldn't possibly build a future together. His career blocked the way. A relationship would never work, so why should she bother to invest more time?

"He only wants to share a meal, Erin."

Gayle's voice lilted amusement. Erin pressed her lips together. She didn't appreciate the humor over her angst.

"He didn't invite you to fly anywhere. He didn't propose marriage. You just need to enjoy a restaurant meal."

"I suppose you might be right." Erin reached for a towel and dabbed her damp face. She stared at the horizon and gulped a shaky breath. "Would you and Dad babysit Saturday evening?" Uncertainty waved a big, red, warning flag. Spending more time with Drew could lead down a very dangerous path.

"Go ahead and make plans. We'll take care of Noah and the dogs."

As soon as she ended the call, Erin fought doubt and anticipation swirling like a prairie wind. She hesitated and decided to place one more call to totally clear her conscience. She hadn't talked to Eric's mom since the blizzard struck. Her mother-in-law lived far away in Victoria but still kept in touch. "Hi, Mom

Hum. Do you recognize my voice?" Her mother-in-law would always be an extra special person.

"Erin, honey, you're the only person in the world who still calls me Mom Hum, and I'd know your voice anywhere. How's Noah?"

"Fine, he's just fine, and he grows taller every day." Warmth flooded Erin's face. "I have so much to tell you." She reported on Noah's progress in school and his growing obsession with airplanes. She described her business challenges and ideas to attract new clients. "I've already talked your ear off, but I wanted to share one more development."

"I have all the time in the world, honey." Mom Hum chuckled. "Keep talking as long as you like."

Erin pictured her plump face creasing into a bulgy smile. "A client stranded with us in the storm, Drew, has become a friend. Actually, he bonded with our whole family."

"We can all use more friends, honey."

"Well, now, he asked me to join him on a date." She hurried to fill the silence on the phone line. "The problem is I'm not sure if I'm ready. He's a jet pilot...but I feel in my heart, Eric...he would understand." She hesitated and swallowed, kneading her middle. "I just wanted to let you know."

"Oh, honey, I'm happy to hear." Mom Hum whooshed a breath. "He wouldn't just understand. He would support your decision. He wanted more than anything to give you and Noah a secure life, and he'd expect you to rebuild a happy family. He always focused on the future and never the past. You need to plow forward, honey."

"Thanks, Mom Hum." Erin's throat narrowed,

strangling her words. Her eyes stung, and she swallowed, her mouth as dry as a soda biscuit.

After the call, she hugged Sam, rested her cheek on his furry face, and let tears flow. She leaned close until she dampened his fur, steadied her breathing, and made peace with her decision. Drew's career still loomed as a giant obstacle, but she would take one step at a time. She'd enjoy his company as a pleasant diversion.

"Come on, Sam, time for work." She headed toward the kennel and sloshed through puddles just for fun. The sun beamed spring warmth, spreading optimism. She'd proceed cautiously, but she couldn't help wondering where the path would lead.

Chapter 17

"This morning's mission clicked." In a brisk wind on the tarmac, Kyle tapped a fist to Drew's left bicep.

"Yeah, we performed like clockwork." Drew squinted and adjusted his pace to match his teammate's shorter stride. These days, life hummed. The rhythm of work and play and the alignment of the team flowed in a more natural and less strained way.

"After we practice a few more drills, we'll nail the routine." Kyle slapped together his hands.

"I agree. The team will succeed." His mantra to trust his teammates worked.

"What did she say?" Kyle nudged him and waited.

He chuckled. Had his teammate read his mind? While on duty, his personal rule blocked thoughts of Erin, but breaks didn't count. When his feet hit the pavement at lunchtime, he daydreamed all he wanted. "She sounded sort of interested, if we can find a free time."

"Okay, how about this Saturday?" Kyle slowed his pace.

"She might be busy." He tensed, averting his warm face. He still hoped plans for a traditional date would work, even if he had to label it something else.

"You know her schedule." Kyle bumped his shoulder.

Drew dodged him and side-stepped. He preferred

to keep private his personal life. Normally, no one coaxed him to reveal his leisure plans. Before he sat facing Kyle in the mess hall, he rushed to finish discussing his social life. "I, uh, wanted to mention something. Erin doesn't know yet about...what happened..."

"If you pay me, I won't say a word." Kyle flashed a wide grin in Drew's direction. "Don't worry, man. The base is like Vegas. What happens here, stays here."

Kyle's gleeful chortle quickly segued into sincere reassurance. "Thanks for the confidentiality. I appreciate your support." Drew relaxed his clenched jaw. He actually trusted Kyle to stay quiet. Eventually, he'd find a way to tell Erin his terrible secret.

****

Erin worked a productive day and couldn't wait to brief Drew. While Noah played at a friend's house, she spent a solid two hours on plans. She listed repairs, painting, and other improvements and detailed a shopping list for supplies. Then she researched promotion options and put together a schedule. Finally, she called more clients to seek feedback and promote her services. Several new bookings added to a steadily-improving outlook.

After dinner, Drew arrived to help with chores.

She met him in the sprawling yard and, with great will power, contained her news a little longer. Heart rate jumping, she breathed deeply.

"I played pilot at my friend's house." Noah jiggled and grabbed Drew's hand. "We flew really fast across the world."

Erin watched Noah burst ahead then gallop, nearly tripping over the dogs, toward the kennel. Her anticipation rushing, finally, she found a private moment to share her update. While her emotions careened like a rollercoaster, she slowed to a saunter and calmed her tone. "By the way, I'm available to get together Saturday evening. Mom and Dad will babysit and handle the chores, so I'm all set." She paused and glanced at his smiling face. "I anticipate a fun, non-date evening."

"I do, too."

His wide grin crinkling his eyes, Drew took jaunty steps. Warmth flooded her chest. He was excited, too.

"I planned dinner and maybe a loop around the park, but would you like to start with a visit to the spa?"

"I might enjoy a soothing soak." She could handle a walk and dinner conversation, but could she put on a bathing suit and relax in the hot-spring pool? In the cool, evening air, her pulse jumped and forced heat to her skin. Surprisingly, right now, she would do almost anything he asked. She just had to pretend he wasn't a pilot, and she wasn't terrified of flying. "Well, back to business." She reviewed her work list. "I need to tackle a lot of repairs and improvements." She paced next to Drew and paused to examine the property.

"A few hours of concentrated work will make a big difference." Drew listened, nodded, and asked questions until they formulated a detailed approach. "If you buy all the materials, you'll keep me busy with assorted chores this week. Then as soon as the weather warms, I can paint."

"I can't adequately thank you. My gift certificate for labor will run out long before I complete the improvements." Her optimism soared, and in the middle of a muddy patch, she swiveled to face him.

"Then I charge big bucks." He lifted his eyebrows.

She giggled at his teasing, ominous tone and resisted the urge to brush a clump of dog hair off his sleeve. Touching him might send the wrong message. "As long as you take payment in the form of meals and cookies, you'll receive compensation." She finished the tour and stood between the house and the kennel. "I better round up Noah for a bath and stories."

"I'll fill water dishes and toss balls for a while." He waved and headed toward the kennel.

Erin scanned the yard and spotted Noah and Sam scrambling without Jake. Usually, the trio stuck together. She squinted and shifted her gaze left and right but couldn't see any sign of the black-and-white dog. Apprehension rose instantly and filled her chest.

"Where's Jake?" Drew hurried to meet Noah.

Noah ran closer, his sobs breaking the evening air.

"Why so sad?" Arms tensing, Erin hugged him. Something was clearly wrong.

Sam nosed in and smothered him with licks to his teary face.

"Hey, Noah. What happened?" Drew rubbed his back.

"I-I-I couldn't catch Jake." He buried his wet face in his mom's waist. "He chased a rabbit. I ran and ran and called him, but I couldn't catch him. He didn't listen."

Drew frowned and searched the horizon. "Which way did Jake run?"

"I-I-I hope he's not lost." Noah pointed toward Ted and Vera's land. Sniffing, he wiped his nose on his T-shirt. "He ran so fast."

Erin gave Noah a tighter squeeze and then squatted

to face him. "I'm sure Jake will find his way here." She struggled to believe her own, reassuring words.

"Everything will turn out okay, Noah. Don't worry, he'll come back. You go inside with your mom and get ready for bed, and I'll find Jake." Drew rubbed his right temple and stared at the open field.

"I'll come and help you." Noah snuffled.

"No, Drew will find him." Straightening, Erin clenched her teeth and squeezed both fists. Losing Jake would be a nightmare. Twisting inside but forcing a brave face, she held Noah's hand and led him toward the house.

Calling Jake's name over and over, Drew sprinted across the yard.

She glanced over her shoulder and cringed. If anything happened to his beloved dog, he would be devastated.

****

Back at home in his dark room, nestled under his cozy, plaid quilt, Drew lay in bed with a very tired Jake sprawling at the foot. If the dog ran toward the road instead of the open field, disaster might have struck. He shuddered and squeezed shut his eyes. The time missing Jake had stretched forever, but in reality, lasted only minutes. Drew dashed over rough ground and soon spotted his beloved Border collie loping across the prairie, back toward Canine Corner.

Jake panted hard, tongue lolling, but fortunately, he suffered no ill effects after his big adventure.

Every pore in Drew's body still oozed relief. As soon as he knew Jake was safe, he had hurried to the house to soothe Noah's worries.

"I'm happy Jake didn't get lost." Noah rubbed his

eyes.

"I'm sorry you had such a nasty scare." Erin shook her head and put a hand on Drew's arm.

"Jake's okay, so everything's fine." His heart rate, just returning to normal, had sped at her touch. Later, when Drew finished working, he stood in the doorway and shared Kyle's invitation for Friday evening.

"I don't want to leave Noah with a babysitter two nights in a row, but we could invite Kyle and his wife here for pizza and games." She tilted her head and tucked a curl behind her ear.

"Sure. I'm not a great bowler anyway." He shrugged.

"Oh, I missed my chance. You mean I would win." Erin flexed her arms and pretended to throw a bowling ball.

"Ha. Don't be too sure." His competitive spirit rising, he had tossed a grin.

He shouldn't let memories of the evening keep him awake much longer. He yawned and ran a hand along Jake's smooth head. Rolling, he adjusted the blankets over his shoulder. Tonight ended on a positive note. Would the weekend turn out just as well?

****

The next couple of evenings followed the same routine with work, playtime, and visiting. Sometimes, Erin and Drew did chores side by side and then switched to individual projects. Occasionally, they compared notes, but frequently, they worked in companionable silence.

Usually, Noah stuck close to Drew, asking questions, handing him tools, and imitating his technique.

Erin gave up on keeping them apart. In some ways, time with Drew unfolded as familiar as a favorite book. She almost believed they had always laughed together, worked in unison, and played with Noah and the dogs. Other times, the novelty and pleasure tingled in a pleasant way through her body.

On Friday evening, Erin waved her guests into her cozy home. "Heather, finally, we get to meet." She reached for their jackets. "Don't worry, I won't put Kyle to work."

"Whew, what a relief." Kyle laughed and rubbed the back of his neck. "Those dogs can wear out a guy."

"Hi." Noah rounded the corner to the entrance and skidded to a stop. "I remember you're a pilot like Drew."

"You're right, and I bet you want to be a pilot, too." Kyle held out his hand for a high five.

Noah nodded and beamed, his face as bright as the moon. She couldn't imagine doing anything to subdue his glowing enthusiasm. After a few minutes, Erin settled her guests in the living room and scooted her son to get ready for bed. "Just make yourselves at home. I'll be back soon."

The frequent talk of flying didn't start as therapy, but she learned to tolerate passing references to airplanes without her body threatening to implode. She still disliked hearing Noah chatter about flying with Drew, but she endured his wishful thinking with achy, rather than stabbing, pain. "Sweet dreams." She gave Noah a kiss and tucked the covers under his chin. No doubt, his dreams would soar high in the sky. She switched on the night light and closed the bedroom door. "Okay, kitchen crew. Let's go." Returning to her guests, she assigned them each the task of adding assorted toppings to homemade pizza crusts.

"I'm impressed you lured Heather into the kitchen." Kyle slung an arm around his wife's shoulders. "She told me allergies forced her to steer clear."

Heather giggled, tossed her full, blonde hair, and tied a colorful, cotton apron around her ample waist. "Kyle does most of the cooking, but only because he's horrible at cleaning. I traded kitchen duties for vacuuming." She sprinkled a handful of cheese over pepperoni. "You forgot to mention that minor detail about our swap."

"Oh, yeah, I guess you're right. Here's to my gorgeous, tidy wife." Kyle grinned and swept his glass in a toast. He stood back and viewed the collection of pizzas. "They turned out pretty well. But if being a pilot doesn't work out for Drew, I can see master chef won't be his next career." He tipped back his head and hooted.

Erin laughed at Kyle's crack and waited for Drew's warm chuckle. Instead, he dropped scraps into the garbage can and gave a bare hint of a smile. He seemed a little on edge, but maybe kitchen work distracted too much to allow him to appreciate the joke. "Now, let's bake these delicious creations so we can eat." Erin caught Drew's gaze and smiled.

For two hours, the foursome ate pizza, played board games, joked, and laughed.

Erin sipped wine and forgot everything on her long to-do list. Clients, bookings, and chores faded to the background. She welcomed the novelty of hosting company. Aside from family, she hadn't socialized much lately. "The evidence speaks. You can't avoid the truth, guys." As Erin gathered game pieces, she grinned and glanced at Heather for confirmation. "The women won."

"Works for me. Keeps my wife in a good mood." Kyle laughed and raised his glass.

Heather rolled her eyes and huffed. Then she winked at her host.

Erin caught her mock exasperation and laughed. Setting aside their friendly competition, she relaxed into a comfortable chair. As she bantered and enjoyed the lively conversation, she reveled in the warmth filling her chest. The companionship of friends was a rare treat.

"I'm a nurse." Heather brushed a stray hair from her cheek. "Luckily, I can work wherever the Forces send Kyle."

Many careers were more portable than Erin's, but of course, her business right here near Moose Jaw was all she wanted.

"We don't have kids yet, but when we do, we'll probably live far from family." Heather grimaced. "I'm not sure how I'll survive."

"I'm very lucky my family lives just a short hop down the highway." Erin nodded and cupped her glass. "I love Moose Jaw, so I'll never leave." The men would perform with the SnoWings for two years and then transfer to another military, flight challenge at another base. Drew could end up anywhere in Canada, a long way from Moose Jaw. Like a persistent doorbell, doubt pinged. Building a closer relationship would only mean another loss when the Forces posted him elsewhere. Her spirits, buoyed by fun, plummeted. She'd already endured enough loss to last a lifetime.

While Drew lowered his gaze and fidgeted, Kyle recounted the intensive SnoWings selection process.

Erin couldn't deny her respect for his role. Clearly, he flew with an elite team who were experts in their profession. The average pilot wouldn't be capable of performing the famous, precision formations. She slammed the door on his pilot life but acknowledged that his remarkable achievement deserved credit. She would tackle one day at a time. Even if their futures clashed, she would still enjoy an evening out. "Excuse me." Smiling and interrupting the guys' banter, Erin pushed herself out of her comfy chair. "I hope I can interest you all in dessert."

"I'll never refuse anything sweet." Kyle chuckled. "Like Heather."

She groaned and reached to swat his knee.

"How long have you and Drew been together?" Heather followed Erin to the kitchen and leaned on the cupboard.

Erin sliced generous squares of carrot cake, richly spiced with ginger and nutmeg. "Oh, we're not together." She widened her eyes. "Didn't Kyle tell you? We're friends but not a couple."

"You're kidding." Heather arched high her eyebrows. "I guessed you've been together for years. You appear so connected, and you even sort of match."

"He's tall, dark, and handsome, so I'll consider your comment a compliment." Arms tingling, Erin smiled.

"Of course, I meant to flatter you." Heather giggled and fluffed her hair. "Well, the only difference is you're tall, dark, and *pretty*."

"Thanks, I appreciate your kind words." She added

a small scoop of ice cream to each plate. "He's a nice guy, but sorry to disappoint you. We're not an item." With their lives headed in different directions, they'd never be a couple. She could pretend their lives melded, deny his high-stakes, flying career, and dream he wouldn't eventually fly away from Moose Jaw. But reality stared her in the face.

"You never know what might happen." Heather smiled. "But hey, what do I know? I'm a nurse, not a psychologist."

Balancing plates of cake, they rounded the corner from the kitchen.

"What did you say about a psychologist?" As he joined the end of the conversation, Kyle smirked.

"I said anyone married to a pilot needs a psychologist." Heather crinkled her nose and winked.

Kyle shook his head and groaned, with Drew echoing.

Erin handed them dessert and returned to the kitchen to pour steaming cups of coffee. Heather had no idea her unwitting irony resonated. Being married to a pilot gave Erin her greatest joy in life. Losing him spun her into a state where she nearly needed professional help. But now, she'd overcome her personal trauma. She had a son to raise, a business to run, and an evening out to anticipate. She also hosted guests, waiting for coffee to complement their dessert.

Life carried on, filled with occasional, pleasant surprises. Still, why did a vague uneasiness tap her on the shoulder?

Chapter 18

Drew woke early Saturday morning to Jake's intense stare. Surrounded by the soothing, blue walls of his bedroom, he had time to loll under the matching quilt, but anticipation lured him to roll promptly out of bed. Even if he wasn't allowed to label this evening an official date, he marked it as a very special occasion and couldn't wait. After breakfast and a long walk, he faced a day that stretched as long and monotonous as a prairie road trip. Bored and restless, he played Jake's favorite hide-and-seek game with a ball. Nothing made the time pass quickly.

He took off the day from kennel work because Erin insisted, so he cleaned the house to prepare for his dad's visit next weekend. He couldn't remember when he celebrated a birthday with a family member. How would he catch up on the lost years? His dad didn't take him for his driver's test. He skipped Drew's graduation from military college. He'd never flown with his son at the controls. Frank missed sharing huge chunks of Drew's life. Did he care or even have an inkling?

Drew couldn't take his dad on a flight using military aircraft, but he could rent a plane for an hour or two from the Regina Flying Club. He'd take him on a tour of the area and demonstrate his excellent, piloting skills. At last, maybe his dad would utter the words he craved—"I'm proud of you, son." He sighed and petted

Jake. He shouldn't get up his hopes.

After he scrubbed the bathroom and floors, he admired his surroundings, gleaming with lemony, antiseptic freshness. Still, an endless afternoon loomed. He took Jake for another long trek, packed his swimsuit and towel for the spa, switched on the TV, and flipped through a magazine. After a few minutes, he slapped shut the journal, tossed Jake's ball, and paced. Finally, he could no longer stand the wait and called Erin.

"You told me to take off the day, but I found some spare time. I'll come and prepare for painting."

"You don't need to give me any more free labor. I've already more than used my credit."

Erin's mild protest only spurred action. "I'm on my way," he insisted, "I could use some fresh air." More than anything, he craved time in her company.

This time, she didn't argue.

Within thirty minutes, he arrived with heat radiating inside his chest and cheekbones. Scanning the yard and outside play area near the red, kennel building, he swung out of the car and waved.

Noah bounded next to Sam to greet him with open arms.

Across the open space, Erin threw balls for a pair of eager spaniels and raised an arm to acknowledge his arrival.

After all the hours he spent here at Canine Corner, he knew her property as well as his own home. Gripping Noah by the wrists, he spun and plopped him on the ground. Laughing, Drew raced him to Erin to get his instructions. The closer he got, the more his chest tingled. Unlike the morning's snail pace, the afternoon sped by. As he and Noah scraped flaking paint off the gate and fence posts, Drew paused occasionally to supervise his eager, young helper.

"How old will you be on your birthday?" Noah looked up.

"Thirty-three." Drew ran a hand along the surface of a fence board.

"Oh, you're pretty old." Noah wrinkled his nose.

Drew covered his smile with a hand and pretended to cough. "I'm not too old to fly."

"What do you want for your birthday?"

As Noah imitated the scraping motion, Drew straightened, shaded his eyes, and scanned the yard to make sure Jake stayed close. He couldn't tell Noah what he really wanted. Cementing his role with the SnoWings and spending time with Erin topped his wish list. "I don't know. What present would you like?"

"I really want a plane ride. Will you come to my party?" Noah stubbed a toe in the dirt.

"We better ask your mom what she thinks." He paused to examine their progress.

Sam and Jake bounded over to lick Noah's cheeks, distracting him from his duties.

"Where do you live?" Noah wiped with his sleeves his cheeks.

"I live in a house in Moose Jaw." He caught a wave from Erin, crossing the yard from the kennel to the house. As always, her presence sparked his heartbeats. He belonged here, pitching in and fielding Noah's never-ending questions.

"What's your dad's name?" Noah climbed onto the bottom fence rung.

"His name is Frank."

"Fr…ank."

The exaggerated pronunciation stretched Noah's mouth wide. "Yes, you said his name right. Do you know anyone else named Frank?" Drew brushed a fleck of paint off his companion's cheek.

"No, I don't think so. When will you take me on a plane ride?" Noah hopped off the fence.

"I don't know. Your mom might not like the idea." Would Erin ever allow a flight? She'd probably never agree. He glanced up and inhaled a sharp breath as she approached, strolling like a model for beauty products. The breeze tousled her hair and tinted her cheeks pink as ripe peaches. Drew swallowed and glanced at the horizon to calm his revving heart rate. He shifted his gaze to admire her lovely face. She grew more beautiful every day.

"Nice work, guys." She stood, hands on hips, surveying their work.

"Yeah, we're making good progress." He smiled and patted the smooth surface.

"I need to head inside to get ready. I've been invited out this evening."

She blinked, tossed her hair, and parted her lips into a wide smile. Jolted by desire, he wanted to kiss her on the spot.

"Where are you going?" Noah tugged on her windbreaker and narrowed his eyes.

"Drew invited me to a restaurant for dinner." She squatted to Noah's eye level.

"I want to come." He popped forward his bottom lip.

Drew hid a smile at the boy's stubborn assertion. He'd never seen Noah less than happy but had no doubt Erin would smooth the situation.

"Remember, I told you Grandma and Grandpa will visit until I get home." She touched his nose with a finger. "You'll play and read stories."

"But I want to go with Drew, too." He swiveled his toe in the mud.

"Sorry, you may not come this time." She held his hand and swung. "Hey, I'll race you to the house. On your mark, get set…"

Before he heard the word go, Noah scurried away with his arms straight out like jet wings cutting the sky.

"Come in for a break. Mom and Dad will arrive soon to babysit." She took off to catch her son.

Drew bent and gathered his tools. The physical work and Noah's continuous chatter tamed persistent waves of uncertainty. The evening with Erin might be a turning point. Maybe she'd give their relationship a chance.

When Brian and Gayle arrived in their white, compact car, they waved.

"Hi, Drew." Brian sauntered with his hand extended. "I'm impressed with your accomplishment."

Drew shook his hand and glanced at the scraped, fence boards. "I didn't work too hard, and Noah kept me amused."

"I don't mean the fence. You convinced Erin to go on a date." Brian slapped him on the back. "Persuading her to join you was no small feat. Besides starring as a pilot, you must be a bit of a salesman."

Forcing a laugh, Drew reached into the car for his gym bag, equipped with a change of clothes. He labelled himself a work-in-progress, not a star. Guilt over the incorrect assumption pulsed in his temples. His SnoWings status still wobbled, but no one outside the

Forces knew. He gripped tight the handle.

While reflecting on the evening ahead, he strode, half listening to Brian's banter. Judging by his vibrating heart, he'd find the time very special—a true, first date—even if Erin resisted the label. He swung his arms high and rolled his tight shoulders. He needed to relax. He hadn't proposed marriage, just an evening out. Still, his body buzzed with anticipation. Finally, he could focus on deepening their relationship. He stepped aside to let Brian enter first and felt immediately at home within the calming, muted walls.

"Hi, Grandpa. Hi, Drew."

Noah flew to the entranceway. He spread wide his arms to hug them both at the same time, even though he had left Drew only minutes earlier.

Pleased but slightly self-conscious, Drew stiffened. How would Erin and her parents feel about Noah's obvious affection?

"I used to be the most popular visitor here." Brian winked. "But now I face heavy competition."

"Oh, don't worry. You're family. I'm just a novelty." Drew returned Noah's half hug. "You helped a lot today, bud."

"I scraped the fence, so we can paint it." Noah demonstrated a scraping motion.

"Atta boy. Keep up the good work." Brian flashed a thumbs-up.

"Will you play now?" He held his grandpa's hand and hopped in place.

"You bet I will." Brian ruffled his tousled hair.

"Have fun with Grandma and Grandpa." Drew smiled and squeezed his shoulder. For a second, Noah's face flickered like a light bulb but stayed bright.

"Come in, boys." Gayle waved them into the living room and plopped on the couch next to a turquoise cushion. "Erin should be ready any minute."

"I better go and change out of these work clothes." Gym bag in hand, Drew headed to the bathroom. Before he left home, he paused over what to wear and settled on dressy, black jeans and a crisp, wine shirt with fine, white stripes. He washed his face and combed his hair. What would Erin think of his appearance? He checked the mirror one last time, straightened his shirt collar, and pulled back his shoulders. Nervous anticipation twinged in his temples. He couldn't wait.

Back in the living room, he nearly gasped. Even in her usual casual jeans and sweaters, Erin grabbed his attention. But now, she dazzled in dark pants, funky boots, and a fitted tunic, swirled with the colors of raspberries floating in cream. A tempting spritz of subtle, vanilla scent wafted in the air. "Wow, you're dressed to impress." His pulse jumped. He was captivated, but maybe in front of the family, he should temper his reaction.

"Thank you." She tilted her head and swept her gaze up and down. "You clean up well, too."

"Hey, you match." Noah quickly pointed at their coordinating outfits. Giggling, he widened his eyes.

A chorus of laughter greeted his assessment.

"He's right." Gayle nodded and swept across a hand from one to the other.

"She must have good taste." The heat in Drew's face intensified. He meant her fashion sense, not her taste in men.

"Of course, I do."

Posing like a mannequin, Erin smoothed the awkward moment. Drew's chest muscles pulled tight, clutching his breath. Witnessing her hug her parents and Noah goodbye, he hungered to be next in the lineup, where only her cherished inner circle belonged. Would he ever enfold her in his arms?

After they patted the dogs and promised Brian to have fun and drive carefully, they got in the car and trundled down the bumpy road. He glanced at Erin's glowing, even profile and gripped the steering wheel. Excitement warmed his chest and arms, but he didn't dare whisper how her natural appearance attracted him. He lowered a window, inhaled the fresh, evening air, and struggled to balance desire with other, more-important demands. Performing to the SnoWings' high standards meant everything. He couldn't afford to get distracted by anything or anyone, not her inner strength nor outer beauty.

"You're deep in thought." Erin turned to face him. "Are you daydreaming about the pool or the dinner menu?"

"Well, not exactly, but I'm looking forward to both. After a dip, I'll be ready to devour a juicy steak." He chuckled and glanced over. Dinner was the last thing on his mind. Other burning thoughts whirled and distracted him. Would he ever convince her to tolerate flying? Could he trust her with his feelings and tell her how much he cared?

****

A mix of anticipation and hesitation swirled inside Erin. At the spa, she parted from Drew in front of the changing rooms. Breathing the warm, moist atmosphere, she squeezed a hand tight around her tote bag. She'd soon let her lingering apprehension drift away.

"I'll meet you in the pool." He swung his gym bag toward the entrance.

Perhaps she should have suggested they save the spa for after dinner so her hairstyle and makeup would stay intact. She couldn't change her mind now, so she secured a high ponytail that wouldn't touch the water and hoped the steamy air wouldn't dissolve her mascara. A few minutes later, she emerged and found him already bobbing in the water. She resisted the impulse to cross her arms, even though he averted his gaze. Her conservative, one-piece swimsuit offered a protective, not-too-revealing cover. The sign on the wall described the pool's healing mineral waters, flowing from a natural hot spring. She sighed, temporarily free of burdens, and relaxed into the warm ripples.

A few other bathers lazed throughout the pool against the soothing backdrop of teal walls. She inhaled deeply, filling her lungs and tickling her nose with humid air, imbued with the scent of minerals.

"Let's go outside." Drew tipped his head toward the passageway to the outdoor section of the pool.

They waded side by side through water which steadily increased in depth. Clouds of steam rose from the pool in the cooler, outside air.

Settling along the edge facing Crescent Park, Erin glanced at his profile. "Soaking relaxes every tired muscle...the perfect ending to a work day." She smiled, and her cares melted into the blanket of warm water.

"I agree." He flicked water off his hand, hesitated, and wiped a water droplet off her cheek.

"You don't know how much I appreciate your help." For a second, she forgot his risky career and allowed her feelings to tug. "And I really enjoyed last evening with Kyle and Heather."

He nodded, and his smile widened into a grin.

"I enjoyed the evening, too." Drew dipped lower, washing the steamy liquid over his shoulders. "Dad will arrive next weekend."

Through the steamy haze, she watched him swish a hand over the surface. "If you don't have other plans to celebrate your own birthday, you could invite him to Noah's birthday party." She glanced at the lines tightening along his jaw. Surely, her invitation didn't trouble him. "Your dad might want to see where the weather stranded you." Her life had changed dramatically since that stormy weekend. She quivered inside and sank deeper into the soothing water.

With his engaging company, she spent an hour soaking and breathing the cool evening air, occasionally sitting on the edge to cool and then sinking into the warm froth. As dusk fell, lights reflected through the windows onto his face. The gentle spotlight lit his dark lashes and deep complexion. Water droplets glistened on his bare, muscular shoulders. She swept her gaze to his chiseled features and smothered a gasp at the striking sight. Desire swelled and lured her closer until she caught herself and floated away.

"I'm hungry. What about you?" He wiped moisture off his face.

"Yes, much as I love this soothing water, I should leave before my skin shrivels like a prune." She nodded and floated toward the archway to the exit. In front of the dressing-room mirror, she examined her reflection to assess what repairs were needed. Her flushed cheeks beamed a healthy glow, but when she released her ponytail, she bemoaned momentarily her unruly curls, spiraling thanks to humidity. Brushing her hair, blotting her face, and smoothing gloss over her lips, she conceded that her relaxed muscles were worth the effort of refreshing her appearance. A light spritz of cologne was the final touch.

After changing clothes, she found Drew waiting in the lobby. Then she joined him strolling to their table at the restaurant next to the spa. Even in the subdued, evening light, she absorbed every detail of his glowing, sculpted face. A background of sage décor and mellow music soothed her slight apprehension over the new-found intimacy she sensed. A sprinkle of other diners murmured conversations.

"To dogs and blizzards." He raised his wine glass in a toast.

She tilted her head, smiled, and clinked his glass. As she opened the menu, she couldn't remember the last time she had dined in such classy surroundings. A meal in a fine restaurant was a rare and welcome treat.

The conversation flowed so naturally she almost believed they belonged together. Last night with friends set the fun tone. This evening, the experience of enjoying his company glimmered with promise. But a relationship would never work when his career was her worst nightmare. Eventually, the Air Force would send him far from Moose Jaw. She needed to stop dreaming of an impossible future. "Excuse me?" She clicked to the present. Meeting his dark, inquiring gaze, she struggled to process his words.

"How will you celebrate Noah's birthday?" Drew

repeated the question and gulped his water.

Despite her growing attraction, she must find a gentle way to let him know their budding relationship couldn't continue. She treasured the way he enriched her life, but she had to protect herself and Noah from getting hurt. "I'll host a casual party with games and cake but nothing elaborate." She spread a napkin across her lap. "Noah would like to invite family, Ted and Vera, and a couple of kids from his class. He also included you. Definitely, he wants you to come. You might not care to join us with your dad here, but if you don't mind hanging out with family and six-year-old kids, you should feel welcome to bring him."

A family event was a harmless way to spend time with Drew, and it might be a unique and amusing addition to his dad's visit. A hint of excitement surged, and she rushed on. "Don't feel obligated, but we always have room for one more."

"We'll come. Rather, I'll join the fun, and I hope Dad will, too." Drew met her gaze.

The server set plates on the table with a flourish, displaying a tempting array of food. Her mouth watered at the scent of a fresh blend of garlic, lemon, and dill drifting over the table. "What will you do to celebrate your birthday?" She tilted her head and tasted a bite of salmon. As she paused for his response, she glimpsed a shadow flitting across his face.

"Dad and I probably won't do anything special. Our family never made much of a fuss over birthdays or any special occasion." Mouth pressed into a straight line, he speared a bite of steak.

She nodded, a birthday balloon bursting in her heart. Their neglect stung. His family didn't even try to honor the day. "I suppose you're accustomed to your family's approach." Her throat tightened.

"Yes, I learned long ago to expect nothing. But I planned a treat for Dad." He smiled and swiped the napkin across his mouth.

"Oh, what will you do?" Erin sampled the almond rice. He had such high hopes for his dad's visit. If she could help in any way by including his dad in Noah's party, she'd feel good.

"He's never flown with me. So I booked a small plane for an hour on Sunday afternoon. I'll show him some sights and give him a flying demo."

"I'm sure he'll appreciate experiencing you in action." Erin sipped water to moisten her dry mouth. The topic of flight surfaced continually. She couldn't avoid it these days, and although she'd increased her tolerance, she didn't embrace the topic. She took a deep breath.

"I told myself I wouldn't even mention flying." Drew sucked in his cheeks and lowered his voice. "But I could take more passengers." He blinked and looked away.

She set down her fork and held the napkin over her mouth. Hearing others talk about flying might be bearable, but contemplating an actual flight was another matter. Fear sent her off balance, rotating the room and fading the clatter of dishes and conversation to a faraway muffle.

"Maybe Noah…" He straightened and sat forward. "If you don't want to join him, I could invite your dad."

His words flew directly across the table, so she couldn't dodge them. Suddenly, he appeared as uncomfortable as she felt.

A deep flush colored his face, and he stared at his plate.

"Thank you, but no, I must refuse." Forcing her lips together in a firm line, she waited for the surroundings to steady. She reached for another sip of water. He couldn't really expect her to enjoy a flight.

"I'm sorry I mentioned the idea." Drew pressed his napkin to his mouth.

"Noah would love the flight, but I would hate it." Her tight throat smothered her words to a whisper.

"You're truly terrified of flying, aren't you?" Frowning, he searched her face and set his fork on the edge of his plate.

Erin nodded. She put a hand over her pounding heart and inhaled a jerky breath. An observation made recently by Noah jumped to mind, and she blotted the memory before it could add to her misery.

"Will you ever face your fear? Do you even want to try?" He brushed her hand with a fingertip.

"I'd like to live my life without fear. Miracles happen." She fisted her quivering hands on her lap. "After you suggested taking Noah to the aviation display at the museum, I forced myself to check it out. I survived, but I'd rather have suffered a root canal."

Drew nodded and sipped his water. "I'm proud of you. You took a giant step, and you proved you're tough and strong."

"I don't question your piloting skills." She gripped and twisted her napkin. "You must be an expert, or you wouldn't be a SnoWings pilot."

"No pressure. I understand." He swirled a piece of steak in mushroom sauce.

"After losing my husband in the crash…" Out at a

restaurant with Drew and talking about Eric, she clamped her mouth shut. Her past and her present shouldn't intertwine. She shook her head.

"Consider the subject dropped. You have your reasons." He chewed a bite of steak and swallowed.

"Thank you. We won't talk about flying anymore tonight." She took a deep breath, enjoyed another savory mouthful, and locked on his chocolate eyes. "Umm…delicious." Did she mean the delectable food or his alluring appearance?

For dessert, he gave her the choice and ordered a single slice of lemon cake because she wanted only a small portion.

When she brushed her fork against his, she recoiled from the intimate act of sharing one dessert. Fond memories of dinner dates with Eric rushed to mind. Curbing a sweet tooth, he frequently refused treats but sampled hers. Sharing food with another man felt foreign and wrong. She dropped her utensil with a clatter and squeezed her shaky fingers. Drew's presence unsettled her world, and she couldn't let it continue.

****

Drew breathed moist, grassy scents and sauntered beside Erin to the car. Stars winked overhead, and a light breeze cooled the evening air. He nearly held her hand, but instead, he leaned close enough to nudge her arm. When she didn't flinch, she gave him hope. Overwhelming warmth rose and swelled in his chest.

Playing romantic music on the car stereo, he took his time driving back to Canine Corner. At the first flash of a yellow light, he stopped to extend the time together. "I enjoyed the evening." He slowed the car in the driveway. "Maybe we can go out again sometime."

He gripped the wheel. He'd do anything to see her again.

"You treated me to a lovely evening. Thank you." She stared at the house lights. "Dad's waiting."

Drew rubbed the twinge in his temple. She didn't agree immediately to another date, yet she had a good time. He had to find a way to convince her to join him again. "I feel like a teen late for curfew." He chuckled at the sight of Brian waving in the doorway.

Sam and Jake burst past him to welcome them home.

"Come in, Drew." Brian motioned toward the entrance. "Gayle just boiled the kettle for tea."

He hesitated and waited for Erin's nod before stepping out of the car and proceeding inside.

"Sit here. Noah's asleep, and the dogs are all handled for the night. We can relax for a few minutes." Brian gestured to a tweedy chair and swiped together his hands. "Ted returns tomorrow, so work should ease a bit."

"What did you plan for your dad's visit?" Gayle carried a tray of mugs into the living room.

"We'll do a few touristy things. I'll show him the base and town." Drew propped his elbows on the arms of the chair. "I might take him on one of the tunnel tours." While they toured, they would have plenty of time to talk and sort out the past. He shifted and pulled back his shoulders.

"Yeah, visitors always get a kick out of hearing about Moose Jaw's bootleggers and the Al Capone connection." Brian settled onto the sofa and cradled a steaming mug of tea. "The local history is pretty colorful with a network of tunnels under Main Street where gangsters hid out."

"I also plan to take Dad on a bit of an aerial tour." Drew rubbed Jake's side.

"Drew has never flown him anywhere." Erin set down her cup and stroked Sam.

"Yeah, this flight marks a first." Uncertainty tapped at Drew's temple. The adventure better work out at last. He hoped his dad actually showed.

"Your dad is a lucky guy. He'll be proud to see you in action." Brian stood and stretched. "Sometime, I wouldn't mind an aerial tour." He nodded at Gayle. "But speaking of travel, before I fall asleep in my chair, I better hit the road with my lovely wife." He patted the dogs and hugged Erin.

"Goodnight." Drew turned to Erin and smiled.

"Thank you for a wonderful evening." She tucked a curl behind an ear.

"I'll come back tomorrow to finish scraping the fence." He followed Brian and Gayle outside. The empty space inside him throbbed. He yearned to caress Erin's arms, draw her close, and brush his lips against her smooth cheek. But he couldn't touch or kiss her now. He risked scaring her off forever. Besides, her parents stood near, smiling and waving.

"Call me." Brian shook his hand before he and Gayle got into their car. "I'll drive over some evening to hang out with Jake and you."

The warmth of Brian's handshake rushed up his arm and filled him like air in a balloon. *He's so interested, caring, and present. He's nothing like my detached dad.* Would Frank ever change? Might he ever show interest the way a father should? As he steered from the blackness toward the lights of Moose

Jaw, he rotated his shoulders to release sudden tension.

He needed to trust Erin and Brian enough to reveal his dreaded secret. They deserved to know his position with the SnoWings teetered, being one mistake away from ending. From what he could tell, he improved every day. Practices usually ran well. The daily missions hummed, grooming the team to perform the new formations and airshow routines with increasing confidence. Kyle's recent friendship helped. So did his determination to trust his teammates, no matter what.

But the *incident* still followed him around like a shadow, fluctuating in size depending on the time of day and success of the latest mission. While he worked tomorrow evening, he would confide in Erin, so he wasn't an imposter, masquerading as a successful pilot. Even though she shunned his career, she should know he still only aspired to be an aerial superstar. For months, he had lugged his terrible mistake like a painful, purple bruise. The unrelenting pressure throbbed in his head and shoulders. Tomorrow, just as sure as he would find the right tools to fix the gate, he would muster the courage to tell her. How would she react?

Chapter 19

Erin checked on sleeping Noah, kissed his forehead, and absorbed the wonder of his smooth, peaceful face. His dad would be so proud. A mix of pride and regret filled her lonely heart. She paused, tucked the blankets under his chin, and tiptoed away.

Whenever she fretted alone, she cleaned. Armed with a sponge and bucket of soapy water, she crouched on hands and knees, nuzzled Sam's droopy face, and crawled to the kitchen floor.

He sighed and flopped in easy patting range.

"Good dog." She rubbed his belly. If only she could scrub away her doubts like muddy paw prints. Her body still fizzed with excitement over the evening with Drew, nearly perfect except for the few minutes of airplane talk. She would even relive the experience if she could, but of course, she couldn't. Pretending their opposing aspirations, his in the sky and hers on land, would meld magically on the horizon wasn't reality.

She would always be safe with his gentle and patient manner...so kind to both her and Noah. But even if, a humungous qualifier, she overcame her fear of flying, she couldn't sell her business to become a military wife. She refused to transfer around the country, imitating her childhood lifestyle. No, as much as she was tempted by his caring approach and athletic body, she couldn't build the future he chose.

Standing, she admired her gleaming floor. The physical work invigorated her, preparing her to tackle anything. She glanced at the clock. Her parents should be home by now, so she picked up the phone. Whoever answered would have something to offer. Her mom would be a gentle supporter. Her dad would be an enthusiastic cheerleader.

"Do you miss us already?" Brian greeted her on the second ring.

"Very funny." Erin groaned. "No, I have a question." She bit her lip. Maybe she should just say goodnight.

"As long as your question is not about knitting, you're okay. You can ask me." Brian chortled.

"Dad, I'm serious." Erin perched on a chair and rubbed Sam's furry side with a foot. Sometimes her dad's wacky sense of humor bordered on annoying.

"Okay, go ahead." Brian lowered his tone. "Give me the burning question."

"If I endured a short ride in a small airplane, would I feel better or worse?" She bent and stroked Sam in a calming, steady motion.

As seconds of silence ticked, she waited.

"You'd feel worse, at first. Then you'd feel relieved and better. For sure, better."

Erin rubbed her middle where doubt and fear stabbed. "When Drew takes his dad on a flight, he can take extra passengers."

"Would you consider going?"

Her dad sounded like he had won the lottery. "I hate flying, but I can't live forever afraid." She stood and stared out the front window. The moon lit the yard and reflected off puddles. She belonged here in familiar, stable surroundings.

"Did Drew pressure you?"

Her dad spoke gently. "No, not at all. Noah jolted me into action." Her voice trembled. "I overheard him tell a friend I'm scared of airplanes. I couldn't deny the fact, so I said nothing, but I just about fell from shock." She wiped a tear off her cheek. "I've never mentioned a word, yet my phobia is so obvious, even a five-year-old boy notices. As a parent, I need to model strength, not anxiety." She sighed. "Now, I'm determined to overcome my terror."

"You can do anything you set your mind on, girl. My dad, your gramps, always taught me the best way to overcome fear is to stare it in the face and never back down."

"Of course, good advice is often easier said than done." She ran a hand from Sam's velvety head down his soft body to his wagging tail. Her furry friend never failed to calm her emotions.

"Mothering a child and running a kennel on your own take courage. You're made of tough stuff, Erin. But you can choose whether to take the flight."

Her dad's tone soothed and encouraged. She was lucky to have such a strong presence in her life, supporting her difficult decisions.

"No one will force you. Take comfort in remembering you have a choice," he said.

"Aw, thanks, Dad." Erin exhaled a shaky sigh.

"Of course, if you decide against the flight, let me know. You-know-who will fill in quite happily."

The lilt in his voice shouted a grin, and she almost smiled. She ended the call and answered another, immediate ring.

"Erin, we're at the hospital in Regina."

Vera's voice wavered, small and distant. "Ted can't come to work in the morning. He…he had chest pains on the flight home from Vegas. As soon as the plane landed, the medics loaded him into an ambulance and rushed straight to Emergency."

"Oh no, Vera, I'm so sorry to hear he's not well. How is he feeling now?" She gripped tight the phone and with her free hand, rubbed her forehead. She fought to tame concerns for Ted, Vera, and her own predicament with an assistant too ill to help.

"He's in bad shape." Vera sniffed. "The doctors can't get his vital signs stabilized. Our family's on the way. I should go now."

"I wish I could give you a hug. As soon as you hear more, let me know." Erin set down the phone, sank to the floor beside Sam, and cradled her head. Poor Ted and Vera. For a man his age, he always appeared so strong and fit. They didn't deserve such a sad ending to their anniversary celebration. She prayed Vera would call in the morning to report a false alarm and assure her he would be fine in no time.

If Ted needed a long convalescence, she'd struggle. Fear clutched her, and she squeezed shut her eyes and hugged her knees. For the foreseeable future, she might be short staffed. She coped for a week without him, thanks mostly to Drew's extra help, but without a steady assistant, she couldn't manage the full load. While reliable when available, her student worker, Oliver, still declined extra hours because of his busy class and extra-curricular schedule. She needed more than a student's sporadic, part-time hours, and besides, she'd need time to recruit and train a suitable replacement. The kennel demanded full-time attention, and she needed an instant solution.

The next morning, Erin woke to a call from Vera's daughter who delivered the sad news that Ted didn't live through the night. Wrapping her bathrobe tight to shield the pain, Erin sank onto a chair in stunned silence. Ted's damaged heart gave out in the early hours of the morning with Vera and family by his side.

Crossing her arms, she rocked back and forth. Her throat stung, and her entire body sagged. The unfairness of his death smarted like a fresh wound. She would miss his reliable work and the friendly companionship he offered Noah. Worst of all, Vera lost too soon her beloved partner. The heartbreaking situation loaded one more challenge on top of everything else. Life could be so cruel and unfair.

She looked up at the sound of Noah's feet padding down the hallway toward the kitchen. Blotting her damp cheeks, she hugged him close and took a deep, shaky breath. "Ted's heart quit working, and he died. He's in heaven now."

"Is Ted with my daddy?" Noah's lower lip trembled.

"Yes, Ted and Daddy live in heaven." She blotted her face and blew her nose.

Noah blinked and swiped a tear off his cheek. "I won't be able to help him anymore. He won't be able to come to my birthday party."

"No, we won't see him anymore. We'll miss him." She hugged her precious son until he squirmed to get loose. The rest of the morning passed in a blur of talking to clients, doing kennel chores, and baking muffins to deliver to Vera.

Noah played with the dogs and zoomed around with his toy plane until an afternoon visit at a school friend's place.

Erin held herself together until she waved good-bye, and then she flopped on the couch and sobbed. Even though she had known Ted and Vera for only a few months, she relied on them not only for his kennel work, but for their neighborly support. Grief shook her shoulders, and a puddle dribbled from her nose. All the hurts she had been holding gushed in a wet, stinging mess. She wept for overwhelming business challenges, the daddy Noah would never know, her fear of flying, and the pain of a nasty blow.

Sam hovered, nudging her with his persistent nose and offering consoling licks.

Finally, she pushed herself upright, wiped her eyes, and blew her nose. She'd find a way to cope. Shivering, she clenched her jaw and resolved to stand strong. With all the challenges she already wrestled, she couldn't possibly encounter more complications.

****

Drew's erratic pulse reminded him of his tough, afternoon task. Arriving at Erin's place, he resolved he must tell her about the *incident*. Hard as he'd find revealing his life-threatening error, he wanted her to know the real him better—a nowhere-near-perfect pilot. He needed to unload the overwhelming burden he'd carried for weeks.

Erin swung open the door and motioned him inside.

"What happened? Did Noah get hurt?" The large, living-room window lit her frowning face. He scanned her puffy, red eyes and nose.

"Noah's fine. A friend invited him to play. I…" Her voice cracked, and she covered her face with both hands, shoulders shaking.

He stroked her forearms, hesitated, and encircled her in his arms. Her breath quivered on his neck, and her hands warmed his lower back. Her body, deliciously firm yet soft, fit like she belonged. Still, he had imagined their first hug sharing a romantic moment, not a sorrowful one. Heat surged in his chest until she stepped away. "Let's sit," he said, "and you can tell me what's wrong."

Erin led him to the sofa and relayed the sad news. "I depended on Ted for help…and he treated Noah like a grandson. I feel sorry for Vera losing her husband." Her voice trembled.

Drew nodded and held her hand. He waited until her voice steadied enough to explain. The sad news opened the tap on an ocean of feelings, and she dared to show him. She must feel comfortable with his presence.

"I didn't need to face another challenge." She sniffed and shredded a tissue.

He didn't say much. Rubbing her hand, he gave her an occasional encouraging nod and murmured understanding.

Finally, she dried her tears and gave him a tiny smile. "Nothing has changed, but I feel better."

In a flash, he wanted to become her man more than anything and offer whatever she needed. He admired her strong independent streak but yearned to protect her in any way he could. She filled the gap in his life with warm, vibrant energy. "Can I hug you again?" This embrace meant something, and he searched her face to gauge her readiness. Reading her nod, he slid closer, enveloped her in his arms, and kissed first her temple and then her full, soft mouth.

Her breathing quickened, and she tensed for an instant. Then she relaxed into the special moment. Quietly, they sat entwined with her head resting on his shoulder. His heart pulsated so wildly, he feared she could feel it, too. He breathed her soft, vanilla scent and eased her closer. Neither spoke for a long time.

Drew savored the intimacy he craved, but now, he needed to unveil his secret. "You should know…" Murmuring, he gave her shoulder a gentle squeeze.

"I need to tell you something…"

Startling him, she jumped in at the same instant. They laughed and squeezed hands at their synchronized timing.

"You go first." Drew leaned back but left an arm draped along her shoulders. He could wait.

"No, you tell me." She swiveled and sat sideways facing him.

"Ladies first." He traced her nose with a fingertip.

"Okay, I'll start but only because you insisted." She turned and stared across the room out the window. "I need to get over once and for all my fear of flying. Apparently, I gave birth to a son who has the love of airplanes in his genes. I don't want him to grow up afraid of adventure and new experiences. So, is your offer of the flight still open?"

"Of course, I'd love to take you for a ride." He squeezed her knee. Inside, he cheered. His wish had come true.

She forced a deep breath. "Noah and I will join you and make his birthday wish come true. He'll love the adventure, even if I won't." She clasped tight her hands.

"Are you sure? I'm honored you'll allow me the privilege." His spirits bounced like a rubber ball, up because she trusted him, yet down because his horrible secret might forever change her mind. He should definitely have confessed sooner.

"Now, tell me." She caught his gaze, lifted her eyebrows, and smiled.

"Maybe I should have told you first. I'll understand if you change your mind about the flight."

"Why would I reconsider at this point? Now, what did you want to share?" Erin put a hand on his arm.

He squeezed shut his eyes. "Let's go outside and talk while we walk." The room closed in, and he craved fresh air and space. Did he really have the courage to tell her this story? Would his confession horrify her? His pain shot to the surface, ready to explode. In the yard, he helped her guide several dogs to the play area and then matched her pace, hiking the perimeter of the acreage.

Sam and Jake bounded in circles, oblivious to their serious masters.

The breeze whisked by with the damp, earthy scents of spring. Drew gathered his courage and rehearsed his confession. After lapping the property twice, he cleared his throat. "A few weeks before I met you, something awful happened on a training mission."

She paced and listened in silence.

Tension cut the cool air. "The team needed to perfect a new formation. We nailed the manoeuver a few times. Then the captain suggested we repeat it one more time. I flew with textbook precision one second, but the next, I nearly caused a disaster." He darted his gaze from the horizon to Erin. A vise grip clenched his shoulders, and hidden inside his jacket, moisture dampened his armpits. Bracing himself, he searched her face and eyes for a veil of fear. When he shared the alarming details, would she spin and flee forever?

****

Erin swallowed, filled her lungs, and swung her arms to match her brisk stride. Movement kept her in control, ahead of the chasing anxiety. She glanced at Drew's solemn profile and back to the pathway. In the distance, cars drove in and out of the neighboring property. Likely a steady stream of friends and family offered Vera condolences. Momentarily torn, Erin would pay her a comforting visit later.

"I made a mistake. I take responsibility and blame no one but myself." He coughed. "I lost focus off my reference point for a split second and sensed another jet flickering into my airspace. I panicked at the threat, and instantly, I adjusted—actually, over-compensated—and suddenly, jets sprayed in all directions. Within seconds, the entire mission aborted."

"But you weren't injured? Tell me everybody survived."

"The team all found clear airspace, stabilized, and landed. The Forces classified the incident a close call or a near miss." He accelerated and swung his arms in short chops. "I was totally at fault."

The terrifying image he painted loomed in dark contrast with the wide, blue sky above. Drew's mistake caused a near catastrophe. Only a split second separated his judgment error from a deadly crash. She plunged into a pool of pain and sped forward in frantic strides. What should she say to console him? Did she want to try?

Birds twittered in the sky while Sam and Jake wrestled in the field. The bright day and gentle breeze brushing her face couldn't lighten his dark, dreadful words. For several paces, she said nothing. If she hadn't already cried herself dry earlier, she might have fought tears. Instead, a muddy mixture of anger and relief surged, and she fisted her hands. Why did bad things happen to good people? Why did fate spare him but not Eric? Just as puzzling, why did she care so much how Drew's terrifying mistake impacted him?

After facing Eric's death, she wasn't easily shocked, but she couldn't find the right words to express her deep empathy for his situation. "Oh, I'm very sorry." She glanced sideways and scanned his pale, sunken face.

He matched her pace, and his breathing quickened. "Nobody sustained a physical injury. Mentally, a major, potentially life-threatening error can really shake a team."

Drew stayed safe. The team survived. Nobody died. Still, she shuddered.

"I received a severe warning from our commanding officer, and I've been on a kind of probation ever since." Drew rotated his shoulders. "If I make another serious mistake, I will get released from the team."

A near miss terrified his teammates but wreaked no physical damage, an outcome infinitely better than the alternative. A blip, Drew's momentary lapse, caused a severe scare but nothing more. Still, the mistake crushed Drew's confidence and put his career on the line. The stakes loomed far from meaningless. She caught the waver in his voice and fought to keep nausea at bay. "You have a tough challenge to manage."

"Ever since the incident, I focus every day on earning the team's confidence." He swung his arms in jerky thrusts. "I need to trust my teammates, too, no matter what."

"I imagine a team like the SnoWings demands absolute dependence on each other." She scanned the play yard where the dogs romped.

"Yeah, and I realize I need work in that area." He glanced up. "I've learned more about trust from your family in the last few weeks than I ever learned growing up. Anyway, I repeatedly drill into myself the same message—to believe in myself and the team."

Beneath the white puff of clouds lazing above, the truth lay exposed. Drew's heavy burden plunged, thrashed, and overtook her personal space like an intruder. She dropped her arms and slowed her pace. He trusted her enough to share his darkest moment, and she could do nothing but offer support. "You can learn. Be confident, and give yourself credit. You will succeed." She stopped and put a hand on his arm.

"Thank you. Every single day, I strive to build my skills and bond with the team, and I show signs of improvement." He searched the horizon. "Anyway, you should know, and I hope you will somehow understand and support me." He followed her to the play yard and helped switch the group of dogs allowed outside. "But Erin, if you don't want to ever fly with me, I understand."

Hand shaking, she bent to pet an overeager terrier. "Well, I don't ever want to fly anywhere with anybody." A quiet afternoon flight paled next to a high-risk, SnoWings manoeuver. His near miss with the team didn't translate into a major flight risk. "I hate the idea of flying, but I still trust you."

"You don't know how much your support means." Smiling, he met her gaze and touched her chin. "But you mean even more."

"Oh, don't...I wish..." Surrounded by a rambunctious trio of Labs, Erin shook her head, spun, and sprinted to the kennel. She couldn't deal with her attraction tempting her to places she must avoid.

A few minutes later, when he joined her and filled water dishes, neither said a word. The rest of the afternoon, she worked at a frantic pace. Drew faced challenges with his career as well as his family. He jolted her with his revelation, but he unsettled her most by sharing his romantic feelings. He cared too much to be a casual friend. She cleaned the kennel runs, poured kibble, and played with different groupings of dogs. But nothing soothed her uneasy heart.

Drew painted the gate and later in the afternoon, helped her post an ad for a new kennel assistant. "Every evening, I'll help out with the daily chores until you hire someone."

Erin's throat ached. Blinking away sudden moisture, she shook her head. "No, you can't give so much time. You're too generous." She must stop seeing him and keep her feelings in check.

Later, after she tucked Noah in bed, she ran a hot bubble bath and sank into the tub to soak away the day's grit and emotion. Her lingering grief dissolved somewhat in the steamy foam. Then she scrubbed the horror of Drew's near miss and rinsed away confusion about their attraction.

Thumping his tail, Sam rested his chin on the edge of the bathtub.

Next to her dog's comforting presence, she steeped in the hot water until her skin glowed the color of watermelon and her eyelids drooped. Then she toweled herself dry, put on pajamas, and made a call. This time, she would seek her wise and gentle mother's advice. Erin poured out the details of the day, starting with Ted's sudden passing. "At once, I lost a neighbor, friend, and employee." Her throat squeezed.

"I'm so sorry, Erin." Gayle clicked her tongue. "I wish I could give you a hug."

"I'll need reassurance for this next update, too." Erin's voice wavered. "I decided I'll take Noah on a plane ride with Drew next weekend."

"I'm proud of you for facing your worst fear."

Her mom's typical, gentle encouragement soothed like salve. Erin couldn't imagine life without such caring, supportive parents. Curled on the sofa with a blanket tucked around her, she steadied her voice and meandered through recent developments, from the kennel improvements she accomplished with Drew's help to her recruiting and marketing efforts. "He's always here when I need him, and when we're apart, I miss him." Finally, she confided the real reason for the call.

"You care about each other, and have you also lost your appetite?" Gayle giggled. "But seriously, does he know how you feel?"

"I haven't told him. He shared his feelings, and I escaped to work." She relived the emotional moment and took a deep breath while inside, persistent butterflies battled.

"Oh, and then what happened?"

"I didn't want to say the wrong thing or lead him

on. I'm afraid of the future." She snuggled under the warm shield. "Melding our lives would not be simple. Love can't change everything. As close as we've grown in many ways, we're miles apart in others."

Reflecting on Gayle's questions, Erin finally made her thorny decision. "I know the best path to take."

"I'm glad. Goodnight, Err Bear."

Her mom hadn't used the childhood nickname in years, and Erin's throat squeezed at the nostalgic reference.

"I hope you feel better."

"I do." Sometimes, the right choice wasn't easy. "Thanks, Mom. You're the best." She ended the call and covered her face while she contemplated her next move. Then she leaned forward to rub her cheek on the top of Sam's soft head. He was a faithful friend, ready to listen and soothe even if he didn't understand.

For now, she'd withhold her decision so she didn't distract Drew from the approaching visit with his dad. She'd spend time in his company but wouldn't reveal anything until the time was right. No doubt, he would find the delay just as difficult. How would he feel when she shared her thoughts about the future?

Chapter 20

Promoting the rebranded Camp Canine on social media created local buzz. Online bookings for the spring and summer months increased, and the phone rang often. Business hummed, and Erin embraced a boost of energy to juggle extra chores, marketing activities, and final preparations for Noah's birthday party. Even though she declined Drew's help, she didn't argue when he insisted on coming to work side by side each evening.

Noah popped in and out, suggesting a game and asking questions.

"Are you excited about your dad's visit?" Erin paused with a handful of dog biscuits.

"Yeah, but I feel a bit uneasy, too." Drew lifted a bag of kibble.

"Oh, what concerns you?" She doled out a dog treat to an eager poodle.

"I hope he follows through and doesn't cancel." He paused and shook his head.

"Would he back out at the last minute?" She squatted and gave a biscuit to a pug. Her dad would never renege on a commitment.

"I can't count the number of times he has let me down." He worked his way along the row of stalls filling food bowls. "I hope he'll follow through and stay open to some meaningful conversation."

"You two don't talk much, do you?" The emptiness in his life clutched Erin's heart. Drew needed support.

"Dad almost never calls. He's never been a steady presence in my life. I keep wishing he might change, or at least, I should finally reconcile the past."

"Moving forward always feels positive." Everyone recited the same advice. She winced at her pat answer.

The day of Ted's funeral, held in a Moose Jaw church, her parents stayed with Noah and the dogs. She dreaded the event and the memories it might stir, but the service healed more than it saddened. Her rawest grief had washed away with the initial news of Ted's death, and she laughed at amusing anecdotes and celebrated his full life. Afterward, she hugged Vera and invited her for tea and moral support anytime. Then at the reception in the crowded church hall, she bumped into Walt, a retired farmer. "Pleased to meet you." Erin extended a hand. "I own Camp Canine, formerly Canine Corner, just across the field from Vera's place."

"I've loved dogs all my life." Walt shook her hand.

He must be a kindred soul. His weathered face wrinkled into an appealing grin. Anybody who appreciated and respected animals the way he did must have a good heart.

"I told Ted and Ray they had the best job near Moose Jaw." He jammed his hands into the pockets of his corduroy pants.

After chatting a while longer, she learned he lived alone, liked to fix things, didn't travel much, and had time to burn. She couldn't imagine finding a better assistant, so she hired him on the spot. He would start on the weekend.

Blasting the radio on the short drive home, she

sang, tapped her fingers on the steering wheel, and practically floated. She solved her staffing dilemma and recruited help she could count on. She could stop begging for favors and remain independent. Her family would be happy to hear the news. She shouldn't care so much, but what would Drew think?

****

The same evening, Drew arrived to work at the kennel. He thrived on his routine of putting in a full day with the SnoWings followed by an evening shift at Camp Canine. Day by day, he settled in, totally at ease helping Erin. As well, he always took time to play with Noah and answer his river of questions.

"I have good news." Standing next to Drew, Erin tossed balls in the fenced, play area. "I hired a new worker, so you're officially laid off."

"I'm what?" He stiffened and stomped into the kennel. He should be happy, but a thicket of jealousy sprung in the way. Now, he wouldn't see her as often.

A few minutes later, she joined him inside. "You can enjoy free evenings." She stroked a whining dog.

"Walt sounds like another Ted." He clunked a pail on the water tap. "I like helping here." He shouldn't snap, but he couldn't restrain his negative reaction. His free time would feel empty. With Noah's cheerful assistance, he filled water bowls and patted dogs, but he didn't take his usual pleasure in the tasks. They would soon disappear from his daily routine. Intense concentration and demanding teamwork consumed his days, and kennel work eased the tension. Erin added an irresistible spark to his life. "I need a steady and reliable worker." She didn't glance up. "The timing works well, too. While I prepare for Noah's birthday

269

party, I can rely on Walt to handle most of the chores. Anyway, you need to entertain your dad." She passed Noah a handful of dog treats to dole out.

"I hope you'll still let me help sometimes." Drew stroked a poodle.

"We can talk later." She wiped a hand on her jeans and stared at the floor.

"I only have to wait two days until my party." Noah balanced on his toes. "I asked Mommy to decorate my cake with a plane."

"A cake with an airplane sounds delicious and very cool. Maybe it'll fly around in your tummy." Drew tickled his sides.

He giggled and dodged out of reach. "Will Frank come to my party?"

"You remembered my dad's name." Drew patted a yappy terrier. "I don't know for sure, but I'll invite him, and maybe he'll come." He clenched his jaw. Frank's erratic preferences were hard to predict.

"Okay." He rubbed his eyes.

"I see a sleepy boy." Erin stood behind him and massaged his shoulders. "Let's get you inside and ready for bed."

"You go ahead. I'll finish here." Drew waved her away. She must be exhausted after a full day of work and parenting on her own.

"Are you sure?" She lifted her eyebrows.

"No, I'm not." He kept a straight face and chuckled at her double take. "Yes, I'm sure." Ever since he expressed his affection, he treaded carefully. She scurried away once, and she might flee again. He couldn't alarm or rush her. She had been open and receptive on their date and especially when consumed by grief after Ted's death, but then she recoiled. He straightened and, as soon as she turned, massaged his throbbing temples. Something had changed. Erin slammed shut a window, and he couldn't unlock the latch.

Before Drew finished for the evening, he double-checked for empty water dishes. Did her feelings mirror his? He had no choice but to be patient and wait for the right time to again broach the sensitive topic. As he trudged toward the house, he longed to learn her feelings mirrored his, simmering rich and deep. He rolled and stretched his tense shoulders. After he said good-bye to his dad, he would talk with Erin about the future. This weekend, he needed to dredge up the past and make Frank's short visit count, so he would concentrate on nothing else. At the back entrance, he sighed and knocked.

Erin swung open the door. "Thank you, again. I don't know how I will ever repay you for all your help."

"Meals, candy, and gifts work just fine. I like them all." Leaning on the doorframe, he delivered an exaggerated smile. When she tilted her head and laughed, her amusement paid all the riches he would ever need. "Come, Jake, let's go." He jingled his car keys and resisted the urge to kiss her cheek. "I'll see you tomorrow."

"Don't worry about the kennel. Your dad will arrive tomorrow." She planted hands on hips and shook her head. "I'll allow Noah to stay up a little later, so I can manage."

"Dad could help, too." Anticipation surged and grabbed his shoulders. He tossed his keys in the air and caught them. This weekend could change everything, but he should keep under control his high hopes. Could he start fresh with his dad? Could he convince Erin to give their budding relationship a chance?

****

The next evening, Noah ran to greet Drew.

"Where's Frank?" Noah peered at the car.

"Probably still driving to Moose Jaw." Drew rubbed the top of Noah's head.

"Your dad hasn't arrived yet?" Erin strolled to join the guys, tipped her head, and wiped both hands on her jeans.

"He got a late start, but he's on his way." Drew shrugged. "He should arrive around midnight, so I figured I had plenty of time to come and hang out with the dogs…and you two, of course." Time with them was much more fun than waiting alone.

"I appreciate your thoughtfulness, but you could take off a night." Erin smiled and shook her head.

Mud streaked her cheek but didn't mar in the least her alluring appearance. Drew lifted a hand and dropped it to his side before he could rub the smudge.

"I need to repay you somehow." She raised her hands to her hips.

"Food works every time." He smiled and swung hands with Noah. "But seriously, enjoy my labor with no strings attached. My time is a gift, and you don't return a gift, so accept it."

"I won't argue tonight." She rubbed her cheek.

Most of the mud disappeared, and he tore away his gaze from her captivating features. "Hey, tomorrow's your birthday, young man." Drew tickled his side.

"I will turn six. You'll come to my party.

Tomorrow is your birthday, too," he shouted and twirled.

"You're absolutely right." Drew imitated his lively jiggle. Following them inside, he helped fill balloons and hang streamers. While he counted the minutes until his dad's arrival, he welcomed the activity to fill the empty evening.

After she tucked Noah in bed, Erin poured glasses of cold soda and flopped on a kitchen chair across from Drew. "Was your dad delayed leaving?" She ran a hand through her hair.

"He always shows up late. I've waited all my life." He sighed and massaged his temple. "I hope we can resolve the past, patch some cracks, and build trust."

She nodded and gazed across the table.

"More than anything, I want to mark a fresh start in our relationship and maybe better connect." If he gathered his courage, he might even confide details of the *incident*. For once, maybe his dad would offer support and encouragement. He could use more than a few confidence boosts.

"I hope the visit goes well." Erin nodded and sipped her drink.

The faint lines in her forehead dipped and rose. With a straight face and a twinkle in her eye, she pursed her lips and scrutinized his face. He chuckled at the attention. She knew how to rev his senses.

"Tomorrow you turn another year older, and you might show more wrinkles." She tilted her head and laughed.

He loved her gentle humor, and as usual, when he departed, he wore a smile and a vest of warmth. He arrived home at eleven o'clock, and by midnight, still saw no sign of his dad. Tired of waiting, he dozed on the sofa with Jake. Finally, a loud knock jolted him upright.

"Hi, Dad." Drew sprang to swing open the door.

"Sorry, I ran late." Frank rubbed his eyes.

His disheveled, gray hair hung in a scramble across his ears and touched his collar. Nothing about his appearance signaled change. Drew hoped desperately that his dad's familiar, scruffy exterior camouflaged a transformed man.

"The trip stretched a little on the long and boring side."

Without covering his mouth, he yawned audibly. "I'm glad you got here." Drew hesitated. He longed to grab his dad's shoulders and squeeze him in a hug.

Instead, Frank stuck out his hand for a vigorous shake.

"Come inside." Drew gestured to the room.

"Not a bad place you've got here." He plunked a small suitcase on the floor, followed Drew to the kitchen, and sprawled at the table.

Frank's cackling voice filled the tidy, white space. While he listened to disjointed details of the trip, Drew served a peanut butter sandwich and a glass of milk.

Frank chomped large bites and slipped the crusts to Jake.

Drew cringed. He avoided feeding the dog human food, but he noticed too late to stop his dad's unknowing infraction.

"Hey, enough about my trip. What about you?" He yawned, groaned, and stretched. "Actually, save your news for breakfast. I'd need a coupla of toothpicks to prop my eyelids."

"Sure. We'll talk in the morning and plan the rest of the weekend." Drew's pulse buzzed in his ears. The visit wasn't off to a stellar start.

"Oh yeah, I didn't mention yet, did I?" He scraped his chair away from the table, stood, and brushed crumbs off his lap to the floor. "Bit of a change in plans. I've gotta take off Sunday morning. But we'll make the most of Saturday."

The sudden change chilled Drew. After he showed Frank to his room, he piled extra blankets on his bed and nursed his disappointment. Some things never changed. Frank always followed his own agenda and disregarded commitments. Without an apology, he planned to swoop away again in no time.

Staring into the dark, Drew condensed plans for a full weekend into one day. Something would need to go. He couldn't skip the long walks, talks, or tour of the base. The gangster tunnels under the city and the drive by the giant moose mascot on the outskirts of town would be fun but not essential. He lay awake for a long time. They would attend the birthday party, whether his dad liked the idea or not. Erin and Noah expected him, and he wouldn't let them—or himself—down. He would do anything to keep her happy. Did she consider his feelings just as important?

****

Noah woke earlier than usual and, followed by Sam, jumped onto Erin's bed.

"Mom." He shook her shoulder. "Today is my birthday."

She opened her eyes and smiled at his exaggerated whisper while he jiggled on his knees. "Happy birthday, Noah. Now, you're my big six-year-old boy." She cuddled him close. Starting with pancakes, she'd make a special day to celebrate her precious son.

After breakfast, Walt arrived for his orientation as the new kennel assistant.

"This place will keep you busy. Meet my son, Noah, and our dog, Sam." She showed him the property and described the daily routine for feeding, cleaning, and exercising the dogs. To her satisfaction, she noted Walt was a natural and quickly grasped the details with no second explanations needed.

"Do you want to come to my birthday party?" Noah stared up at Walt.

He popped his unruly, gray eyebrows and grinned. "Happy birthday, young man. Thank you for inviting me, but I bet your friends will come to celebrate. Maybe you could save me a piece of cake. I'll see you again this evening." He winked at Erin.

"Can we give him cake?" Noah spun in a circle.

"Of course, we'll set aside a big piece." She smiled and nodded.

Walt hit it off with Noah, showed a natural way with dogs, and welcomed physical work. Confident of her new helper's ability, she bounded into the house to spread thick, chocolate icing on two birthday cakes. She wanted Drew to have a special day, too, and choosing the right gift had taken a while. The present needed to show she cared without appearing too personal or lavish to send the wrong message. At one of the quaint gift shops on Main Street, she selected the perfect choice.

At least two hours ahead of the party, Noah fidgeted at the window and watched for his guests to arrive.

While Erin set out chips, drinks, and hotdogs for

the barbecue, she smiled at Noah and Sam, zigzagging from the front step to the gate and across the yard. Spurred on by their contagious excitement, she quickened her pace. The weather warmed, and she smiled under the beaming sun. Erin's family arrived first, followed by Vera and two school friends.

Vibrating with excitement, Noah greeted his guests with generous hugs. "Where are Drew and Frank?" He didn't wait for an answer before he sprinted to chase his cousins and friends in a game of tag.

Puzzled and slightly concerned, Erin checked her watch. Noah had a point. They should be here by now. Unlike prompt Drew, they were late. If they didn't show, they'd disappoint the birthday boy. She had to admit she'd feel let down, too. Drew always kept his word, but had Frank interrupted plans?

****

On Saturday morning, Drew walked Jake and sizzled bacon on the stove before he saw any sign of his dad.

Frank's late travels must have tired him, because he didn't wake until close to nine. "I smell coffee. I need coffee." He strolled into the kitchen, yawned, and stretched. "Oh, happy birthday, by the way." He slapped Drew on the back. "I couldn't come up with anything you needed, so I'm your present." He jammed his thumbs into his chest.

Drew nodded and forced a half smile. He wasn't surprised, but disappointment still tensed his shoulders. His dad never bothered much with presents, but a card with an uplifting message would have added a nice touch.

"You're right, Dad. Your visit makes a great gift."

Over breakfast, he filled him in on the day's itinerary.

Frank nodded, his mouth too full of toast and eggs to speak.

After breakfast, Drew drove to the Armed Forces base where he trained. Nervous anticipation pulsing, he finally gave his dad a first glimpse of his professional life. Glancing over, he strained to spot even a hint of pride in his dad's gaze.

"Captain Dixon, eh? Has not a bad ring. So, you're a bigshot SnoWinger now." Frank punched his shoulder.

"Yeah, being selected to the team was a big honor." Heat shot to Drew's face. He didn't intend to brag. First, he better make sure he secured his position.

"Congrats, Drewzer. You worked hard and hit the jackpot." Through the car window, Frank surveyed the base.

Drew waited for the words he craved but didn't hear anything close to "I'm proud of you, son." He shook off disappointment even though he would treasure a deeper affirmation. "Thanks, yeah, when I made the team, I almost couldn't believe the news." A wave of fear caught his breath. He better not blow the opportunity. He slowed to give a better view of the buildings and the tarmac in the distance. "The thing is…" The band of tension gripping his shoulders stretched to clutch his back and chest. Could he tell his dad he faced huge challenges and fought daily to prove himself? He struggled to muster the right words.

Then Frank jumped to a new topic.

The abrupt change forced Drew's unfinished confession to float away like a helium balloon.

"Who's the kid with the same birthday?" His dad

drummed his fingers on the armrest.

"Noah. His mom runs the kennel where I take Jake…the place I got stranded in the storm." He glanced at his dad's smirking profile. "They want to meet you." Surely, he'd behave.

"Okay, I'll humor them." He shrugged. "As long as I don't have to play ring-around-the-rosy, I can cope." Frank rasped a laugh and slapped his knee.

After steering slowly around the base, he circled Moose Jaw past the infamous moose statue on the edge of the city and took his dad to tour the tunnels under downtown Moose Jaw. Then they headed for the party.

"Don't worry that you didn't feed me lunch. Almost five hours ago, you filled me with a decent breakfast." Frank chuckled and smacked his lips.

Drew forced a laugh through his tight jaw, but his dad's sarcasm bit. "I'm sure we'll find lots to eat at the party." So far, their conversations mainly centred on the sights of Moose Jaw interspersed with Frank's stories about his card and shuffleboard buddies in Phoenix. Drew planned to initiate more-personal topics later. Drew drove into Erin's yard just a few minutes past two and caught sight of flashes of color darting around the yard.

In the back seat, the dog barked and paced.

"You've arrived at Camp Canine, Jake's new home away from home during airshow season." He swung an arm across the dash at the view. Erin's tall form crossed the prairie backdrop, and his pulse took a flying leap.

"Check out all the little boogers running in circles." Frank pointed. "Better get ready to deal with all the noise and action."

"They're nice people, Dad." Drew slowed the car

and parked. So far, his dad showed few signs of change. Drew never had to guess his opinions. He took a deep breath and wiped his brow.

Frank yawned and stretched. "Don't worry, Drewzer, I packed my best behavior." He chuckled and flicked his eyebrows up and down.

"You better promise." Drew plunked a hand on the wheel for emphasis and swung open the car door. He gulped fresh air seasoned with a hint of barbecue smoke. "C'mon, let's go." He couldn't control his dad's unpredictable behavior. He couldn't help him fit in, and definitely, he couldn't muzzle him. Sighing, he jutted his chin. Erin's opinion mattered. Would the stern warning prevent Frank from saying or doing anything embarrassing in front of her family?

Chapter 21

"Good to see you." Erin stepped away from the barbecue and held out a hand. "Hello and welcome. You must be Frank. My name is Erin. I hope Drew didn't promise you a relaxing afternoon." The older man gripped her hand like a baseball bat. Overlooking his smirk, she noticed instantly the contrast between his unkempt hair and Drew's neat cut.

"Hi, Erin. Yes, he warned me a few, little monkeys would run loose around here, and he didn't exaggerate." He scanned the yard and chuckled.

She laughed at his raspy assessment and glanced at Drew's flushed face. Frank didn't immediately charm her. "Go in and help yourselves to cold drinks or coffee. Oh, first, you can meet my parents." She waved them over to greet Frank.

"So, you're the grandparents responsible for this unruly crew." Frank hooted, crossed his arms, and rocked on his heels.

"They keep us busy and entertained." Brian chuckled, watching the kids running in circles.

"I need another shot of caffeine to keep me going. I gotta find the coffee." Frank smothered a yawn and scratched his head. "I'll be right back." Soon, he reappeared, slurping and sloshing his beverage.

While Erin watched him talking to the others, she studied his animated face. Drew might have inherited his chiselled profile, but the similarities ended there. Frank appeared weathered, plainer, and garnished with a splashy bow of a personality.

Pretty soon, Frank and Brian leaned with their elbows propped on the deck railing, razzing each other about their favorite football teams.

Her dad could get along with anyone. Drew mustn't feel comfortable joining the conversation. He stood to the side, shoulders hunched. He wore a serious expression except an occasional smile at the kids' antics. With Mitch's help, Erin organized a game while Vera, Gayle, and Claire sizzled a batch of hotdogs in a cloud of savory smoke. So far, the party ran smoothly, and all the kids and adults—except maybe Drew— appeared to be enjoying a good time. After games and a picnic lunch, she carried out the presents and cakes. Her stomach fluttered with anticipation that both guys would be happy with her choices.

"Thank you." Dropping to his knees on a blanket spread on the ground, Noah squealed and, in an excited flurry, tore the paper from his gifts. He received a dress-up captain's uniform from Drew, a new bike from his grandparents, and assorted games, books, and action figures from his cousins and friends. "I love all my presents." He shouted and threw both arms above his head.

Erin saved her gift for last. Riding a wave of ambivalence, she set it on his lap and pressed her tumbling stomach. Normally, she maintained a consistent, parenting approach, so her change of heart in gift choice marked a big exception. She wrapped her arms around her middle, bit her lip, and waited. As he unwrapped a book on airplanes and reached for his big surprise, Noah's face glowed. She had pondered how best to unveil the flight, and finally, she taped his picture to the side of an airplane with Sunday printed over the top.

He immediately deciphered the code and leaped, shrieked, and hugged her. "I get to go on a real plane ride." He hollered, bounced, and clapped.

What had she done? Hands shaking, she gripped the table. A whirl of emotion blurred and spun her guests and yard. She sipped a mouthful of earthy, spring air and settled her pounding heart. Now, she couldn't stop the plan she'd put in motion. She searched for reassurance, and across the picnic table, Drew flashed a thumbs-up. Her mom placed a warm, comforting hand on her lower back.

"He's one spoiled kid." Frank smothered a burp and picked a crumb from a tooth.

"Oh, Dad, I disagree." Drew shook his head and frowned. He clenched his jaw and lowered his head.

Erin wished she could set a hand on his arm. He didn't need to worry about what anyone thought. No one expected him to control his outspoken dad.

"Noah's just loved and lucky." Brian hugged his grandson and rubbed his head.

"Now, let's give Drew his gift." Erin held out the bright parcel and studied his face. His expression folded into narrow lines. He didn't want to be the center of attention but glanced up and down, beaming at the contents.

"Thank you, Erin, Noah, and Sam." He lifted the contents one by one. "These gifts suit me perfectly." He cleared his throat. "You know me well."

Erin knew he'd appreciate her choices—a coffee

table book of inspirational messages, artfully designed around pictures of Border collies like Jake, and a key ring with a paw-print fob.

"That little beast tails you all day, so anybody could guess you're stuck on black-and-white dogs." Frank tossed his head toward the dog.

His chuckle might have been intended to ease a bit of the sting, but a shadow, like a solitary cloud, crossed Drew's face. Instantly, she wanted to hug him and squeeze away the strain. His dad sure knew how to offend. "I hope everyone's ready for cake." Erin led, and everyone sang "Happy Birthday." "Now, make a wish, guys." Warmth radiating in her chest, she savored the celebration.

Noah and Drew blew out their candles and high-fived.

Everyone devoured the huge slices of chocolate cake she served.

"Not bad at all." In the chorus of compliments floating over the picnic tables, one voice rose above the rest, and Frank held out his plate for seconds. "I might even choke down another piece."

As Erin sliced another wedge, she marveled at the differences between gentlemanly Drew and his boisterous dad. For Drew's sake, she wanted to like the man, but she didn't exactly feel a natural bond.

Holding a plate next to Erin, Claire leaned close. "Good thing Drew didn't learn his father's manners."

Erin lifted her eyebrows at her murmured assessment and nodded agreement. A dad like Frank would be a handful. She glanced at Drew's handsome face and hard jaw. Definitely, he wasn't enjoying as much fun as usual.

Before departing, Drew talked for a few minutes with Brian, gave Noah a high-five, and thanked her for including him in the celebration. "Dad plans to leave early tomorrow, so I invited Brian to take his spot on the plane." He touched her arm. "I'll swing by to get you around one o'clock."

"Nice meeting all you Moose people." Frank waved to the group.

"Thanks for the catchy, new nickname, Frank." Erin's face burned to match Drew's, and she caught her mother's wide-eyed glance. She scanned her sensitive, caring family, and her eyes welled. While Noah giggled with his cousins and Brian kissed Gayle's cheek, she blinked away tears. Thankful for her loving support network, she wiped the table and picked up the cake plate. The party proved a huge success. She wasn't so sure about Drew's time with his dad. How would he react to the visit and, more importantly, the message she would soon share?

****

"Haven't been to a kid's birthday party in years." As he rode toward Moose Jaw, Frank yawned and rubbed his eyes. "The company and food were okay, though."

"We could hike Crescent Park now." Drew waited in vain for his dad to suggest a personal, birthday celebration. He glanced at his dad's open mouth. "If you're not too tired, we could take a brisk walk and talk. I want to tell you a few things and hear your thoughts." They could finally connect on a deeper level.

"I appreciate the offer, Drewzer, but you'd need to wheel me in a cart. Before I do another thing, I need a nap."

Frank stretched and exhaled another loud, groaning yawn. The signal was unmistakable. He didn't want to talk. Drew clenched his jaw and drove home. When would he finally get a chance to broach tough, personal topics?

With Jake curled beside him, Frank napped until dinner time.

While Drew waited for his dad to wake, he flipped TV channels. If anything, his loneliness magnified, not disappeared, with distant Frank being here. Over a dinner of takeout pizza, he attempted to steer the conversation deeper than his dad's social life in Phoenix, but nothing worked. Either his dad missed the hints or wasn't interested. Drew chewed slowly, rotating his aching shoulders.

"Food's not bad." Frank chomped another slice of pizza.

"I'd like us to get closer, Dad." Maybe a more direct approach would make an impact. He ached to hear Frank reflect on the past, share feelings, or apologize for being an absent father.

"Do you think the Forces will set up a base in Phoenix?" Frank chuckled and hiccupped.

"Dad, I meant what I said. I want to build a closer relationship…like Erin's family." He could have bitten his tongue the moment the words escaped. His dad would never understand.

Tipping back in his chair, Frank shrugged. "I'm happy you're a bigshot SnoWing and all. I'm glad I finally got to the Jaw." He folded his arms across his chest. "And it's a darn shame while you were a kid, I spent so much time with my drinking buddies."

Frank came close but avoided a true apology. Drew

swallowed and rubbed his temple. His dad had quit drinking, but he retained his old personality.

"But let's be realistic. You can't change the past, and you can't teach an old dog new tricks. Face the facts." Frank poked his chest with both thumbs. "At the best of times, this old hound learned slowly. You might dislike reality, but you got stuck with a cheap imitation of the family at the birthday party."

Drew blinked hard, and his throat closed on any words he could possibly muster. Pain raced to every single body part, and he rubbed his left arm. His dad could be direct to the point of harshness, and he would never change. He didn't want or expect to be anyone different. "Sorry to hear you don't want to grow closer, Dad. But if you're happy, I guess I better adjust."

Jolted by the candid assessment, Drew had no choice but to accept the entire, rough-hewn package. He needed to give up the dream of turning Frank into a guy like steady Brian. He couldn't change him or erase decades of distance in a day or two. He cleared his throat. Reluctantly, he pushed away from the table, stood, and cleared the dishes. The rest of the evening loomed long and depressing. Now, he needed Erin and her family more than ever. Was she ready and willing to support him?

****

Erin rubbed Noah's back to calm him to sleep and then lay awake for hours drenched in dread. Tomorrow morning, she'd face her worst fear. She shivered under her quilt and rolled from side to side. She forced herself to take slow deliberate breaths, but after three steady breaths, she fought a ragged, shallow gasp.

Pure torture threatened. She visualized herself

boarding the flight with confidence—buckling up, squinting out the window, and squeezing Noah's hand. The motor rumbled into action, the propellers spun, and the plane sped down the runway. Then as the plane lifted, a wave of fear slapped her and wiped out the image. She pictured soaring over Regina, Moose Jaw, and the patchwork prairie, but her imagination refused to cooperate, and the vision dissolved. Finally, she fell into a dark, restless sleep.

The next day, riding with Drew to Regina, Erin stared ahead at the road while Noah fidgeted in his seat in the back. She couldn't block her nervous brain from splatting graphic, crash images.

"You threw a great party yesterday." He smiled and glanced her way.

"Thanks." She swallowed and wrung her hands. None of Drew's cheerful comments lessened her misery.

"Are you okay?" He kept his gaze forward.

Chatting to himself, Noah wouldn't overhear Drew's murmured concern.

"Okay might be a stretch, but I'm surviving." She sipped water from an insulated bottle to moisten her sawdusty mouth. Nervous energy somersaulted down her spine. Why had she invited this torment?

At the air terminal, Brian waved and beamed brighter than Noah. "Atta girl." He put one arm around her shoulders and squeezed.

As she approached the small plane, she gulped air and fought vertigo. Her arms, legs, and fingers fizzed like soda pop.

"Yay. My first plane ride." Trailing Drew, Noah shouted and bopped up the airplane steps.

While her dad's steady hand braced her back, Erin gripped the rail and dragged her legs up each step. She couldn't turn and run.

"You can handle this test, Err Bear." Settled on the plane, her dad reached to pat her shoulder.

Cream walls with small oval windows threatened to suffocate her. On either side of her shaky legs, she pressed on the blue cloth seat.

In the pilot seat ahead, Drew adjusted dials.

A red light grabbed her attention, and she flicked her gaze to the floor. Pulse racing, she blotted her moist palms on the thighs of her jeans.

"Mommy, I can't wait to fly." Noah squirmed in his seat across the narrow aisle and behind his grandpa.

She forced a smile at his oozing excitement, nodded, and buckled him in place. Hands shaking, she fastened her seatbelt and took a deep breath.

"Everybody ready?" Drew revved the engine, glanced over his shoulder, and signaled a big thumbs-up.

Accelerated by adrenaline, her heart thumped wildly in her rib cage. She gripped the armrests, blinked back tears before Noah could notice and, for a few seconds, almost floated outside her body. Her son's thrill of a lifetime shouldn't cause such agony.

With a roar, the plane took off and circled Regina.

Stretching to peer out the window, Noah kept up an animated commentary.

Drawing strength from her dad's steady influence, she focused on breathing and stared below. Repeatedly, she wiped damp palms on her jeans.

Drew flew above the football stadium, Wascana Park, and strips of houses and roads. Navigating west toward Moose Jaw, he passed fields with hints of green and a potash mine. Over Moose Jaw, he pointed out the Air Force base, the spa, and the shops along Main Street. "What do you see down there?" To the west, he swooped over a landmark. At the curving dip, her stomach lurched.

"I see our house. Hey, I see Sam and Jake running." Noah waved out the window.

The two dogs frolicked in the yard below.

Swinging a pail, Walt crossed toward the kennel.

She surveyed the familiar, calming landscape below, and a sliver of pride wedged beside the fear. She owned that patch of land and business. Breathing steadily, she chased away the tingling in her limbs. She might survive the trip and show Noah the power of determination.

"See the airport. I'll circle and land." A few minutes later, Drew pointed below.

"Aw, we flew back too soon." Noah thumped his armrest and frowned.

"Remember to be grateful. Airplane rides cost a lot of money." Erin touched his arm. He would have stayed in the air all afternoon, but she couldn't wait to plant her feet on solid ground.

Drew performed a slow, smooth descent and set them down like a carton of eggs.

"Good work, pilot," Brian cheered and led their applause.

Erin's relief hit in such a hot rush she nearly melted into a puddle, but she stayed strong, exhaled, and even echoed her dad in a weak cheer. She survived her worst nightmare. "What should you say to Drew?" She tapped Noah's shoulder.

"Thank you." Noah beamed and unbuckled his seatbelt.

Momentary peace filled her chest, and she sagged against the seat. Moistening her lips, she studied Noah's glowing face. Her son's expression shouted more joy than words ever could.

Like an official, commercial pilot, Drew stood at the bottom of the steps. "Thank you for flying, ma'am." He tipped his head and smiled.

"I appreciated the ride, sir." Erin nearly smiled. Setting off a pang, she absorbed every detail of his striking face lit by the sun. She gripped the hand rail and steadied her jelly legs. When she sensed his fingers brushing her elbow, she stifled a gasp. Still, his steady, attractive presence reassured. She paused, stepped onto the tarmac, and hugged Noah to celebrate. She accomplished her goal. Palms damp the whole flight, she despised nearly every moment but still faced her worst fear.

"I'm proud of you, Erin." Brian met her gaze and nodded.

"Can we go tell Grandma about the plane ride?" Noah tugged on his grandpa's sleeve.

"Yes, as long as your mom agrees." Brian took his hand.

Erin nodded. She welcomed time to decompress, and he could celebrate his adventure with his grandparents. Besides, she needed to converse alone with Drew.

"You and I will go to our house." Brian swung Noah's hand. "Maybe your mom and Drew want to go somewhere else for a while."

"Sure, we'll join you later." Erin needed a soothing

cup of herbal tea and a chance to speak privately. Within a few minutes, she settled into a comfy chair opposite Drew. The rustic coffee shop's warm, moist air enveloped them in a sweet cloud of cocoa and sugar.

"Way to go, Erin. Did you hate the whole experience as much as you feared?" He narrowed his eyes, reached across the table, and touched her forearm.

Mesmerized by his intense, dark eyes, she could feel the depth of his concern. "Yes, I detested every minute. I shook and practically hyperventilated the whole time, but at least, I stayed conscious." She breathed out in a whoosh, narrowed her eyes, and twisted her napkin. "In the past, I loved flying."

"I know, and I'm sorry your fear forces you to suffer." He held her gaze without a waver.

She nodded. "The flight was torture, but I proved I can fight pure dread. To set a good example, I needed to confront terror. But nobody said I had to enjoy the flight." Sipping lemon tea and nibbling an oatmeal cookie, she squirmed under his intense scrutiny. "I need to share something else." Her mouth dried, and her throat ached. She struggled to swallow and find the right words. Despair weighted her chest, creating a sharp, physical pain. "Oh, Drew, I saved all my hardest tasks for today."

"What do you mean?" He glanced down.

"Drew, we need to talk." His expression stretched in tight lines. "I care about you, more than you know." She pressed a hand to her chest to calm her heartbeats, speeding with dread.

He nodded, and cheeks paling, his expression hardened.

"But... Drew, we both know a serious relationship

will never work. We spend every possible hour together now, but we've ignored reality. Our lives point in different directions." She raised her napkin and dabbed her eyes.

"Erin, stop. You don't know what you're doing. Don't say another word. How can you possibly believe we're not meant to be together?" He blinked and searched her face.

"I put down deep roots in Moose Jaw. You'll eventually fly away." Her throat squeezed her words into broken syllables. She glanced at his eyes, glazed to shiny glass, and twisted her napkin then blotted her cheeks.

"You feel a strong connection, too. We belong together. Admit you agree." He touched her arm.

"You're right." She swallowed a small sob. "Noah and I both love your company…but I need to cut ties before we get hurt. Flying causes only part of the problem. Even if I adjust to life with a pilot, I know you won't stay in Moose Jaw."

"I'll never hurt you." He shook his head and placed a hand on hers.

His warmth seared her skin. "You would never on purpose hurt anyone. But you will leave eventually and wound my heart." She slipped away her hand and clasped her mug. "You'll stay in Moose Jaw with the SnoWings for two years, and then you'll transfer to another base far away. You'll abandon us." She struggled to swallow the boulder in her throat. "I've made my life here, and even if I wanted, I can't pack Camp Canine in a suitcase."

"What do you mean? You won't even give us a chance? You'll give up everything we share, all because the future frightens you?" Drew stared and plunked down his mug so hard the beverage sloshed. "Your choice doesn't make sense. We would both be crazy to sacrifice the attraction and trust we share."

"You might call my decision crazy, but I call protecting myself and my son wise and realistic." She wrapped her arms around her middle. "I know the future I want." She avoided his gaze, reflecting pools of pain. Sniffing, she wiped her nose. "I'm sorry, Drew. I really am." How could she reject him when he meant so much? Her moist eyes blurred his face into a sad oval across the table.

"You need to reconsider. I've never wanted anything—anyone—more. I value the time I spend with you and Noah every day." He leaned closer. "If you send me away, I will miss you more than you know. You'll crush me."

Sharp lines carved his pale cheeks. "I'm so sorry." Hearing her own voice shatter, she covered her face.

"I just don't understand. But I respect your decision." Drew put his elbows on the table and rubbed his temples.

His eyes welled, and she lowered her gaze. She couldn't stand to witness his raw pain. Without saying another word, they finished their drinks and drove to her parents' place.

Gayle had dinner ready for the whole family and insisted everyone stay.

Erin resisted but spent a couple of hours putting on another brave front. Soon after dinner, she yawned and announced they should head for home.

"After your adventure, I'm sure you're exhausted." Gayle hugged her. "Come again soon."

"I'm proud of you, sis." Mitch patted her on the back. "For once." He laughed.

She mustered a playful punch and headed out the door. Her brother teased, but he always showed support. He had no idea that her suffering extended beyond the flight.

"Give me a call, Drew." Brian called from the doorway. "We need to get together again for guy talk."

All the way back to Moose Jaw, Noah jabbered. His plane ride, cousin fun, and birthday party memories bubbled, and his monologue filled the car.

Erin listened somberly and nursed the sharp pain stabbing her heart.

Back at Camp Canine, Noah jumped out and laughed at the licks on both cheeks from Sam and Jake.

"C'mon, Jake. Jump in." Drew gestured toward the back seat.

"Won't you stay to play?" Noah frowned and swiveled his toe in the dirt.

"Sorry, I can't stay tonight, bud. Jake and I need to go home." Drew shifted and barely smiled.

"Say goodnight, Noah." Erin placed a hand on his shoulder. She couldn't drag out the farewell any longer.

"Goodnight." Noah straggled toward the house with Sam nudging his side.

"Are you sure you mean good-bye forever?" Drew closed the car door behind Jake and turned to face her. His forehead drooped to his eyebrows, and his mouth quivered.

Erin nodded and blinked back tears. Her throat gripped too tight to speak.

"If you change your mind, let me know. I hope…at least, will you still board Jake while I'm away?" He stuffed his hands in his pockets and stared toward the kennel.

She hesitated and nodded. Sorrow clutched her chest and smothered her breath. Even though she needed to avoid him, she really couldn't afford to refuse a paying client. "If you insist, I will." She blinked and met his glassy eyes. "Drew, thank you for everything you've done. Take care." She stood frozen.

Drew bowed his head, lifted a hand, and swiped his eyes.

Regret chased Erin into the house and followed her everywhere that evening. Maybe she had made a terrible mistake. She missed him already. How could she ever forget his gentle companionship and electric touch?

Chapter 22

As he processed the weekend's events, Drew hardly slept. His spirits sank, heavy with the realization his dad would never change. At the same time, losing Erin and Noah jabbed like a pointy stick. An image of Erin's flashing eyes and perfect oval face floated past, shooting hot embers to his chest. Never had he wanted more to love and protect someone. He said he would accept her decision, but how could he? How would he adapt to life missing her and Noah? How would he fill the big, gaping hole?

He punched his pillow, flipped, and rested a hand on Jake's warm head. Opening his eyes, he stared at the ceiling. Scenes played in his head like a movie—Erin laughing at his quips...Noah playing airplane...the trio together cleaning dog pens.

Unable to stand the memories any longer, he threw back the covers, leaped out of bed, and paced. Before long, he tripped over Jake and decided to take him out. Striding along the dark street, he kept time with the name reverberating through his head—Er-in, Er-in, Er-in. He needed her in his life, but how could he convince her to give their relationship a chance? Could he do anything to change her mind?

Driving to work the next morning, Drew massaged his throbbing temples and blasted the horn at birds clustered on the highway.

"Why so glum, chum?" Heading to the jets, Kyle gave him a playful shove.

"Didn't sleep much last night." Drew rubbed his neck where tension grabbed his head. He'd slept better the night the *incident* happened.

"Dealing with girlfriend trouble?" Kyle swung his arms and glanced over.

"I suppose." Drew clamped his mouth into a firm line and struggled to process the sobering truth.

"Don't worry, the issue will blow over." Kyle smacked him between the shoulder blades.

"Maybe." Erin stood firm and didn't act on impulse. She chose her words with care, and she meant them. His head smarted with the painful memory. Maybe he'd tell Kyle the details eventually but not now, with distress bruising his heart blue.

"Speaking from experience, I would say definitely," said Kyle. "Girlfriend problems never last."

Erin's decision was no lover's tiff. He replayed the scene, and nothing changed. He must forget her. As he roared his jet engine into action, he switched into pilot mode and focused only on the complex manoeuvers ahead. Right now, staying precisely synchronized mattered most. After work, he joined a few of the guys bowling. He attacked his anguish with every ball and pounded his full strength into every throw.

"Hey, man, you blew out the back wall with that shot." Kyle slapped his hand in a high-five.

Drew threw three strikes in a row, and at the end of multiple games, he chalked up the high score. But he still lugged a lump as heavy as a bowling ball in his chest. How would he cope without her?

****

The night after she broke the news to Drew, Erin couldn't rest. She did everything possible to relax and prepare for a solid night's sleep. She took her time with each step—a warm bath, a light snack, and a boring novel—but nothing soothed her. Drew's wounded expression haunted her, stirring her pain.

Maybe tomorrow would look brighter. She would adjust to his absence, not sharing the workload and laughing about little things. But tonight, nothing cheered her aching heart. He fit like a missing puzzle piece, yet she'd thrown him away.

In the morning, she scrubbed the kennel runs, exercised the dogs, and posted promotional material on social media. The day passed quickly enough, but she couldn't anticipate his visit after dinner. When Noah asked about Drew, she simply said he and Jake stayed home.

The next day, after Walt took over and Noah boarded the school bus, she picked up Vera to do errands. "I'm glad you wanted to get out today. Do you find coping difficult?"

"Ted's passing shocked me, and I'm not sure I've fully absorbed my loss. But I've lived through grief before, and I'll get through it again." She sighed. "I need to make some decisions about the future, but I'll stay put for a year to give me time to adjust. So, I plan to stay your neighbor for a while."

"I'm very glad. You're a great friend to live near. If you ever need anything, let me know." Erin patted her arm.

"Thanks, dear. I couldn't ask for a better neighbor." Vera wiped one eye.

At the grocery store, Erin chose a cart and parted

from her neighbor to shop. "I'll meet you by the door when we're through."

Thirty minutes later, Erin led the way back to the car.

"You're sad, dear." Lifting her groceries into the trunk, Vera touched her arm and gazed at her face. "What problem upsets you so much?"

Erin slid into the car and wrung her hands. "I told Drew I couldn't continue to see him." She lowered her trembling voice to a near whisper. "I will either miss him now or later, and I decided to face the pain now."

"How does Noah feel?" Vera clasped her hands.

Her wrinkled brow and obvious concern offered little solace. "He doesn't know yet." Erin stared out the window at the carts cluttering the store parking lot.

Vera listened and lowered her window to let in the soft, spring air. "Do you want my opinion?"

"Yes, of course, I want to hear your wisdom." Erin bit her lip. Vera would deliver tough, honest advice. She glanced at her neighbor's wrinkled profile. Grief aged her, even though her attitude stayed positive.

"Life is too short to cut meaningful relationships out of our lives." Vera rubbed her eyes.

"But..." Erin shook her head and squeezed the steering wheel. The tragic crash cheated her out of her loving relationship with Eric. The situation with Drew was different. She could foresee challenges and control the outcome. Vera couldn't be right.

"From what you've told me, I believe you and Drew belong together like bread and butter." Blinking fast, Vera sniffed. "Your young man sounds ideal, even if someday, his career might take him away."

"I don't know if I can talk about the situation

anymore." Pain burned her chest like a nasty, hot ember. "Try to understand…"

"Erin, please, let me finish." Vera set a hand on her arm. "I just said farewell to my soul mate against my will, so I don't know why anyone would say good-bye to love for no valid reason. Why deprive yourself of the chance to be happy? You can use the next two years to figure out logistics." She fumbled in her purse for a tissue and blew her nose.

"I want you to support my decision," Erin whispered and wiped a single tear off her cheek. "Excuse me. I need fresh air." She leaped out of the car, grabbed a stray grocery cart, and trundled across the parking lot to the store. Attacking her raw emotions, she rammed the cart into place and rounded up two more from the far corners of the parking lot. Finally, she sprinted, panting, back to the car.

"Welcome back. Now, where did we leave off?" Vera dabbed at her nose. "I am on your side, dear. I won't say any more. But do consider my advice." She folded her hands on her lap.

"I will. Drew almost never leaves my mind." Voice wavering, Erin blasted the music and steered toward the pet-supply store. Vera's insights shook her to the core. If she followed her friend's advice, would her life change forever?

****

The next evening, Drew arranged a walk with Brian.

"You work all day, so no worries. I'll come there." After dinner, Brian met him in Moose Jaw.

Skirting the perimeter of Crescent Park with Brian and Jake, Drew broke the sad news. "I understand if you don't want to continue our friendship…" Talking about Erin's rejection flooded hurt through his veins and locked in his jaw. Usually, he felt better surrounded by trees and fresh air, but not now.

"Erin has her own ideas about things, but I enjoy your company. Let's stay in touch." Brian gave him a couple of pats on the back.

"I appreciate your friendship." Still, Brian's reassurance offered little consolation. Drew fought to steady a waver in his voice. Brian enveloped his family with the fatherly qualities he craved. Staring at a budding branch, he paused to let Jake sniff a bush.

"How'd your dad's visit go?" Brian waited, hands in his pockets.

"Okay." He tugged the leash and continued along the path. "Dad never changes. We had a few laughs but no real serious conversation. I shouldn't have hoped for anything different."

"Were you disappointed?" Brian stared at the path ahead.

"At the time, yes, but I concluded he's not really confidant material. He didn't want to dredge up the past or talk much. So I decided to bury all the junk and get on with life." He raised a hand to the future. He'd survived so far without a devoted dad—even become a pilot—and he would thrive, with or without paternal support.

Brian nodded. "Sounds like a wise approach."

"Thanks." Drew quickened his pace. Missing Erin overshadowed everything. Losing her ripped him to pieces. He inhaled the green, spring air but couldn't dilute the anguish stalking him day and night.

They paced in silence for a while until

conversation switched to the hockey playoffs and the football team's latest signings for spring training camp.

The visit with Brian didn't solve anything, but at least, Drew didn't feel so alone. He needed moral support to attack the issues still plaguing him. Could anything help win back Erin?

****

The next time Noah asked for Drew, Erin faced him and held both his hands. "We can't hang out together anymore because...we want different things." She winced. Her explanation sounded weak. Even she hardly believed it.

"But why can't he come play? I miss him." He frowned and stuck out his bottom lip.

"I'm sorry, Noah. Drew is busy doing other things." She missed him, too. Each day, she exhausted herself working but still couldn't sleep.

The next week, Noah's teacher, Mrs. Jansen, called. "I'm concerned," she said. "Recently, Noah's spark disappeared. He changed from excited, future pilot to quiet, subdued boy."

Erin swallowed and waited. These days, her son was a different child. The woman didn't exaggerate.

"He says he lost two of his best friends. Is anything going on at home you can share?" said Mrs. Jansen.

"He experienced some changes and is still adjusting." Erin fought to steady her voice. Noah's grief and the teacher's concern tormented her. She would give him extra attention to help him rebound.

The breeze blew warmer than usual for early May and tempted her to plant flowers in the pots around Camp Canine, but she held back. The prairie rule to avoid frost delayed planting until after the long weekend later in the month. Instead, she and Noah picked weeds, added topsoil, and raked stray leaves lingering from the fall. She told herself each day would improve, but life without Drew faded to humdrum and didn't get any easier. Memories stalked her everywhere. He'd painted the fresh coat of stain on the gate. He'd laughed at Noah's foibles. He'd praised her latest marketing idea. She even missed Jake chasing Sam around the yard.

Nobody supported her decision. Vera advised her to give love a chance. Her mom and dad listened and said little, but their creased foreheads contradicted their silence.

"Mitch and I wondered if, well...you and Noah don't smile as often." Over lunch one day, Claire leaned forward and touched Erin's arm. "Would you ever give Drew a second chance?"

Erin shook her head and sipped water to cool her burning throat. Forcing him away protected them. Still, on more than one night, she cried until she fell asleep. No matter how much she missed him, she couldn't risk an uncertain future. But were her family and friends right? Had she made a huge mistake? Should she stifle caution and reconsider?

****

On a bright, sunny morning, the commanding officer called Drew into his office. They stood facing each other in the stark space, surrounded by unadorned walls.

Drew held high his head, jutted back his shoulders, and directed his gaze to the man's hard, olive eyes. Heart racing, he readied himself for the news that could change the course of his career. His probation was over, and he awaited his fate for better or worse.

"You can plan to travel with the team this summer."

The CO didn't waste words on positive feedback, but Drew floated all the way home. His dream lived. If only he could tell Erin, hug her, and see her smile, but she'd slammed the door and locked him out.

His dull ache never eased. He played with Jake in the park more than ever, and when evenings dragged, he practiced his cooking skills. Erin could diagnose why his roast dried and muffins flopped, but she wasn't available to consult. Most of all, he missed her lovely features, funny stories, and Noah's spout of questions.

True, their futures headed in opposite directions. She cherished her Moose Jaw roots, and he would eventually fly off to another base. But the more he quashed memories, the more he remembered. Nothing filled the big, yawning hole. He'd tasted a morsel of family life, and now, he wanted the full course meal. Could he find a path to a future together? She clung to her lifestyle in Moose Jaw, and he loved his military career. Could anything change? He needed to find an answer. Over lunch at the mess hall, he floated an idea.

"It might work." Kyle chomped a burger and nodded. "Give it a shot. You have nothing to lose."

Drew didn't wait. He took hope from Kyle's endorsement and explored options. If the opportunity materialized, it could transform his life. "Yes," he hollered at Kyle, when the life-changing news arrived.

"You go, man." Kyle grinned and pumped a fist.

Heart rate jumping, Drew considered his next move. Airshow season approached, so he booked space at Camp Canine and then counted the days like a child anticipating Christmas. Besides dropping off Jake, he would share some tremendous news. When Erin heard, would her beautiful face light like his passion burned?

****

When Erin finished kennel chores, she found an email from Drew. Did he know he was constantly on her mind? Eager yet hesitant, she couldn't contain the rush of anticipation that danced along her spine. But she shouldn't feel this way when she knew their blossoming relationship was over. Scolding herself and preparing for whatever he might say, she stared out the window. Maybe he would ask her or even beg her to reconsider. No, he respected her and would never ask her to compromise. As she opened the message addressed to the Camp Canine account, she jiggled her tingly arms and slowed her rapid breaths.

His brief words simply confirmed his booking and drop-off arrangements for Sunday afternoon. Her eyes welled, and her throat ached. The message stuck to business. She better prepare Noah for a short visit, nothing like the full, fun afternoons they once enjoyed. She also better get more rest before he arrived. The hallway mirror reflected her dull, shadowed eyes.

On Sunday, the sky beamed bright blue with a few cotton-ball clouds. The breeze lazed, and the sun smiled real warmth on a perfect day for a picnic lunch. With Noah's help, Erin made ham-and-cheese sandwiches and packed potato chips, carrot sticks, lemonade, watermelon, and cookies in a basket with a checked cloth liner.

Vera couldn't join the picnic because she already had lunch plans with friends in Moose Jaw.

Noah added a handful of dog biscuits for Sam, who

sat drooling next to their preparations, and followed his mom outside.

Erin spread a blanket on a patch of lawn between the house and the kennel and set out the food. The lawn hinted green, and the land stretched as flat as the picnic blanket to the horizon. The old prairie joke you could watch your dog run away for days held a grain of truth. She lifted her sandwich and took a generous bite. She belonged right here, planted on this little patch of prairie she owned.

"Here comes a car." Noah selected a carrot and pointed.

Sure enough, a cloud of dust hung over the gate, marking the arrival of a vehicle.

"I see Drew." Noah dropped his carrot, jumped up, and ran.

Drooling, Sam took a last glance at the food and trotted toward the car. Heart springing into erratic beats, she stood and waved.

Jake ran to greet her, circled back, herded Noah like a sheep, and knocked him over.

Drew laughed, helped Noah stand, and brushed off the dirt.

He sported a light suntan, and his eyes shone dark and bright at the same time. In his T-shirt and cargo shorts, he stood strong, fit, and more muscular than she remembered. "Hi, Drew." She flushed and ran her fingers through her hair. "I see Jake hasn't changed."

He chuckled and adjusted the sunglasses perched on his head. "Maybe some time with you will burn his extra energy. Feel free to teach him more manners."

"I gather the airshow season has arrived." She nearly gasped. How could he have grown even more handsome? A rush of affection nearly tipped her off balance. Why had she ever rejected him?

"Yes, I locked my spot on the team." Beaming, he lowered his gaze.

He was as modest as ever. "Congratulations. You've worked hard, and you deserve the opportunity." Her knees trembled.

"Mommy." Noah tugged her hand. "Can Drew stay for the picnic?" He hopped into Drew's arms. "Do you want to eat a picnic lunch?"

Erin hesitated for a split second. "I made extra." Drew's face lit, fuelling even more-deeply her affection.

"I'd love to stay." He swung Noah's hand. "I'm glad to see you, buddy." He dropped, sat cross-legged next to them, and dug into the food.

The dogs stared and drooled until Noah fed them dog biscuits.

Crunching, they devoured the treats.

Noah radiated excitement and told Drew about school, the puppy in the kennel, and the baby geese in Crescent Park.

"Remember to eat." Erin smiled and handed her son a sandwich.

"Will Jake stay here?" Noah chomped a large bite. His voice scrambled through his food, and his gaze fixed on Drew.

Her son hadn't appeared so happy in weeks. She knew the feeling. The same surge of delight filled her, and she pressed a shaky hand on her chest. Maybe the invitation was a foolish idea. She toyed unnecessarily with her yearning heart. "Yeah, you and your mom will dog sit while I go away to an airshow." Drew munched a carrot stick.

"What's an airshow?" Noah copied and selected a carrot.

"You see lots of different planes fly, and the pilots do tricks. The jets zip fast and make fancy patterns in the sky." He swooped his carrot in a circle.

"Oh, an airshow sounds cool. I want to go." Noah jiggled on the blanket.

"I can't say for sure, but maybe sometime, you'll get the chance." Drew bit into a sandwich and glanced over.

"Maybe someday you can go." She didn't make any promises, but the idea didn't totally horrify her. One day at a time, she faced her fears. Right now, missing Drew every day hurt worse than any phobia.

"Please, can I have more lemonade?" Noah held out his cup for a refill.

Erin steadied his hand and poured. She swept her gaze to Drew then the prairie backdrop. She couldn't stand to torture herself with the welcome sight of the man she forced away.

"How's business?" Drew munched on a pickle.

"Bookings keep growing." She tilted her head from side to side. "The new name and dog photos on the website attract attention. Calls and online inquiries have increased."

"You'll revitalize the business, guaranteed." He smiled and nodded.

Stomach rippling, she served cookies and watermelon. His vote of confidence counted. He understood the challenges and solutions he helped design.

While the threesome ate dessert, Noah blurted

details of the school hamster's escape.

She giggled at his rapid, exaggerated description and caught the light in Drew's crinkled eyes. Memories of the good times they had shared flooded her entire being. Laughing often and chatting easily made her feel more alive than she had in weeks.

Noah swallowed his last bite and jumped to his feet. "I want to find my airplane." He ran to the house with Jake and Sam frolicking behind.

"I've missed this place."

As Drew removed his sunglasses, his complexion deepened beneath his tan. He still cared.

"But most of all, I've missed you."

Erin's breathing quickened, and warmth flooded her face. She shifted on the blanket just as he turned his head. He sat so close that she breathed his irresistible, spicy scent. "I've missed you, too." Joy and confusion swirled her heart into a cartwheel. She should resist the invisible tug but couldn't.

Then he leaned forward in slow motion. He smiled, placed a finger under her chin, and touched his warm, moist lips to hers.

Closing her eyes, she trembled, and love rose from deep within and overflowed. But she couldn't give in to desire. This closeness couldn't continue. She snapped open her eyes and pulled back, pushing away gently. "No, we can't…"

"Yes, we can." Drew lifted a forefinger and brushed her cheek. "I have something to tell you."

Forcing ragged breaths, she focused her gaze on his dark eyes and nearly melted.

"I can fulfill my commitment to the SnoWings and then become a flight instructor at the training school in

Moose Jaw. I will stay." Swallowing, he bowed his head and then swept his gaze over her face. "If you'll accept my commitment, I'll never leave you."

Erin let her mouth fall open. She gasped, and her eyes misted with tears. "I never believed a pilot could make me the happiest woman in Moose Jaw." She smiled through her sobs and tipped her teary face, inviting him to kiss her one more time. How could life get any better?

Chapter 23

A few months later, Drew granted Noah's wish and invited Erin's entire family and Vera to the special airshow for military families and friends.

Blazing sun baked the runway, pesky mosquitoes buzzed, and erratic grasshoppers jumped in the field, but nothing could spoil the festive mood. Erin climbed onto the bleachers and waited with the rest for the show to begin. She placed a hand on Noah's shoulder and breathed hot, dusty air infused with grass and dandelions. Finally, she would see Drew perform the famous, aerial stunts. Anticipation and fear paraded up and down her spine. Earlier, she forced down only a few bites of cereal for breakfast.

"How're you doing, Err Bear?" Her dad squeezed her shoulder.

She squinted and caught him winking at her mom. "I'm okay. A bit nervous, but nothing I can't handle." Erin set a hand on her fluttery stomach and sipped water. They didn't need to worry so much. She'd survived a flight, and she needed to see Drew in action with the SnoWings team. She turned just as Mitch and Claire exchanged smiles. "Hey, I told you I feel fine. You don't need to stare." She adjusted her cap brim lower, shielding their scrutiny. She had total confidence in Drew's piloting skills, but tension still whirled.

Vibrating energy and excitement, the spectators'

conversations and laughter filled the air.

Squinting at the sky, she brushed away the perspiration dotting her nose. Since the picnic, when she and Drew agreed on a new path toward their shared future, they spent as much time together as his schedule allowed. He travelled to airshows much of the summer, but long phone calls and emails helped them grow even closer.

"When will the show start?" Noah wiggled on the bleachers beside his cousins.

"Should be any minute. Having fun, sis?" Mitch adjusted his cap to shade his eyes.

"I can't say for sure. I'll let you know later." Erin tilted her head, bit her lower lip, and twisted her hands. The thought of watching Drew's jet acrobat across the sky still shook her to the core. She believed he'd soar safely through his dangerous maneuvers, but in the air, surprising things could happen.

****

In the cockpit, Drew focused on the task ahead. His entire body tingled, excited yet calm and confident. His lovely Erin might be nervous in the bleachers, but did she have any idea what would soon take place?

Kyle had first suggested the idea and convinced the team to agree. They kidded around, and the idea simmered and grew.

Finally, the commanding officer considered their plan and approved it with a bare hint of a smile.

Then before he finalized details, Drew consulted two important people. Brian's and Gayle's blessings meant the world. This morning, adrenaline pulsed through his veins while he exercised Jake. The path ahead would change his life forever.

In the late morning, Erin called to wish him a good flight. "I'll watch every swoop and hold you safe in my heart."

Excitement zinging in his shoulders and temples, he counted down the minutes until he departed for the base to prepare for the show. In the car, he caught sight of his eyes reflected in the car rearview mirror. They had matched the intensity beating in his chest.

"Is everyone ready?" Before takeoff, the lead pilot checked in with every member of the team.

"Yes, I'm ready." He straightened and expanded his chest, already filled with radiating heat. He had never felt surer about anything.

****

Music blared out of the speakers, the master of ceremonies delivered opening remarks, and the show flew into motion. The crowd applauded, and a few people fanned themselves with event programs.

"Watch the sky. The show will start any minute." Erin put her hand on Noah's arm.

He bounced and clapped, his joy almost contagious.

Absorbing his excitement, she inhaled calming breaths in time to the music.

The SnoWings team flew upward in perfect formation. They zigzagged across the sky, slicing red and white streaks over the blue backdrop.

Almost enjoying the spectacle, she traced every dip and plunge. Her heart beat double time, and nervousness tingled across her shoulders. Then suddenly, she strained to hear an announcement blaring from the speakers.

"Erin Humphrey…"

She jumped and clasped the brim of her hat.

"…Captain Drew Dixon speaking from jet three."

"Pardon me?" Heartbeat rushing, she glanced left, right, and up. He soared above, yet his deep voice rumbled her name. She fanned her hot face and let her mouth fall open. Why did he call her name from the sky? While the burning sun and passion sizzled her skin, she absorbed vaguely the action around her.

Noah jumped and waved. "Hey, I hear Drew!"

Her entire family beamed and stared.

"Erin, I love you, and I love Noah. Will you marry me?"

Drew's voice crackled into the crowd, and a clamor arose. High in the sky above, two jets split, curved, swooped, and traced a fluffy, white heart.

"Oh, yes, yes, definitely, yes." Tears streaming, Erin crossed her hands over her pounding heart, leaped, extended both arms, and waved. The man of her dreams—even if he was a pilot—wanted to marry her, and without a doubt, no one could make her happier. Surrounded by hugs from her family and friends, she gazed at the dramatic symbol of his love that floated high above.

A word about the author...

Margot Johnson lives with her husband, Rick, and their two dogs in Regina, Saskatchewan, Canada. She has written magazine articles and children's stories. *Love Takes Flight* is her first novel.

She welcomes email from readers at:
authormargotjohnson@gmail.com
or contact her on Facebook at Margot Johnson Author.

Thank you for purchasing
this publication of The Wild Rose Press, Inc.

For questions or more information
contact us at
info@thewildrosepress.com.

The Wild Rose Press, Inc.
www.thewildrosepress.com

To visit with authors of
The Wild Rose Press, Inc.
join our yahoo loop at
http://groups.yahoo.com/group/thewildrosepress/